Dating on the Dork Side

Also By Charity Tahmaseb and Darcy Vance

The Geek Girl's Guide to Cheerleading

BY CHARITY TAHMASEB

The Fine Art of Keeping Quiet
The Fine Art of Holding Your Breath

Praise for The Geek Girl's Guide to Cheerleading:

"This novel is contemporary, laugh-outloud funny, and positive."

—Florence H. Munat, VOYA

"Sweet, funny, and heart-warming, *The Geek Girl's Guide to Cheerleading* truly makes you want to cheer!"

—Elizabeth Scott

Dating on the Dork Side

CHARITY TAHMASEB AND DARCY VANCE

COLLINS MARK BOOKS

DATING ON THE DORK SIDE

Published by Collins Mark Books
www.collinsmarkbooks.com
Cover art copyright © 2015 by Creativeye99/iStock Photo
Cover design copyright © 2015 by Aaron Andersen

ISBN-13: 978-0-9987938-7-0
ISBN-10: 0-9987938-7-6

Dedication

To my mother, Luanne Jarvis, and to my daughter, Sara Vance,
for teaching me to be strong.

~ D.V.

For the strong women in my life: Karin, Ulla, Abby, and Kyra.

~ C.T.

Epigraph

If people do not believe that mathematics is simple, it is only because they do not realize how complicated life is.

~ John von Neumann

Dating on the Dork Side

Chapter One

♡

'VE HAD ELEVEN YEARS to think about this (twelve if you count kindergarten), and if you ask me, the first day of school should come with a checklist:

- **Your best guy friend manages to wear matching socks?**
  A good sign.
- **Your homeroom teacher turns out to be a drama king?**
  Proceed with caution; hilarity may ensue, but so may humiliation.
- **You find a jock in the tutoring room?**
  A sign of the apocalypse.

On my last first day of school, I counted the minutes to the final bell, then took the stairs to the tutoring room on the third floor two at a time. I paused at the threshold and sucked in a breath.

The monitors inside the room, at least the ones that I could see, were spotless. I had new pencils sharpened to deadly points. My notebooks were filled with blank pages and promise. Everything was still first-day fresh. Through the open windows came the wondrous sounds of the Olympia High School football team warming up.

"O-L-Y-M-P-I-A!"

Anything was still possible.

"Switch!" Coach Cutter's voice, amplified by the megaphone, rode the breeze through the windows. The trip seemed to soften all the hard edges, making him sound like someone you might actually want to talk to.

"O-L-Y-M-P-I-A!" the siren song came again. I loved it when jocks spelled. I loved the first day of school. I really, *really* loved my view of the football field from the windows of the tutoring room.

But Jason "The Ab" Abernathy was ruining all of it.

Jason was one of those A-list jocks you'd hope would only exist in stereotypes, the kind with big muscles, a small brain, and a long list of downtrodden victims. He was captain of the baseball team, but in the fall, he also headed up the Yell Club, probably because it put him up close and personal with the private parts of Olympia High's varsity cheerleaders. Or maybe I was being unfair. Maybe Jason truly had loads of school spirit demanding to be unleashed.

I took in the sight of him in the tutoring room, his tall frame hunched over a computer, typing something with a slow, two finger hunt and peck. Why didn't he just use a smartphone, like everyone else in this century? I thought about leaving. It would be easy to turn around and slink away. But without my skybox view I'd have to hang off the chain link fence and watch football practice like some sort of fangirl. *That* was dance team/pom squad territory. I was *so* not pom squad. I was so not dance team, either. Plus, in my ancient jeans, a vintage *Star Wars* t-shirt, and wrists full of bracelets that had started life as string, I wouldn't exactly blend in.

So I inched into the room. Just in case, I pulled one of those deadly pencils from my book bag.

"Uh, hi," I tried. Tried and, I might add, failed. My voice barely reached my own ears. Except for a muted peck, peck, peck, Jason remained motionless, his eyes still locked on the screen. Outside, the football team moved from stretching to speed drills as I took a few more steps into the room. The newly waxed floor felt slick beneath my Chuck Taylors.

I drew in a breath and said, "Hello?"

Jason jumped. If he'd been going for a fly ball, he would've caught it. Not that we get a lot of those in the tutoring room. My heart rate doubled when he crashed back into his chair, his hands fumbling over the keyboard. That's when he tried it: the screen switch.

I know a few computer geeks (my best friend Rhino, my dad) and I've witnessed more than my fair share of screen switches. One minute, the swimsuit model is there; the next, poof! She's a spreadsheet detailing the mechanical specifications of the Millennium Falcon.

Jason might be a gifted athlete; he might have some amazing batting average, but he couldn't pull off a screen switch to save his life. Whatever he'd been looking at was still on the screen. He went straight into full panic clicking mode, until at last, his finger landed on the computer's power button.

"Don't—" I said.

"Huh?"

Too late. The monitor shimmered and turned black. I sighed. "Never mind."

"Sorry, I was just—" Jason pointed at the screen like I could somehow figure out the rest. Then his expression changed. He lifted one eyebrow and started studying me, like he'd never really seen me before. That might have made sense except he'd sat behind me in homeroom all last year. And the year before that.

"Do you need tutoring?" I asked.

"Do I ... what?"

"Do you need tutoring? Help with schoolwork?" I waved a hand at the computer lab and then the side area with the long tables and individual carrels for studying. "It's what I do."

"That's okay." He pushed back his chair. "I was just leaving."

But when he reached me, he halted, his blue-eyed gaze raining down on the top of my head. I had to crane my neck to look up at him. I wondered where the safer view was. His pecs? Or his face?

"Tutoring," he said, like he was trying out a new word in a foreign language.

Outside of homeroom, I'd never stood this close to Jason before. It was almost like we were having a moment, except he was an A-list jock and I was an A-list ... nothing.

"I might have to try that," he added.

And then, as if the situation wasn't already strange enough, he leaned in closer and inhaled. Deeply. It was almost as if he was *sniffing* me. Then he was off, charging down the corridor, body slamming the lockers on one side of the hallway, then the other, morphing back into the athlete that half the school loved—and the other half feared.

When I turned back to the room the space felt oddly vacant, as though Jason had taken something crucial with him when he left. But I had what I wanted now: a blissfully empty room.

Strange as it sounds, I *like* tutoring. I started in middle school as a homework buddy for the little kids at Olympia Elementary three days a week. It was fun. Then, the year my parents' marriage got rocky, it felt almost like compensation for the little brother or sister I'd probably never have. When my group kept acing all their spelling tests, the guidance counselor suggested peer tutoring as the next logical step.

But there was one more reason I liked spending time in the tutoring room. In those first weeks of school, when it was too early for anyone to need serious help with their schoolwork, it was mostly just me and the sights and sounds of football practice. Those were the moments I lived for. Up there, I was free to watch as long as I liked. And watch I did.

I focused my gaze on quarterback Gavin Madison warming up his arm. He looked good this year. Oh, who was I kidding? He looked good every year. When he launched a pass to one of the wide receivers, my fingertips tingled in anticipation, as if the ball were headed straight for me.

That's not as crazy as it sounds. Once upon a time, I'd played in the same youth football league as Gavin. My body still remembered how it felt to reach for the ball, to grasp it and tuck it in tight, to run with it down the field. But my football career had ended in eighth grade at the bottom of a pile-up. I sighed and resisted the urge to touch the scars on my knee.

As much as I was enjoying the view, something gnawed at me. Instead of admiring Gavin's form, the spin he gave the ball, or—okay, I'll admit it—the way he looked in those tight football pants, I turned toward Jason's blank monitor. It was like a dare, just sitting there, taunting me. With a click and the fizz of static, I turned on the computer.

The more I thought about it, the stranger Jason's appearance in the tutoring room seemed. I mean, really—jock + tutoring room + first day of school? The combination didn't add up. It was like he'd brought a negative integer into the equation. At least, that was what my friend Rhino, the math genius, might say.

Surely Jason hadn't felt an overwhelming urge to start a research project on the first day of school. So why else would he have sought out a computer? A few unsavory options entered my mind. Did I really want to get an eyeful of cheerleader types modeling their Spankies, or whatever skeevy fantasy tripped that boy's trigger? What if it was worse? What if I got caught looking at something that could get us *both* in trouble?

The first option was a definite possibility; the second, not so much. Sure, Rhino had hacked the school's firewall. He could do the same to the grading system if, through some bizarre twist in the space/time/school continuum, he ever needed to. But he was not only good at math, he was a techno-genius. I was pretty sure something like that was beyond the abilities of anyone nicknamed The Ab.

That didn't stop me from checking the browser's history files. The listing was short: the school home page, this year's open gym schedule, the Minnesota High School Athletic League. Those last two made sense. Jason was an athlete. Maybe they'd changed something about high school baseball rules over the summer. According to Rhino (who knew everything about the sport), Jason was devoted to the game.

I was about to give up when a final site caught my eye.

The Hotties of Troy.

True, the mascot for Olympia High was a Trojan warrior. But pulling up a website called *The Hotties of Troy* on a school computer? I knew better than that.

I did it anyway.

All I got for my daring was a login screen.

But one with a familiar name in the user ID field: *jasona*. Oh, it was just too tempting. My fingers itched to try, and I quickly filled in the password field. *Baseball? Cheerleader?* I even tried the old standby: *password.*

Nothing. Then the obvious hit me. I typed *theab.*

Bingo.

I squeezed my eyes half shut, finger over the mouse to close everything … just in case. When nothing raunchy happened, I opened my eyes all the way, feeling a bit of pride swell in my chest. Hacking? It was kind of fun.

The site appeared to be the sort of place where a group of people contributed information, a wiki: a living, breathing (well, virtually) encyclopedia. The sidebar contained a list of pages: recently updated, most-accessed, hottest of the hot. Every single page was labeled with a girl's name. A girl who went to Olympia High, which made her, I guessed, a Hottie of Troy. So, what we had here was a living, breathing girl encyclopedia?

Of all the chauvinistic, sexist, and utterly stupid things.

Stunned, I sat back, not sure what to do. I clicked the home icon. The main page contained instructions for the computer illiterate and a general chat board, with messages like:

bro, Call of Duty throwdown tonite at teh abs

Yeah, it wasn't exactly a brain trust. Returning to the home page refreshed the sidebar as well. The girls' names rippled and changed position. At that moment a new one popped up on the recently-accessed list.

Camy Cavanaugh

I'm pretty sure my heart stopped. For several seconds I sat, frozen, until footfalls in the hallway yanked me back to reality. Matching Jason's earlier panic, I minimized the browser and brought up Excel. The footsteps got closer, a clipped stab against the linoleum. A teacher, I guessed. I plugged a fake formula into the spreadsheet. It took every ounce of willpower not to look at the wiki, not to click the *Camy Cavanaugh* page, not to see what someone had written about *me*.

I hit right click and closed the browser just as Ms. Pendergast and her deadly sharpened high heels clip clopped into the room.

She glanced around, a small frown on her face. It was as if her super-secret teacher sense had alerted her that, just minutes before, a jock had invaded the tutoring area, one focused on hotties instead of academic assistance. One who maybe had been looking at a page named after me?

"Oh, Camy, you're here?" Ms. Pendergast said, but her tone was more: *Why are you here?*

I shrugged. It wasn't like I could tell her how much I liked the view.

"I guess so, but I think ..." I let the sentence trail off, not sure *what* I was thinking. That I wouldn't be here long? That I couldn't wait until she left so I could check out the strange girl wiki? That I had, in general, no clue what was going on?

Ms. Pendergast adjusted her leather tote, then shot me another look.

"I admire your dedication, but I don't really think you need to stay. Is that"—she pointed a manicured finger at the computer screen—"something you could do at home? I was thinking of locking up and leaving early."

"I'm just checking to make sure the new video tutorials got loaded on all the computers this summer. As soon as I finish, I'll shut everything down and turn off the lights."

Ms. Pendergast sighed and dropped her bag onto a desktop. "Camy, you know what they say, don't you?"

If by "they" she meant Jason and the rest of the users of the *Hotties of Troy* wiki, then no, I didn't know what they said. But I was bursting to find out and would, if I could just get Ms. Pendergast and her tote bag to leave the room.

"All work and no play makes ..." She gave up, apparently deciding I was too lame to understand. "There'll be plenty of time for that later," she said as she walked toward the windows. "It's a beautiful day. Get outside. Enjoy yourself."

I could hear Gavin calling a sequence of numbers on the football field below. How could I explain that being alone here, with my skybox view, counted as enjoying myself? I couldn't. As if to prove her point,

Ms. Pendergast pulled the last window closed and flipped the lock just as Gavin called, "Hut!"

She turned toward a row of computers next and stabbed at the power buttons. Her eyes were on her task instead of me when she said, "You can't just watch life from the sidelines, you know."

On any other day I might have marveled at the stiletto-shod Ms. Pendergast tossing out sports metaphors. Today that seemed no stranger than the rest of it. It was no weirder than finding Jason in the tutoring room, and definitely less odd than my name turning up on the *Hotties of Troy* website.

I closed Excel and logged off before powering down the other computers on my side of the room. All the while, I wondered: What was the URL of the wiki? Could I remember it so I could log in from home later? And was I really so pathetic that even a teacher could sense my loser status?

Ms. Pendergast locked the door behind us, dashing any hope I might have had of sneaking back in once she'd left. She shifted her tote from one shoulder to the other.

"It really is good you're so ... dedicated," she said again. "But it's your last year of high school. Don't forget to enjoy it."

She left me with those words ringing in my ears. I waited until the last click, click, click of her heels had faded, then tried the door, but the handle rattled under my grip.

I thought about texting Rhino. I'd never seen him pick a lock, but I bet he could do it. I imagined his lanky frame stooped over the doorknob, dark strands of hair falling into his eyes. Rhino would come if I called. He always did.

We'd been friends since preschool and we'd seen each other at our worst. I was sitting in the front row of the bleachers at the T-ball game when Rhino struck out, lost his helmet, and knocked himself unconscious with his own bat. In eighth grade, he came to my rescue after the girl I thought was my best friend ditched me in the restroom at the Spring Fling, leaving me half naked and with no way to get home.

What now? My plans for a perfect first-day-of-school afternoon were completely blown. Should I walk to Rhino's and ask for his help, or head home and hack *Hotties* by myself? Hang off the chain link fence and gaze at Gavin?

Maybe Ms. Pendergast was right, I thought as I headed down the stairs. So far, I hadn't enjoyed a single minute of senior year.

♡ ♡ ♡

I wouldn't say Rhino hated school. The word *hate* requires far more passion than Rhino had ever worked up about an educational institution. Dislike, maybe. Disdain. I'm sure he could conjure up a dozen other D-words to describe how he felt. So of course, in a cruel twist of fate, he lived just a block away from Olympia, Minnesota's only high school.

On crisp autumn nights, you could hear the football games from his house. Every year, the homecoming committee used his street as a staging area for the parade. Last fall, as convertible after convertible arrived to carry homecoming royalty, Rhino had turned to me and said, "I'm being punished for something I did in a past life, right?"

He forgets that when we were little, we loved it. All of it. Rhino wanted to be the drum major. I yearned to wear a long gown, to sit on the trunk of a convertible. Once, Rhino wove a paper chain crown for me. With it on top of my head, I practiced waving at an admiring crowd.

Middle school had quickly demolished what was left of those wispy fantasies. I was never going to be popular enough to make it into the homecoming court. I'd even convinced myself that it didn't matter. But I still didn't see the point of treating school like it was a jail sentence.

Things could be worse. Much, much worse.

And today, they were. Because standing in Rhino's garage was … Jason. Yes, *that* Jason, the one with the stupid nickname. For a second I considered Mr. Dawson's opening lecture in Advanced Earth Sciences that morning. He'd talked about the Butterfly Effect, the theory that an insect flapping its wings in the Amazon jungle could cause a tornado thousands of miles away.

I stared, open-mouthed, and couldn't help wondering: Just how big would a butterfly's wings need to be to make the jocktastic Jason appear both in the tutoring room and in my nerdy best friend's garage on the same afternoon? In most cases, pretty freakin' huge, I thought. But in this case, you had to account for Darren.

To really understand Rhino, and why Jason "The Ab" Abernathy might be standing next to him, you don't need to know much about earth science, but you do need to know a little about Rhino's family. It was Rhino's older brother Darren who defined the Rineholds. Darren, the superstar athlete who'd led Olympia High to not one, but two state baseball championships.

If you took everything that was Darren and held it up like a photograph, Rhino would be the negative. He was dark where his brother was light. He shined in ways most people didn't notice. The saddest part? Hardly anyone could see Rhino for the amazing person he was because they kept expecting to see Darren instead.

No matter how different the brothers were, there was one sacred thing that connected Rhino to Darren, and both of them to Jason. That thing was baseball. I always wondered if Rhino loved the game the way I love football. Maybe he simply loved his brother. For the record, Darren *is* pretty cool.

Whatever the reason, Rhino started keeping team stats when he was just a seven-year-old tag-along and Darren was a Gopher League

All-Star. When his big brother joined the middle school and then the high school team, Rhino followed with his scorebook. After Darren graduated four years ago, Rhino kept at it. He can do things with statistics that make my brain hurt.

Over the years, Rhino and Jason developed an odd sort of friendship. At first, I cringed whenever I saw them together, certain Rhino was being set up for a massive fall. But then I figured it out. There's one thing I know about athletes: they're superstitious. As long as Rhino was the one keeping track of RBIs and extra bases, then Jason would no more body slam him into a locker than toss out his own pair of lucky socks.

That afternoon, the two of them were huddled over a card table strewn with printouts from Rhino's computer. Neither boy noticed me standing there in the driveway. And standing there.

At last, I tried, "Uh, hi?" because that had worked so well in the tutoring room.

They both jerked back. Rhino recovered first.

"Hey, Cams," he said. "Jason stopped by to pick up a pair of Darren's old cleats and we decided to look over the stats for the incoming freshmen."

"State," Jason added. "We want to go to state." He didn't sound all that pumped about the prospect. Jason gave the printouts another look, stroked his chin like he was considering something earth-shattering, then he said to Rhino, "See ya, bro."

They did that fist bump thing boys do, then Jason wandered down the driveway, a haphazard path that put him close enough that he could—I swear I'm not making this up—*sniff* me. Again.

It was getting kind of creepy.

Jason's SUV belched to life, the engine loud, the blast from the stereo even louder. He felt the need to leave a patch of burnt rubber behind as he rumbled down the street.

"So," I said to Rhino once the exhaust had cleared. "You guys." I crossed my fingers. "Like this now? BFFs? I bet you're planning to room together in college next year. He's probably penciled you in as best man at his wedding already."

"Shut up," he said in typical Rhino fashion. "You *are* aware that I would never attend any school that would accept the likes of The Ab, right? Besides, there isn't a girl on the planet dumb enough to marry him."

Rhino might be a genius, but he didn't know much about girls. Just one day into the school year and Jason already had a posse of freshman flirts following him through the cafeteria. I thought of the girls in my own class. The shy ones he never noticed, the popular ones he both flattered and tormented.

There was *something* about The Ab, though. He was big and goofy, with dark blond hair and slightly darker eyebrows, which, combined with those killer blue eyes, was actually kind of cute. I'd never crushed on him, but I knew plenty of girls who had.

"Last first day of school?" I asked, just to get a rise out of Rhino.

"Four years too late."

I stuck out my tongue at him. "Come on, did you really want to go off to college without me?"

He didn't smile, but his eyes narrowed in a squint that I knew, from years of studying his face, was affection. That squint was also, in part, how he'd gotten his nickname. I should mention that his parents did give him a perfectly normal first name. It's Ben. But back in grade school, before glasses, Rhino squinted all the time. And his nose? Well, he still hasn't grown all the way into it, though it was looking more Romanesque. He's kind of grumpy too, if not actually wrinkled like a rhinoceros. And when he charges? Even I get out of his way.

The nickname fit, so it stuck.

Just then, something tiny and red flashed in his tangled hair.

"Hold still," I told him.

I stepped closer, just a breath away from him, and went up on tip-toes. I parted the strands with my finger, half expecting to find that Amazonian butterfly, but a ladybug crawled onto my nail instead.

I showed her to Rhino. "I think that's good luck."

He held out a finger, and the ladybug clambered over to him.

"It's a real one, too," he said, "not one of those heinous Asian beetle imposters." The ladybug preened, testing her wings, then took flight, a tiny spot of red against a blue September sky.

"Ladybug, ladybug, fly away home." Rhino turned to me. "What about you? Are you flying away home or can you stay a while? Need help with calculus yet?"

Thanks to Rhino and my pride, I'd managed to cling to the accelerated math track. Unlike Rhino, who raced through mathematics the way some kids leveled up in video games, I had to claw my way past each new theorem and function. The only upside was that once I understood something, I could almost always explain it. That I was the most requested math tutor in school was an irony not lost on me. Or Rhino, for that matter.

"Maybe by the end of the week," I said. "You're on my speed dial."

"In that case, stay. The Twins are playing tonight."

I didn't know why he thought that would tempt me. Baseball bored me, and Rhino knew that. I opened my mouth, not so much in response, but to tell him about that afternoon in the tutoring room. About Jason, and the wiki. Then, in my mind's eye, I saw my name in the recently-accessed list and a fierce flush flooded my cheeks.

"What?" Rhino asked, a hint of amusement in his voice.

I never blushed around him. Well, almost never. Rhino could help me hack into the site, but that would also mean he could read about me on *The Hotties of Troy*. Was it worth it?

I shook my head, both in answer to his question and my own. "Nothing," I said.

If I didn't get anywhere with it at home, I'd log in tomorrow from the tutoring room. There was no need to involve Rhino at all, no need to expose him to what were sure to be unflattering remarks about me.

If I knew one thing about myself, it was this: I was no Hottie of Troy.

"Okay, then, Ladybug, fly away home." He turned back to his printouts.

Rhino was not a touchy-feely kind of guy. His self-containment was legend and his personal space sacred. That he let me inside his bubble, close enough to pluck an insect from his hair, said a lot. I still wasn't getting a hug from the deal.

I waved as I left, but with his head down, his focus on baseball stats, Rhino didn't see me. I walked home, equally focused on the wiki.

♡ ♡ ♡

I couldn't remember the website address. I couldn't find it in Google either. Someone had made sure that search engines didn't pick up the site. I shut my eyes, trying to visualize the address field. It was like a test, and I was good at those. *Wiki*, I thought; that was part of it. The rest were letters. Initials. T-H-O-T?

All I got was a blank page. Then I smiled and swapped numeral 0 for the letter O, and I was in!

I glanced over my shoulder. My room was at the opposite end of the house from the driveway. Any minute, Dad could pull up, walk in, and be up the stairs before I realized it. I eased my bedroom door closed. A girl couldn't have too much privacy, especially when she was about to hack into a website called *The Hotties of Troy.*

Back at my desk, my fingers shook so hard that the first time I tried the login, I messed it up. I tried again, hoping Jason hadn't gone all security-conscious since that afternoon.

He hadn't. For several heartbeats, I stared at the girl wiki in all its chauvinistic glory. Enough time had passed that my name no longer came up on the recently-accessed list. And let's face it, no way would I pop up in any kind of hottie list. I used the box at the top of the page to search for myself.

My name appeared, and all I had to do was click on it to get to my page. I pushed away from my desk again, cracked the door, just an inch, and listened hard. Then I rushed back, clicked on my name, and hid my face in my hands.

I had all of four entries, two from last spring and two from today.

Admin: She always smells good.

Oh. Well. Let's hear it for hygiene.

Adm*n: She smells f**king fantastic.

Okay, really good hygiene.

jasona: UR rite. She smells like a chick should ... not all perfumey and fake. And bro, she was totally checking me out in the tutoring room today. I'm going to have to fail something this year, get some up close academic help, if ya know what I mean.

Only someone with an ego the size of Jason's would assume any girl who glanced at him was checking him out.

Adm*n: Dude, how's failing this year different from any other year?

I snorted, starting to like this Adm*n with an asterisk guy. I clicked on the home page again, but then I sat back in my chair and thought: What now? I felt like I should tell someone. The principal? Ms. Pendergast?

Or maybe the person who had the most at stake in all this, the one who topped every list, recently-accessed, recently-updated, hottest of the hot: the one and only ... Elle Emerson.

I clicked over to her page and read the first comment:

jasona: Bro, totally hot, but completely lethal. I don't have any pics from today's cheerleading practice cuz she tossed my phone into the bleachers and I lost the battery.

Well, that explained why Jason had been in the tutoring room, using a computer instead of his phone. And that was Elle, all right. She had all the intelligence and ambition of a Hillary Clinton packed into the body of a Victoria's Secret model. Elle was student council president, star performer in the debate club, captain of the cheerleading squad, and when I say she ruled the school, I mean she literally Ruled. The. School. No one crossed Elle and escaped unscathed.

More comments littered her page, way more than my measly four. There seemed to be nothing about Elle that wasn't being discussed. Her class schedule was posted, along with a list of her favorite school lunch entrees. Someone who called himself *mchottie* pointed out that Elle hadn't eaten broccoli since sixth grade, when it got stuck in her braces. Another boy disagreed. He'd witnessed her eating it with cheese sauce on a baked potato at Wendy's last year.

That led to a thread about her eating habits in general. Things went downhill when someone started a debate about whether Elle might be a secret scarf 'n' barfer. They took an even more disgusting turn when several boys volunteered to hold her ponytail the next time she puked, especially if they could perform this act of gallantry in the girls' locker room.

i don't know, one boy added. **she's really not that special. have u ever tried to make out w her? girl is totally made of ice.**

Adm*n had stepped in at that point, which was good. I guess. But why couldn't he have stopped things sooner? And why did these boys think it was okay to talk about girls like this in the first place?

I clicked on Elle's photo page next. It took forever to load, thanks to endless pictures of her: at parties, at last year's prom, in the center of an epic cheerleading pyramid collapse, adjusting her bra strap in front of school this very morning.

Wow. These guys were dedicated. Total creepers, but dedicated.

Elle needed to know about this, but I wasn't sure how to tell her. Except for surviving three years of French with Madame Bourg-Schmidt (who was also Señora Bourg-Schmidt, the Spanish teacher) together, we barely knew each other. But thanks to French club, I did have her email address. I opened my mail program and started typing.

> **Elle,**
> **This is going to sound strange, but I think you should look at this website. Log in using jasona and theab.**
> **Camy**

I included the website address, started to click send, then went back and added my last name, just in case she had no idea who I was. I waited, wondering if the seismic boom of her anger would shake my windows. Then I wondered how often she even looked at her email. I could be in for a long wait.

Nothing was lamer than checking email every five seconds, so I made my bed and stacked my new textbooks on the shelf next to the desk.

When my mail program chimed, the calculus book slipped from my fingers and thudded on the floor.

Her message contained two words:

> **K. Thanks.**

That was it? No seismic boom? No anger? No … nothing?

A thought crept into my mind. Maybe everyone else in school already knew about the wiki and I'd just walked into a world of humiliation.

I closed my email program, then shoved my feet against the desk. My chair careened backward into the wall and I'd hoped the jolt would knock some belated sense into me. All it did was give me a headache. Then I went downstairs, pretending I hadn't just committed the first social blunder of the school year.

Chapter Two

♡

I FOUND DAD in the kitchen, staring into our refrigerator. He did that sometimes, like he expected the food to parade out and prepare itself. Even so, he was a pretty decent cook, a pretty decent housekeeper, and all around a pretty decent dad. Of course, these days, he did a lot of the mom stuff too.

After the divorce, Mom moved to Iowa City to accept a teaching position at the university there. My summer visit with her had ended two weeks ago. When I got back to Minnesota, the sight of extra gray in Dad's hair had startled me. When had that happened? It had always been thick and nearly black. We shared that, the same dark, unruly hair and matching dark eyes.

"Hey, Cams," he said after I'd tapped on the fridge door. "What about fried egg sandwiches for dinner?"

One of the great things about living with Dad was all the dad-type food. In Iowa with my mom this summer, it'd been all vegan, all the time. If I snuck out to get a cheeseburger, I had to bring along one of those travel toothbrushes so Mom wouldn't smell my evil, carnivorous ways on my breath.

"So, how was the first day of school?" Dad asked, piling the butter and cheese slices on top of the egg carton.

"Okay," I said. Well, except for the whole girl wiki part of it, but it was probably best not to get into that.

"I got an email from your mom," he said, maybe a little too casually.

"Oh?" It wasn't completely weird that Mom would email Dad. They had me in common, after all. And they were pretending to have the friendliest divorce in the history of the world.

Dad unloaded the food onto the counter. "You know those writing samples you did over the summer?"

While I was in Iowa City, I took a teen writing course while Mom taught summer school. That way, she'd told me, I could experience "an authentic workshop environment" (group humiliation is fun!) and "real college student life" (with my mom three feet away!) while "exploring my issues about the divorce" (no comment!). I'd told Mom, more than once, that I had no issues about the divorce. To which she always said, "Nonsense."

Dad turned up the heat under the frying pan. "She showed the samples to one of her colleagues, who was impressed," he said, a hint of pride in his voice. "You might have a lock on getting into Iowa."

"Wow," I managed.

"I've never doubted it." He cracked one egg, then another into the pan. The whites sizzled and buttery steam floated in the air, making everything smell warm and rich. I pressed a hand against my stomach to keep it from growling and rolling over on itself. I'd applied to just two colleges: University of Iowa, where I could be near Mom, and the University of Minnesota, where I could be near Dad.

Sometimes I pondered what would happen if both schools accepted me and I had to choose between them. I missed my mom when I was with my dad. But I missed my dad when I was with my mom.

I didn't want to deal with all that, not now, so I set two places at the table, then opened the fridge.

"Orange juice or milk?" I asked.

"You decide."

My decision. Right. I hesitated long enough that Dad, on his way to the table with the frying pan, rolled his eyes at me. He doubled back, pulled the OJ from the fridge, and plunked it down on the table like a centerpiece. I sat across from him, sopping up egg yolk with the crust of my toast, pretending we could go on like this forever.

♡ ♡ ♡

After dinner, I loaded the dishwasher so Dad could watch the Twins game. Back in my room, I ignored my laptop for a good five minutes. It helped that I had a text from Rhino. It read:

Your boyfriend is about to take the mound if you want to come over for the rest of the game.

One time, just one time, I had mentioned that the Minnesota Twins relief pitcher was kind of cute, and Rhino had teased me about it ever since. The downside to having a guy as a best friend? Talking about other boys, cute boys, *any* boys, was off-limits. Rhino had been working this particular joke since May, and it was getting old. I deleted the text and switched to email.

All I had was a message from my mom, recapping what Dad had told me earlier. She signed off with:

Love you and see you soon. (Like on campus next fall!)

Mom had a way of making difficult problems all the more impossible. The second I closed her email, a new one popped up, this one from Elle. My hand froze on the mouse. For a moment, I just sat there. Then, I opened it.

Camy,

Sorry about earlier. I was dealing with ... a problem. I think it has something to do with what you sent me. Don't want to do this in email. Call me.

She listed her number. In the seconds before I picked up my phone, the obvious, and most embarrassing, scenario flashed through my mind. The cheer squad gathered round, hands clamped over their mouths, giggles stifled, my voice broadcast on speaker, saying all sorts of stupid things.

But that wasn't Elle's style. At least, not that I'd ever seen. I wouldn't put it past a few girls in her crowd to do something like that (I'm talking about *you*, Clarissa Delacroix) but Elle didn't usually rule through intimidation or mortification. I woke up my cell phone and dialed.

"Hey," Elle said. "Great. You called. This is going to sound dumb, but you know how some of us went on that student trip to Greece this summer?"

Oh, of course. Some of us went to Greece, some of us went to Iowa City. Therein lay the difference.

Elle took a breath. "Anyway, we were at the beach, following local custom, and apparently some asshat snapped a cell phone pic."

"Wait. Explain 'local custom.'"

"You might say we forgot our bikini tops."

No bikini tops + cell phone. The only answer to that equation was: Oh. My. God.

"Oh," was all I managed to get out.

"Anyway, I think it has to be Aiden, since he was the only guy from Olympia on the trip, but really? It could've been someone from Prairie Stone, or anybody. Now I think Jason has the photo. Click over to my Facebook page. It's all there."

I waited a beat, then another, wondering when Elle would figure out the obvious, and astoundingly humiliating, fact.

"Hang on," she said a moment later. "I'll friend you."

It took only five seconds, but it felt like five hours.

Sure, I had a page on Facebook and maybe thirty friends. Ten of those were family. And yeah, your dad reading your Facebook entries is So. Not. Fun. But Elle? I clicked through and joined her nearly six hundred friends.

Jason had posted five comments in a row on her wall, things like:

Can we see more of you?

And:

Wow, no tan lines.

"He didn't do anything helpful, like post the photo and tag you, did he?" I asked.

"Not that I can see. But if this gets out, there goes ... everything. I swear, if I lose homecoming court over this, he's dead. I'll make sure he doesn't play baseball in the spring, one way or another."

"Do you think he's sending the picture around?" I asked.

"Maybe, but I was wondering about the link you sent me."

"The wiki?"

"Could it be on there?"

"I didn't see anything like it on your photo page," I said, then rushed to add, "I hope you don't mind. I was trying to figure out what it was."

Elle laughed. "No worries. I'm doing the same thing. What is it, anyway?"

"Technically, it's a wiki. You know, like Wikipedia? It's supposed to be a place where a group can share knowledge."

"Talk about an over-share."

I logged in to the wiki and took another look around. If I wanted to hide something, where would I do it? Not somewhere obvious, like Hottest of the Hot.

CHARITY TAHMASEB AND DARCY VANCE

On the main page, I tried a link I hadn't before, one called Site Statistics. I'd figured it led to some dull readout on site use. I was both right and wrong. Below a table detailing time of visits, length of visits, and so on, I saw a few more links. I picked the one with the most boring label: Disclaimer.

Another login screen popped up.

"Uh-oh," I said.

"What? Did you find something?"

"I think so. It looks like there's a second layer of security."

"Huh?"

"I have to log in again. I'm hoping whoever set up the site gave Jason access to this page. Hang on."

I set the phone down to type in Jason's information. The screen dissolved, or seemed to. All I could see was a shaky image of bright sunlight, immaculate white sand, a blue, blue sea, various shades of suntanned skin ... and not a whole lot of bikini tops.

Not that you could tell, really. This wasn't the sort of photo that would destroy Elle's career as student council president—or her eventual run for the U.S. Congress. You probably couldn't tell it *was* her without prior warning. But still ...

"Hey," I said to Elle. "Found it." I directed her to the link and waited.

"Balls," she said, then fell quiet.

"It looks like Aiden posted it, from what I can see." Fewer comments littered this page. Someone controlled this site, maybe even removed messages when things got out of hand. Add in that second layer of security, and we definitely weren't dealing with an amateur.

"Can we delete it?" Elle asked.

"I think so, but the question is, do we want to? We're logged in as Jason. Someone might ask him why he pulled the photo."

Static buzzed on the connection. I drew a breath and waited for Elle to speak.

"I like the way you think," she said at last. "Even before all this, the guys in this school needed to be taken down a notch ... or twenty. Remember that prom deal Jason started last year?"

Remember? Kind of. I hadn't attended a dance, or paid too much attention to them, since a traumatic experience with Clarissa in the eighth grade. But rumors had gone around for weeks last spring. For fifty dollars (or an unspecified sexual act) you, too, could have an A-list jock as your prom date.

"I wasn't really involved," I told Elle.

"Yeah, well, you didn't miss anything." She paused. "The guys in our school are tools. But it's more than that. It's their whole attitude. They have some serious entitlement issues."

I couldn't disagree. After all, Jason now thought he had the right to sniff me whenever he pleased.

"I mean, honestly," Elle continued. "*The Hotties of Troy*? Is that supposed to be some play on Helen of Troy? They want Greek? I'll be more than happy to make their lives a freaking Greek tragedy."

I snorted at that.

"You want to help?" she asked.

"Do I *what*?"

"Want to help. I could use it."

A chill zipped down my spine and I sat up straighter. I could hear it in her voice: Elle had a plan. "What do you need?"

"A list of all the girls with a page on the site. And we need our target list too. Do you think you can find the names of every guy who's posted a comment?"

"It could take a while," I said. "Whoever set up the site was probably smart enough not to give Jason administrative rights."

"Yeah, clearly not an idiot. But can you do it?"

"I might miss one or two."

"I already have a good idea who the culprits are," Elle said. "I'd like to make sure, though."

"You know," I said, wondering how to approach this subject, "Gavin Madison will be on that list."

Elle and Gavin had been a couple since last year's prom. And no, it hadn't been a pay-to-date swap, but the real deal.

"Yeah," she said. "I know."

"He hasn't said anything bad." From what I'd seen so far, Gavin's posts were downright mild-mannered; polite, even.

"Here's the thing," Elle said. Her voice grew intense. "Every boy who's ever logged in to the wiki is guilty. There are no innocent bystanders here."

I nodded, not that Elle could see me.

"So, do you think you can do it?" she asked.

"Yes," I said, my voice catching.

"Will you?" she added.

She'd picked up on my hesitation. Really, it wasn't like I thought the wiki was okay. It was awful with a capital A. I could imagine Dad's reaction to my name on that site, or worse, my post-modern, ultra-feminist mom's. (Not that either of them needed to know about it.) But still, a girl like Elle Emerson could take on half the boys in our senior class and survive. For someone like me it was a much bigger risk. I could lose the tiny speck of popularity I'd managed to carve out for myself.

Of course, if I went against Elle, I'd lose that anyway.

"I'll do it," I told her at last, blowing out a breath afterward.

"Good. Thanks. And, hey, ask Pendergast for the tutoring room this Friday. Tell her we need the space for a homecoming project."

"Sure, easy."

Name-dropping Elle would get us the room and the privacy she wanted. Ms. P would be all, *"Oh, Elle is such a good influence on everyone. She'll draw you out of your shell."*

Barf.

"Oh, and Camy?"

"Yeah?"

"This is a secret. You can't tell anyone about this."

"Of course."

"I mean no one. You haven't, have you?"

"N-no."

"Not even Rhino?"

"No, not yet."

"Not ever. Got it? I don't want any boys knowing about this."

I almost said, "Rhino's not a boy," but I stopped myself in time. What I meant was, Rhino wasn't an Olympia High asswad or whatever word Elle was using for them.

"I haven't seen any comments on there that sound like him," I said.

"I don't care. There's something very wrong about this site and about these guys."

I laughed. "Come on, Elle, this is Rhino we're talking about."

Silence stretched between us, long and hollow. A muted cheer came from the television downstairs. When Elle didn't speak, I broke the silence with, "I think the Twins just hit a home run."

"And if I have my way, none of these guys will be making it to first base for a very long time."

"Including Gavin?" The question left my mouth before I could reel it back in.

Elle coughed. "Let's not go there. But, yeah, I'm willing to make a sacrifice or two to set things right. What is it the guys say? Take one for the team? How about you?"

We both knew I didn't have an A-list boyfriend to sacrifice. But the truth was, I understood what she was asking, and what it would mean. Rhino wasn't some guy I'd been going out with for a few months. We'd grown up together. We had a sixth sense about each other. We were the kind of friends who finished each other's sentences. Still, I saw Elle's point. I also saw, all wrapped up in the pretty package of helping, a threat.

"Okay," I said. "I won't tell Rhino."

♡ ♡ ♡

How do you know your day is going to be bizarre? When the queen of Olympia High sidles up to you … and sniffs. Twenty minutes before first bell the next morning, that was exactly what Elle Emerson did.

"Damn, girl," she said. "You do smell good." She lowered her voice an octave and, in a dead-on impression of Jason, added, "Like a chick should." Then she rolled her eyes. "Seriously, though, what do you use?"

I shrugged. "Burt's Bees, a little Suave, some organic stuff my mom bought me."

The downside to living with Dad: He didn't see the need for more than one kind of product, of any sort. Like plain ChapStick was going to cut it, even for me.

"So?" She nodded toward my binder.

I glanced up and down the hallway. Over Elle's shoulder, I caught sight of Gavin, star quarterback to Elle's head cheerleader, the other half of their perfect couple.

Elle tapped on the notebook, demanding my attention. "So?" she said again.

I sucked in a breath and banished Gavin from my mind. "We have a list, minus two."

By ten o'clock the previous night, I'd scoured all the pages of the wiki and had:

- A definitive list of the Hotties of Troy, every last girl, including myself, who had a page on the site.
- A list of perpetrators, minus the identities of **Admin** and **Adm*n**.
- A whole new perspective on a large number of my classmates.

I slipped Elle both lists. "I think," I told her, "that the admin IDs are two different guys, and I'm guessing that they might have regular IDs as well, but unless they slip up—"

"Don't worry. We rattle these guys enough, and I'm sure they'll slip up. In fact, I'm counting on it."

Down the hallway, Gavin was leaning against a locker. Jason was standing in front of him, hands swooping through the air, a mock windup and a pitch, last night's Twins game on instant replay. Neither boy looked all that rattle-able.

"You get the tutoring room for Friday?" Elle punched something into her phone, her attention half on me and half on the screen.

"Pendergast wants to know what we're doing, but yeah, we got the room."

She flicked a hand through her hair, brushing aside such mundane annoyances as teachers. "We might have bigger problems if everyone shows. It's going to be crowded, and—" She narrowed her eyes and took in the hallway and the students around us. "Pull out your calc book," she said in an undertone. "Pretend to be helping me."

I almost laughed out loud at that. "Blind leading the blind," I told her.

We huddled against my locker, book open, me with a pencil so I could pretend to walk her through a problem.

"That many girls in one place could look suspicious," she continued a moment later. "These guys aren't stupid."

Down the hallway, Jason was fading back to catch a phantom fly ball, complete with play-by-play ("*Back ... back ...*").

"Okay, *most* of these guys aren't stupid," Elle conceded. "Anyway, do you know how to project what's on the computer onto a screen?"

I nodded. "Easy."

"Can you do that in the tutoring room?" Her voice held an edge.

Again, I nodded.

She pulled out her phone and started tapping. "I'm sending you links to some of the juicier comments I found on the wiki. Some of these guys really have a way with words." She raised her eyebrows at me. "We might have to do the hard sell, and we have to be ready."

Not that I knew what the hard sell was, but a roomful of girls, plus a way to project the wiki up on a screen? Well, even I could figure that much out.

"Oh, *thanks*, Camy," Elle gushed, her words high-pitched and sudden. "You're a lifesaver." She slammed my math book shut and shoved it back at me. Then she whirled, facing a newcomer to our little group. "Hey, Aiden. What's up?"

My heart thudded against my chest. Between Elle and the distraction of Gavin down the hall, I hadn't heard or seen Aiden Tuttle approach. He frowned at Elle, the crease between his eyebrows deepening when his eyes landed on me.

"Student council," he said. "We need to meet before Friday, to hash out some stuff for homecoming, things like that."

They stood in front of my locker, trapping me there. I started to pull out the binder I needed for that day's block of classes, then decided it was more fun to eavesdrop.

"It's Tuesday," she said, her voice all honey and homicide. "And we're meeting tomorrow. Soon enough for you?"

"I'm talking about you and me, without the others."

"Oh, you mean vice president." Elle slipped the pencil from my hand and pointed at Aiden. "To president?" She pointed to herself.

In that moment, when the light left his eyes and his lips went thin, a thought struck me. He might be the mastermind behind the wiki. After all, Aiden Tuttle excelled at school: in the academic decathlon, in cross country, and at being a jerk. He was, in fact, the worst combination: a guy with all the brains of Einstein and all the charm of a Neanderthal.

I slid a glance toward Elle, but if she was thinking the same thing, it didn't register in her expression.

"I'll be in my office after school and before cheer practice," she said.

Everyone knew Elle's "office" was the third row of bleachers next to the football field on sunny days. When it rained, she commandeered the stairwell next to the lobby.

She tapped Aiden's shoulder with the eraser. "I'll be sure to pencil you in."

"You do that." He pushed his glasses up then, which might have been a reflex, except he used his middle finger.

Elle stared at him until he really had no other choice than to turn and leave. Aiden never glanced over his shoulder, but he walked like he knew we were watching him, steps slow, neck rigid.

"I swear, if I could," Elle said, her eyes still locked on Aiden. "I'd have surveillance on that kid, twenty-four seven."

"You don't suppose he's the one behind the—" I began.

"Yeah, I do."

I felt the air shift around me. Near the end of the hall, I caught sight of Rhino. He was slouching toward homeroom, gaze on nothing in particular, but I swore he saw me talking to Elle.

"How much do you know about hacking?" Elle asked.

"Not much. Just what I've picked up from my dad." I stole another look down the hall. "And Rhino. We could always—"

She arched a brow. "Do we really need to have the Rhino conversation again?"

I sighed. "I searched, but I still can't tell who set up the site. Maybe we should just tell someone," I suggested. "Pendergast, the principal?"

Elle whirled on me. "And why would we do that?"

"Because what they're doing is wrong?"

"Right. Agreed. But telling on them is the least effective thing we could do." Elle shook her head. "No one will really do anything about it. The boys will just get angry. They'll be even more obnoxious, and they won't learn a thing, either. I want to take them down myself, in a way they won't forget."

Even if she had to take the rest of us with her.

"You're not tired of it?" she added.

"Of what?"

Just because I happened to have four little comments on the wiki didn't mean I was a full-fledged member of the Hotties of Troy. I wanted to tell Elle: Welcome to my world. The place where you were just a means to an end, whether it be a better GPA, an easy A on a group project, or an object of ridicule. Even Rhino's baseball statistician mystique went only so far. He'd taken more than one tumble over someone's outstretched foot, resulting in a face plant on the cafeteria floor.

After a moment, Elle said, "It's just..." Her voice trailed off, and her gaze unfocused. "The way these guys treat girls. It's really disgusting."

"Yeah," I said. "I know."

"And?" she prompted.

"Okay."

"Great. We'll need a PowerPoint presentation by Friday, so ... I mean, could you *please* put a presentation together by the end of the week? I want to do some techno-whiz stuff, but you're better at that than I am."

I stifled a laugh. "A PowerPoint presentation?"

"Yeah." She grinned. "Trust me, it'll be great. I'll text you later."

Elle left then, gliding effortlessly into the pre-bell crowd, as if a red carpet was perpetually rolled out at her feet. No one ever stuck a foot into her path, but no one was beneath her notice either, from the loners to the stoners to the lowly freshmen; she had a smile or a nod for everyone. Except for today.

Today she walked right past Jason and Gavin without acknowledging either of them. Gavin stared after her, looking a little confused. He surveyed the hall as if that would help him pinpoint the source of Elle's distraction. His gaze fell on me, and my cheeks burned.

No matter how hard I tried, even the barest glance from him sent me back to eighth grade. It always reminded me that whatever I'd done back then, it had made him refuse to speak to me for three whole years. And now? Somehow I had his complete attention. Then Jason stepped in front of him, blocking my view.

I gathered the rest of my books and shut my locker. By the time I looked back, Gavin was gone.

Chapter Three

♡

FRIDAY AFTERNOON, after last block, I didn't bother to stop at my locker. Instead, I took the stairs two at a time, hoping to find the tutoring room still empty. The varsity football team had their first game in a couple of hours. They wouldn't be practicing today, but I didn't discriminate; I also liked to watch JV and the ninth grade reserves. Not to mention that I needed a few extra minutes to set everything up for Elle's big campaign.

The first thing I saw when I walked into the room was Clarissa Delacroix standing at the window—*my* window—using the reflection to guide some thick-looking gloss across her lips. I'd braced myself for this. Even so, my stomach tightened.

Back in eighth grade, for exactly five months, she'd been one of my two best friends. The thought, that she'd been neck and neck with Rhino, sparked a flash of heat across my face. Sometimes I could still feel the footprint Clarissa had left on my back during her climb up the social ladder. Sometimes I thought about getting a tattoo of one, just so I'd never forget.

She continued to admire herself, patting a stray golden tress into place and smoothing the straps of her top against her chest. I couldn't help noticing the color of her blouse: jade, the same rich shade as her eyes. I bit my tongue to keep from reminding her that black was really her color, the perfect match for her heart.

Sophie Vega and a few of her crew were slouched in chairs nearby. Sophie was a pretty girl, if you could find her underneath all that hair dye and glitter. The stuff was everywhere: on her eyelids, her cheekbones, her lips. Once upon a time a warehouse full of sparkles must have exploded in her vicinity and now they were permanently embedded.

Not that I'd say that to her face.

Or to the face of anyone who might repeat it to her.

The truth was, Sophie scared me. She had a reputation for being tough and in her skinny jeans and serious black boots, she definitely looked the part. I'd tutored her for a couple of weeks last spring. She'd been nice enough to me then. That still didn't mean I felt comfortable around her.

I slipped into the chair at the first computer. The night before, I'd saved everything I'd need on a thumb drive. I plugged that in, then reached over the monitor for the cable that would hook the computer into the overhead projector. My fingers strained, meeting nothing but air.

"Looking for something?" Sophie had switched chairs and was now straddling one directly across from me and my monitor. In one hand, she held the cable, in the other, the remote control that turned on the projector.

"Could I—" I began.

"Only if you tell me why we're really here."

More girls arrived, in twos and threes. The A-list girl jocks padded in, ponytails twitching. They were like caged tigers and just as dangerous. Lana Greene, their leader, raised her head as if she smelled blood in the air.

"We have volleyball practice," she said. "Coach Taylor will have chickens if we're not there. This better be good."

"Could I?" I said again to Sophie, trying to ignore the rumble of discontent in the room. "It takes forever to warm up."

She handed me the cable, but clutched the remote close to her chest. "Just tell me what buttons to push. I'm good at that."

I bet she was. "Try the one that says On," I suggested.

Sophie snorted. From above, the whirr of the overhead projector made us both glance up.

With her eyes still locked on the ceiling, she said, "You tutoring again this year?"

I laughed, but Sophie continued to stare upward, her profile sharp and fragile, like the edge of broken glass.

"Of course I'm going to tutor," I said, my words rushed, in case she took my laughter the wrong way. "I've been tutoring, like, forever."

She lowered her gaze, but kept her eyes forward.

"What classes?" I started to ask, but the door opened again. Elle crossed the threshold, and the room fell silent.

Sophie swung around in her chair and her shoulders tensed, just slightly. Elle crossed to the desk at the front of the room and pointed behind her.

"Chair. Now."

One of the cheerleaders sprang up (no, really, she sprang) and dragged a chair across the floor. She shoved the back against the door, then plopped into the seat. Meanwhile, Elle directed a few other cheerleaders to pull the shades while another looked like she was sweeping the room for covert listening devices.

Sophie sat up straighter. From the hallway came the clang of a locker shutting. Elle sat on the desk so the skirt of her cheerleader uniform fanned out around her. She crossed one leg over the other and planted her palms on the surface behind her.

"In case you haven't noticed, the guys in this school are tools," she announced. "And I don't know about the rest of you, but I'm sick of it."

A few girls shifted in their seats. Elle gave me the tiniest of nods, my cue to start the PowerPoint presentation. I clicked the mouse and the presentation lit up the screen just as one of the cheerleaders hit the lights. Elle, now standing to one side, fired up a laser pointer.

The first slide contained a list of sins committed by the boys in our class through the years. The list started with bra snapping in fifth grade and ended with the prom date scandal last spring.

"Any of this ring a bell?" she asked. "Make you the teeniest bit angry? Anyone? How many of you seriously considered paying for a date?"

In the dark, I sensed a few involuntary arm jerks. A few fierce whispers floated in the air, but no one raised a hand.

"And what did you think when these guys, who we've known since kindergarten, went over to Prairie Stone and found dates there? How many of you ended up alone at the dance?"

This time, a chill settled over the group. Prom hadn't really been on my radar, but I'd heard the stories of dresses bought, boutonnières ordered, and no-show dates.

"What's your point?" The question, sharp and angry, came from Clarissa. She'd been stood up too, and had only had a date for prom because Elle had arranged a last minute substitute, her own cousin, from Prairie Stone of all places.

"My point." Elle shook out her hair. "Is that the guys in this school keep their brains in their butts, and I think it's time we did something about it."

Somebody snorted. I suspected Sophie, but whoever it was captured the doubt swirling in the room.

"You don't think we can?" Elle faced the room, hands on hips. "I'm not saying it's going to be easy. But I have a couple of ideas. I got more than this fabulous tan in Greece this summer."

Here's the thing about Elle Emerson: She was the kind of girl who could say a thing like that and you still couldn't hate her. She pulled a slim paperback from her messenger bag and waved it for all of us to see. In the dim light, the picture on the cover blurred into something Medusa-like and a little frightening.

"My parents made me take a few enrichment sessions on the trip," she said, holding the book in front of her now. "Language lessons. The Classics. Those Greeks, they had some interesting ideas."

"Wait a minute," Sophie said. "You went halfway around the world … *for summer school*?" Her voice cracked with the shock of it all.

"A small price to pay," Elle said. "But I'm not paying because of some turd seed and his iPhone."

"Wait—" Clarissa's voice wavered, its usual strength and bitchiness masked by fear. "What happens in Greece stays in Greece, right?"

"I guess not." Elle tucked a lock of hair behind her ear as if to calm herself. "Photographic evidence exists."

"Are you sure?"

"Positive." Elle pointed to me. "Check this out."

I switched the view so the only thing on the screen was the *Hotties of Troy* login page.

"Camy," she added. "Will you do the honors?"

I logged in as Jason. We'd debated about this, about giving away one of the user IDs. But we figured if any of the girls read the on-screen comments closely enough, they could guess at this piece of information. Anyway, they still wouldn't have a password.

"That didn't stop *me*," I'd pointed out.

"A calculated risk. I want to prove to the girls that this site is real.

To do that, they have to see you log in." Elle had shrugged then, like the matter was settled. "Who knows? We might even get lucky and see a few live updates."

Now, in the tutoring room, the site's main page flashed onto the screen, and as if Elle had custom-ordered it, a message popped up in the chat box, something about scoring beer after tonight's football game.

"This," Elle said, her laser pointer skipping across the screen, "is a girl wiki."

"A girl who?" Sophie shifted in her chair. She hunched forward, like she was trying to get a better look.

"A girl wiki. It's like an online encyclopedia, only instead of articles, this one has a page of information for each girl in this room."

Elle crossed her arms over her chest. The light from the projector turned her blonde hair blue and cast shadows beneath her eyes. She looked truly tired of the guys at Olympia High. Murmurs rose around me.

"Wait a minute." Clarissa stood. She craned her neck toward me. "We're talking *every* girl in this room?"

"Yes," Elle said, the word clipped. "Every girl."

"Whoa, Camy. Way to go!" Sophie crowed, raising her hand. The room erupted in laughter as my fingers grazed Sophie's palm in what was probably the lamest high five ever. My whole face burned.

"And this"—Elle's voice sliced through the noise—"is our hit list."

My hands fumbled on the keyboard, but I managed to switch back to the PowerPoint presentation and the list of guys Elle and I had pulled together.

Sophie relaxed, crossing one ankle over the other on a chair in front of her. "Oh, mmmm," she purred. "I'd hit that."

A word rang out in the room, clear and cold. *"Slut."*

Elle shot a look into the darkness before nodding her head at Sophie. "Let me rephrase that. Think of this as our *anti*-hit list. Every boy here"—her laser pointer jumped over the names, highlighting each one—"has contributed to the wiki in some way. If he's on the list, he's a full-fledged member of the anal cranial society."

When some of the girls looked confused, she tried again. "They, uh, wear their sombreros on their gluteus maximi."

A clacking sound pulled our attention to the doorway, where cheerleader Mercedes Washington had popped up from her seat. The beads in her braids were still swinging and even the harsh light from the projector couldn't keep her deep brown skin from glowing.

"Oh," she said. "You mean they're buttheads?"

"Exactly," Elle said, and it was if the room got a little brighter from all the light bulbs popping on above the pom squad members' heads.

"Hello." Clarissa was still standing. "Gavin's on that list too." This time she didn't just sound mean; her voice was full-on cruel.

"You think I don't know that?" Elle tilted her chin, just slightly, in Clarissa's direction. They were the best of frenemies, and Elle knew a power play when she saw one.

Elle settled back on the desk, picked up the paperback and flipped through the pages like she was getting ready to tell us all a bedtime story.

"This is *Lysistrata*." She waved the book again. "It's a Greek play by Aristophanes about this ancient girl who gets tired of all the fighting between Athens and Sparta. To get the men to end the war, she gathers all the women together from both sides and convinces them to hold a strike."

"So they stop going to work?" a cheerleader in the back called out.

Elle's eyes narrowed against the glare of the projector. "No. It's more of a boycott."

One of the girls from the pom squad raised her hand. When Elle nodded at her, she began, "Like in history class? When they threw all that tea in the river?"

Elle sighed.

My tutoring genes kicked in before my social stupidity genes could click off. "Actually, they threw it into the *harbor*, and the Tea Party was a different kind of protest. But yes, the American colonists boycotted English goods, including tea. A boycott just means you refuse to buy or associate with … something."

At that moment I realized that every girl in the room was staring at me like I had a giant neon *dork* sign flashing on my forehead.

"Okay. Uh, thanks for the clarification, Camy." Elle said. She looked around the room, holding every girl's gaze for a second or two. Then she went in for the kill.

"Until the boys at our school make this right, we boycott … them."

The girl with the sketchy grasp of American history raised her hand again. "I still don't get it," she said. "We don't buy anything from the boys, so what is it we're supposed to stop doing?"

Elle pressed her lips together and I saw her mouth the words, *Oh, honey.* Out loud, she said, "We stop doing *it*. And not just that. There will be no kissing, no hugging, no handholding. No contact of any kind."

Silence. Then whispers. *That won't work. They'll find some other girls. They'll find some … skanks. Prairie Stone skanks.*

"But we can still hang out with the guys, right?" Clarissa began, her words pushed together in one long ramble. "I mean, if it's just—"

"This is stupid." The heels of Sophie's boots cracked against the floor one at a time. "It won't work. Some guys will always be assholes. It's the way the world works."

Elle surveyed Sophie before turning her sights on Clarissa. "So, you want to keep hanging out with these boys? Are you sure about that?"

"It's just a stupid website, and homecoming's only a few—"

"Would you like to see your page?" Elle asked.

"Would I ... what?"

"Like to see your page on the wiki," Elle repeated. "Would you like to read what these wonderful specimens of the male gender have to say about you?"

I held my breath. The previous night I'd made an awful (although Elle had called it wonderful) discovery. She'd wanted me to find more evidence of what she termed "asshattery," so she'd asked me to concentrate on Clarissa's page. Thanks to their on-again, off-again, who-knows-what-again relationship, our prime suspect, Aiden Tuttle, made a regular appearance there.

At the beginning of summer, things definitely had been on again between Clarissa and Aiden. With the page littered with endless comments to each of Aiden's posts, I had a hard time deciphering what exactly had happened. Then, as I minimized the comments, it became clear. During one of their dates, Aiden had posted live and continuous updates about his "progress" on the wiki. I stripped out the comments and sent the whole thing to Elle. Two minutes later, my cell phone rang.

"Oh, my gosh," Elle said, over and over again.

"I know," I responded, each time.

I had my own reasons for not liking Clarissa. She was one of those girls most people happily admitted they didn't like—as long as it was in quick whispers behind the locked doors of bathroom stalls. Because all Clarissa had to do was wrinkle her nose in your direction for your social status to plummet.

But no one, not even Clarissa, deserved Aiden's messages. Not even the mild one posted at 10:26 p.m.:

Dude, I'm in, up close and personal with victoria's secret.

And no one deserved the eighty-seven lurid messages in the comment thread beneath it, either. So when Elle asked Clarissa if she wanted to see her page on the wiki, I knew just how serious that question was.

"Yeah, sure." Clarissa tossed her head and added, "Bring it on."

Elle nodded to me. "Camy, why don't you show everyone what happened on June twelfth?"

Clarissa jerked her head toward me. I think, maybe, she knew what was coming. She stood there and took it anyway. For a moment, I felt sorry for her. For a moment, I almost liked her again.

Up on the screen, the new slide came into focus. Elle had told me to title it "The Date."

"Damn," someone whispered.

"That isn't—" Clarissa began, but something that sounded like a sob swallowed her words.

"True?" Elle suggested. "Would it matter either way?"

"What's the big deal?" Sophie said. "Guys were saying way worse things about me in sixth grade."

"Camy?" Elle said.

My second cue. Elle had reasoned right. We needed both Clarissa *and* Sophie on our side, or the whole plan would fail. A few girls squirmed in their seats and a few got up to comfort Clarissa. Everyone stopped when Sophie's wiki page flashed on the screen.

It wasn't pretty. While innuendo and speculation were present on most of the pages, the comments on Sophie's page read like a scoreboard of sexual favors. After the first couple of entries, I'd stopped reading, and believing, most of what was posted there. There simply weren't enough hours in the day to do that many things with that many boys.

If Sophie was bothered by what she read on the screen, she didn't show it. Not at first, anyway. She kicked up her feet again and rested them on the chair. A second later, her boots hit the floor. She leaned forward, then stood and clomped over to the screen as if she needed to see the words up close.

"What the ever-loving hell?" She traced the comments with a finger, lingering on the names of each guy, snorting and shaking her head. Then she turned toward the girls in the room.

"I'll go through your list and I'll be glad to tell you who I've done," she said. "I'll even tell you which one of your boyfriends I want to hook up with next. But I'm telling you this right now. I never touched The Ab. If it were up to me, I wouldn't even show up in his dreams."

"Oh, please." This from Clarissa, who'd recovered her voice.

Sophie spun on her. The girls sitting in front of Clarissa ducked. "You got something to say, Delacroix? Then come over here and—"

"Ladies." Elle held up her hands. "You're venting your anger at the wrong gender. We could keep going through examples, or…"

"Or what?" Sophie spat.

Clarissa's gaze traveled the room, each girl, one by one, falling under her scrutiny. "Or we could go through the list," she said.

Sophie glanced at her. Something passed between them, a brief moment of understanding, and Sophie nodded.

By four thirty, we'd read through dozens of comments. Some recounted tales of hanging boogers and various embarrassing wardrobe malfunctions that had occurred through the years. One thread covered leg shaving—or lack thereof—and came complete with Photoshopped images of girls' heads atop Sasquatch bodies. An entire page of comments listed who wore padded bras. Another suggested who *should* wear them. Quite a bit more time was focused on who would do what and when. Finally, there was an especially painful discussion of Lana Greene's allegedly hairy nipples.

No girl in the room was left unscathed. Not even me and my fantastic smell.

Sophie, back in her chair, leaned across the desk and whispered, "You've got to lend me your deodorant."

"So, what do we do?" The question came from Clarissa, who sounded like she'd had all her normal bitchiness knocked out of her.

I felt as shell-shocked as she sounded. We'd just gone through a lot of words about a lot of girls. In the aftermath, we now had this one thing in common. The wiki was some sort of secret guy tribunal, judging every girl's worth by her smile, eyes, hair, and assumed body measurements.

"I'm going to show you what we do," Elle said.

That was my third cue. I hopped up from the computer and let Elle sit. My heart fluttered uncontrollably. She logged in to Facebook, everything still projected on the screen for all to see.

"Good," she said. "He's online."

She opened a message session with Gavin, a single command that said:
Watch my profile.

Then she changed her status from *In a relationship with Gavin Madison* to *Single*.

"What are you doing?" one of the cheerleaders said. Actually, she shrieked, her voice rising with her next words. "We have a game tonight!"

"He's a big boy," Elle said, her voice impassive, almost bored. "He can deal."

A message from Gavin popped up on the screen.
Gavin: wtf?
Elle: You saw it.
Gavin: are we breaking up?
Elle: way to keep up. Are you on the honor roll?

I braced for a string of obscenities, but they never came. Gavin's icon just vanished. When Elle checked his status again, he was no longer online.

"Uh," said Clarissa. "That was a little harsh, don't you think?"

Elle closed Facebook and *The Hotties of Troy* reappeared.

"Should we see what happens to my page?" she asked. She clicked on her name. There on top was a new entry with just one word:

bitch

♡ ♡ ♡

High school football in Olympia is a big deal. The whole town (minus Rhino) comes out for every home game.

Maybe it was habit. Maybe I was superstitious. I don't know. But before each game, I walked row three of the track that surrounded the field. I can't remember ever not doing it. Tonight, I'd gone a quarter mile when Mercedes Washington dashed up to me. She was perky and petite, but came equipped with a powerhouse engine. The rows of braids on her head swayed and danced with her every move. She never stopped—cheerleading, gymnastics, and in the spring, tennis.

"Oh, my gosh, Camy." Mercedes clutched my arm. "I did it. I dumped Lukas right before he went into the locker room, and now I can't breathe." She waved her free hand in front of her face. I wanted to suggest that if she paused between sentences, the whole breathing thing might work itself out.

Before we left that afternoon's secret meeting, Elle had extracted a promise from each girl with a so-called significant other: All dumping would occur before first bell on Monday.

Oxygen deprivation aside, Mercedes didn't look too broken up about the breakup. Lukas had been another one to give play-by-plays of dates. He was also the second string quarterback for Olympia High. Something told me tonight's play-by-play would suck, on so many levels.

"So." Mercedes caught her breath. "Are you okay? Did you dump Rhino yet?"

Did I ... *what*? My mind churned for a few moments before I found the right combination of words.

"One," I said. "I'm not going out with Rhino. Two, he wasn't on the list." Yeah, like Rhino would ever be on that sort of list. I imagined his disgust if he heard about the wiki. The rant would almost be worth breaking my promise to Elle.

"Oh!" Her face lit up. "That's right. He totally wasn't on the list. Wow. An actual nice guy. I don't think I know one of those."

Nice? Rhino? Sure. Only if Machiavelli was nice. I tried to hide my smile, but Mercedes took my look as complete agreement.

"I'll be sure to tell him that," I said.

"Great. You know, I—" Her eyes darted sideways and I followed her gaze.

In the center of a group of cheerleaders, Elle was sending Mercedes her own eye message.

"Gotta go. My leader, she beckons." Mercedes did a little bow with a flourish and ran off.

I laughed. Who knew Mercedes Washington was so clever?

The air cooled. I felt it on my cheeks, that first cold bite of autumn. I untied the fleece hoodie from around my waist and slipped it on. Dew came next, the night heavy with it. I tipped my face toward the sky, closed my eyes, and felt the weight of it against my lashes.

I slipped through the people jostling for food and seats before the kick-off. Sometimes I played a game where I worked on guessing the stops and starts of those around me. When I was "in the zone," I could sneak through a crowd without ever bumping or brushing up against anyone.

I was so busy dodging others and searching for a spot in the stands that I only noticed Clarissa Delacroix when she planted herself in front of me. We stared at each other, her jade eyes flinty under the stadium lights. I had never understood her attitude whenever we landed within three feet of each other. If anyone should have issues, it should be me.

"So," she said to me now. "Can you get me in?"

"In where?" I asked, not knowing what she meant and feeling like a moron because of it.

"The wiki." Her voice dropped to a whisper. With the crowd swarming around us and the marching band clattering into the stands, I barely heard her. "*The Hotties of Troy*. I want to ... I want to see for myself."

No, I couldn't. I had suspected this might happen, and so had Elle. We weren't giving out Jason's password. That way, not only could we keep tabs on all the guys, but if a girl strayed with anyone on the anti-hit list, we'd be sure to know about it.

I didn't bother to explain all that. I simply said, "Talk to Elle."

"Are you taking orders from her now?" Clarissa spat the words. "That's not the Camy I knew."

The Camy *she* knew?

"You don't know me at all." I turned from her and immediately bumped into someone. I didn't care. I was out of the zone now. "But," I added under my breath, "I know you all too well."

Talking to Clarissa had soured my mood. I bought a Cherry Coke then spilled half of it on my feet, soaking my Chuck Taylors all the way through to my socks. After I got mustard on my jeans, I considered leaving early.

But I always stayed until the game clock ran out. Until three years ago, I'd been in the same youth football league with these boys. I hadn't been the first girl to play. I was probably the only one with a career-ending injury, though: a spectacularly blown-out knee. I got the same surgery the pros did and spent most of eighth grade on crutches.

And I never played football again.

Even if most of the players on the field were also on the anti-hit list, that didn't mean I could abandon those guys. So tonight I did what I always did at Trojan Warrior football games. I settled into the stands and watched the Olympia High School football team, and Gavin "Mad Dog" Madison in particular, play.

Gavin had been a star player since third grade but you couldn't tell that tonight. He overthrew; he underthrew. Coach Cutter called time-outs and took him to the side for pep talks. I was too far away to hear anything, but I could tell the vibe was less *Gee, son, what's wrong?* and more *What the hell is your problem?*

The only time Gavin resembled his old self was when he ran the ball up the middle, charging through the other team's linebackers. It was his signature move and the reason behind the nickname Mad Dog. He always pushed through without caring whether he got hurt.

Tonight, it looked like he *wanted* to get hurt.

At halftime, Coach pulled Gavin and put in Lukas, who threw even worse than Gavin had, proof that a forward pass could actually sulk. We lost with one of those spectacular, cringe-worthy scores that, years from now, fans would still talk about in hushed tones. Through it all, the cheerleaders kept up their relentless stunts and chants, but I'd never seen a more miserable group of peppy girls. They managed to depress the crowd even further.

After the game, I still sat huddled on the frigid aluminum bench, wriggling my numb toes. Once the crowd had cleared, I stepped down from the stands and headed for the field. I walked the fifty-yard line, placing one foot in front of the other in the center of the white line.

I was halfway across when I spotted someone else heading for the center of the field. My feet stopped moving. My heart did too. I stood there, in my sticky shoes, and waited for Gavin.

"I thought I was the only one who did this," he said when he caught up to me.

I shrugged and he fell into step beside me, his hands shoved deep into the pockets of his letter jacket. We walked in silence with only the rumble of the closing concession stand door and our quick breaths to keep us company.

"Thanks for not saying anything about the game," Gavin said at last.

"What game?" I asked, and he laughed.

When we reached the other side, he said, "Can I give you a ride home?"

Gavin had barely spoken to me since eighth grade and now he was offering to drive me home? As much as I would have liked to settle in beside him, in his car, or anywhere—Elle's spectacular dumping this afternoon, and the equally spectacular loss tonight, sent warning sirens firing through my brain.

Besides, I didn't need a ride. I wondered if I could speak without stuttering.

"I'm just going over to Rhino's," I said finally. "It isn't very far."

"Oh, yeah. Of course you are."

His words stung me, but I couldn't say why. "What's that supposed to mean?" I asked.

"Nothing." He scratched his head, then looked not at me, but past my shoulder. Maybe at the field and the fifty-yard line behind me. "It means nothing."

Gavin walked off, following the asphalt path to the parking lot. I stared after him. Halfway there, he stopped, turned around, and stared back. Although I couldn't see his expression, this time I knew he was looking straight at me.

♡ ♡ ♡

The light from Rhino's garage glowed yellow and warm. It cast strange shadows across my jeans, highlighting the mustard stain and my ruined Chuck Taylors. Rhino wouldn't care if I showed up looking like a mess. Chances were, he wouldn't notice my clothes at all. But he'd notice me. Even though he was leaning so close to the huge computer screen he could give it a kiss, he turned around and waved when I walked in.

"I love nights like this," he said. "Cold enough that there aren't any bugs, but I can still keep my door open."

Yes, Rhino lived in his family's garage, with his row of self-built computers lining one wall, and his bed—a single mattress on the floor—up in the loft. It may sound weird, like one of those "orphan beneath the stairway" kind of stories, but it was totally his choice. He'd begged his parents for months before they finally relented.

I'd helped him move, lugged all his books from his bedroom. We'd whitewashed the walls together, spread cement paint across the floor and found carpet squares to cover the oil stain the paint couldn't hide.

Now, when I came over, his mini-fridge was always stocked with Cherry Coke (my favorite). The garage felt like a second home, and Rhino like a brother.

"We lost," I told him now.

"Huh?" His eyes darted toward me, then back to the screen. "You lost something?"

"No," I said slowly. "The football game. We lost."

"So?"

There was no point in talking to Rhino about the sucky game, the breakup drama at school, or my strange encounter with Gavin on the fifty-yard line. Rhino wouldn't care, but I didn't have anyone else to share this stuff with. Sometimes I missed having a best *girl*friend.

"Elle dumped Gavin today," I said, "right before the game."

"Eh." To my surprise, Rhino swiveled in his chair, abandoned the screen, and rolled closer. "The world's a better place if they don't reproduce."

I opened my mouth to protest, then shut it.

"Besides." He rolled over to the mini-fridge. "It's not like they were really into each other or anything." He tossed me a Cherry Coke.

I set the drink on a side table and tried to understand what Rhino had just said. "And you know this … how?"

He rolled his eyes. "I'm stating something that should be obvious to anyone with an IQ above fifty."

"Oh," I said, groping at the knowledge that my IQ must be, at best, forty-nine.

"It was an image thing with them. You know, like a marriage of convenience. Not that they hate each other, but it was just easier that way." He shrugged. "They could accomplish all the social stuff without any relationship drama."

Well, we had drama now.

"Mercedes dumped Lukas too, right before the game."

A spark of curiosity lit his eyes. "Is there some sort of cheerleader conspiracy going on?"

I shrugged. Then I started to expand on the subject. "Actually," I said, but Elle's words pinged my conscience so hard that I stopped.

It wasn't like I told Rhino everything, anyway. For one thing, I'd never confessed my mixed-up feelings about Gavin. Rhino would tell me I was just being a dumb girl. That was something I didn't want to hear.

"Actually, what?" he prompted when I didn't say anything more. "You drinking that?" He pointed to the Coke, and I shook my head.

"I guess there was something that happened on Facebook, with Jason and some photo."

"The beach one? He didn't actually post it, did he?"

I blinked a few times, taking in this new bit of information. "Wait. You saw it?"

"Jason sent it out to the baseball team. At least he was smart enough not to include the coach. Too bad it was so blurry."

I crossed my arms over my chest and glared.

"Hey." Rhino held up his hands as if warding off an attack. "All I'm saying is, the composition of the shot was way off."

"I'm cold," I said.

The truth of it struck me as I spoke the words. I folded my arms against my chest and hunkered down on the couch. I couldn't pinpoint exactly when the feeling had come over me, but it was before I reached Rhino's. It was before the game, even.

"I can pull out the space heater," he said.

I shook my head. "I think I'll just go home."

Rhino stood, an unspoken offer to walk with me, but I waved at him to sit. "It's okay. I'll be fine."

"Cams." He marched over and placed both hands on my shoulders. "It's after dark, and we have no idea where The Ab is."

"I think I'm safe from him."

"Trust me, no one is. Now, come on."

So I waited while he buttoned something flannel over the Chicken Butt T-shirt I'd given him for Christmas and then I let Rhino walk me home. When I got there I said goodnight to Dad, climbed the stairs to my room, considered studying for Monday's calc quiz, then stared at the laptop on my desk instead.

Something kept me from lifting the screen and turning it on. I crawled into bed and opened my math book, but ended up gazing at the ceiling. The word that had appeared on Elle's page moments after she dumped Gavin played in my head.

bitch

It burned against my eyelids. At last, I couldn't stand it and got out of bed. I huddled in my robe and pushed the power button. I went straight to the wiki, and then Elle's page.

The message remained, only now it had one of the longest comment threads I'd seen on the site. I didn't bother to read any of those. One thing I'd learned about the Internet: For better or worse, it would still be there in the morning. But I needed to check something I'd been wondering about all evening: Who had posted the message?

It was Aiden, not Gavin. I released a breath I hadn't realized I'd been holding, and almost smiled.

Chapter Four

MY CELL PHONE woke me on Saturday morning. I fumbled for it on the nightstand and squinted at the clock. Six. Six a.m. I touched the answer icon, guessing it was Rhino.

"This better be good," I said.

"Of course." It wasn't Rhino, but Elle, on the other end.

I sat up. "What is it?"

"Phase two starts now." She sounded way too calm for someone who'd dumped her boyfriend just the day before. I remembered what Rhino had said about her and Gavin, and wondered at the truth of it.

"There's a boatload of comments on the wiki since last night. Most of them are about me."

"Did you call me this early so I could get a head start on congratulating you?" I asked.

"You're so funny," Elle said. "I was thinking about making a backup of the website, or at least the pages with the most action. Actually, I started to, but ... help?" The last word came out kind of pathetic.

"Yeah, I can help with that. There's probably an app that will do it automatically. I don't know how, but Rhino—"

"You've got a one-track mind about that boy."

"He's my best friend."

"Whatever. No Rhino. No guys, period, can know about this."

"Got it," I said.

"And the backup?" she asked.

"It shouldn't be too hard."

"By the way, have you been on Facebook this morning?"

"You woke me up," I said, trying not to clench my teeth.

"Sorry. I have to leave for a debate tourney in fifteen minutes. I wanted to make sure to catch you first. You might find a little surprise. That's all I'm saying."

And with that, Elle hung up.

I couldn't face the wiki, Facebook, or anything on the Internet without coffee. Really, I was pretty sure no one should log on to *any* form of social media without a good dose of caffeine.

I brewed a full pot so I could pour a giant mug and leave plenty for Dad. I tiptoed back upstairs, eased my door closed with a foot, and leaned against it.

"Okay, Internet," I said aloud. "Here I come."

I was trying to decide between starting a wiki backup versus Facebook when my email program pinged. And pinged again. *Loading 15 of 103 messages*, the status bar said. I almost spewed coffee all over the keyboard.

Finally, the last message arrived. I clicked through to find endless friend requests, and game requests, and things on Facebook that I didn't even know existed.

It took me five whole minutes to confirm all the friends Elle had sent my way. There were cheerleaders, pom squad girls, the dance team (minus Clarissa Delacroix, of course). Mercedes Washington had sent me a ton of virtual roses, kittens, balloons, and bouquets. She'd left a message sometime last night that said:

OMG! I didn't know you were on Facebook or I would've friended you before now.

Only with more words, creative spelling, and about a hundred extra exclamation points.

Girls I'd never even met, who went to other schools, wanted to be my new best friend. Someone named Chantal Simmons from Prairie Stone had even sent me a pair of virtual designer shoes. It was like Elle had waved her hand and cured me of my social leprosy.

It took me most of the next two days to figure out the art of multitasking, but by Sunday afternoon I could accept friend requests, make backups of the wiki, and do my homework all at the same time.

"Have you seen the sun at all this weekend?"

Dad's voice made me jump out of my chair. I'd been so focused, I hadn't heard a single creak on the stairs. For five awful seconds, I had that crazy tunnel vision. I couldn't tell what was on my laptop screen. Was it the wiki? Was some disgusting jock comment right there, where Dad could see?

"Easy, Cams," he said. "You okay?"

"You scared me."

He took a step back and held up his hands. "Just checking on you. You didn't go to Rhino's last night. You didn't come down for the Vikings game. You haven't gone for a walk or anything." He shrugged. "Dads worry about stuff like that."

He was right. I hadn't done anything I normally did on the weekends.

"They're really killing us with homework this year," I said. "And calculus—"

When he stepped closer and peeked at the laptop screen, I seriously thought I might hurl.

"I don't think the fine citizens of AcreRage are going to be able to help you with your math," he said.

Mercedes had sucked me into that one. I already had a henhouse full of chickens and three sheep to take care of. Who knew virtual farming could be so hard? At least *The Hotties of Troy* was minimized. I let out a breath and said a silent prayer of thanks to the patron saint of the Internet. (Saint Isidore of Seville.)

"I'll switch back to the math," I told Dad.

"Why don't we take a jog in a little bit?" He checked his watch.

I straightened my leg and flexed my knee. My fingers traced the scars through my jeans.

"Are you hurting?" He got that worried Dad look of his again.

"No, it's just a little stiff," I said. "A jog is just what I need."

A second after Dad had left, a message popped up from Rhino.

Rhino: Why do I have friend requests from cheerleaders?

I started to type "Elle, through me, I guess" but thought it might raise suspicions.

Camy: Opposites attract? They're trying to woo you to the dark side? I dunno.

Rhino: I've been invited to a virtual pillow fight. I have no idea how to respond to that.

Camy: You don't?

Rhino: It's like I stepped into the dream world of the average American teenage boy. Somewhere, there's a jock in wtf-mode cuz he just got an IM from Bill Gates.

Camy: That's *your* dream world?

Rhino: I'm not dignifying that with an answer.

Camy: I'm sure your fantasy life is very rich.

Rhino: Bite me.

Camy: Wanna help me with calc?

Rhino: See above response.

I sighed. Only Rhino could get crabby over a bunch of pretty girls pestering him for a pillow fight. Really, it wouldn't hurt Mr. Antisocial to interact once in a while. Maybe I'd tell Mercedes to send him an AcreRage request.

Half an hour later, the wiki backup was almost complete, but I still hadn't figured out the first calculus problem. My phone rang and Rhino's number popped up on the screen.

"Do I need to talk you back from the edge?" he asked.

"Not really."

"That's because you haven't been trying, have you?"

"I've been trying." *Just not very hard.*

"Sure you have." His words were still grumpy but his voice was soft and patient. "So," he said. "What do you need help with?"

I refreshed the wiki, then turned back to my math book. I was reading the problem to Rhino, so it took me a few seconds to notice the recently updated pages. The list hadn't changed much all weekend. Elle's page was always on top. It was filled with massive complaints, like this one:

She cost us the freaking game. What a bitch.

Just then a new comment appeared at the bottom of that thread. Adm*n wrote:

We played like sh*t. That's what cost us the game.

We? I thought. Was that admin with an asterisk guy someone from the football team? I opened my email and sent the link to Elle.

"Uh, Camy, you there?"

"Still here," I said. "I got a little—"

"Hey, Cams!" Dad called from downstairs. "You ready for that jog yet?"

"That's my dad," I said into the phone. "I promised him we'd go jogging. Just a sec."

I told Dad I needed fifteen more minutes with Rhino and math. When I sat back down, I found a message from Mercedes on the screen. I sighed. I didn't think I'd ever been so busy on a Sunday afternoon.

> **Mercedes: Whats up?**

I typed back:

> **Camy: homework**
> **Mercedes: O. Thats rite. UR a brian.**

A *brian*? Maybe that was cheerleader-speak for *loser we now tolerate*. Then it hit me. She meant *brain*.

> **Camy: Not really. I just study a lot.**
> **Mercedes: Wow. I should totally try that.**

Speaking of studying, I was ignoring Rhino, and he'd noticed. I didn't hear anything, so I said, "Hey." But he was ignoring me back. I refreshed the wiki again. The guys were busy on the main chat board:

> **lukasn: Mercedes just told me she's staying home to study. STUDY!? Girl hasn't cracked a book since 6th grade. I thought she was just playin with me before the game, but now I think I've really been dumped.**
> **mchottie: Lana's not taking my calls either. Guess I'll have to hit up "Old Reliable" if I want a little bow chicka wow wow tonight.**
> **rickman: Don't bother dude. I saw Sophie at the gas station. Asked her if she wanted to hang out. She said, "Sorry, but I'm already doing nothing tonight." wtf?**

I sat back and admired the genius that was Elle Emerson. She was right. It could work. No, it *was* working.

"Camy?" Dad called up the stairs again. "You ready?"

I tried to get Rhino's attention on the phone again. And failed. Calculus wasn't happening; not that afternoon, anyway. I might as well get some exercise.

"Let me change," I called downstairs.

Five minutes later, I plopped back down at my desk to pull on my shoes. I decided to refresh the wiki one more time. More comments had appeared in the chat box, including one from Aiden:

> **aident: Yeah, well Clarissa is taking a "me" day. Right. Like every day isn't a "me" day for her? Does anyone else think they planned this or something?**

Uh-oh. Aiden was way too smart. He'd been on the same trip with Clarissa and Elle this summer. Had he read *Lysistrata* too?

I held my finger over the mouse to click everything closed. That's when I saw it. My page. Recently updated. My heart fluttered so fast, it felt like I'd already gone for that jog.

"Camy?" Dad called.

"I'm coming!" I said, but I didn't move anything except my finger. I clicked the mouse and found two words.

> **Adm*n: She's different.**

That was all. It was weird knowing that someone was thinking about me. It was weird being a Hottie of Troy.

At the time, I didn't realize just how weird.

Chapter Five

MONDAY MORNING, I threw on some jeans, an old Avengers t-shirt, and a random pair of Chucks. I stopped by Rhino's on my way to school, hoping to get a little calculus help before the quiz. I was asking him about the Squeeze Principle when we walked into Olympia High.

His eyes narrowed, and I followed his gaze to the main lobby. Elle Emerson was standing there chatting with the chess club president, Dalton Reese. Or rather, Elle was chatting. Dalton was mostly fidgeting. He took off his glasses and put them back on so many times I thought he might break the frames.

"What the—?" Rhino said. Then he shook his head and marched forward. "Come on. He needs our help."

"She isn't really doing anything wrong," I pointed out.

"That's just it. She doesn't have to. Jeez, Camy. Look at him."

Now that we were closer, I could see that Dalton was sweating.

"He may be going into shock," Rhino said.

"So this is like a medical emergency?" I said.

"It's a humanitarian mission. Hurry."

I followed, because that's what I always did when Rhino charged.

"Oh, hey, Rhino," Dalton said when we got there. "Camy." He nodded at me.

His cheeks were already pink and getting pinker. He shook so much that he almost dropped the old-school *Star Wars* case that teetered on top of his books and held his prized collection of pens.

"How's the chess club doing this year?" Rhino asked.

"G-good." Dalton blinked a few times, as if his own voice had scared him. He looked at Elle, swallowed hard, then blinked again. "We've got two new freshmen and a junior who moved here from another state."

"Hello?" Elle planted an impatient hand on one hip. No one interrupted the queen of Olympia High.

Well, almost no one interrupted the queen. To Rhino, it was like she didn't exist.

"When are you guys meeting?" Rhino asked. "I'd like to check it out."

In the middle of sophomore year, Rhino had dropped every extracurricular activity except baseball. Somehow, that had earned him a weird celebrity status, at least with the geekier crowd. If Ben "Rhino" Reinhold attended a chess club meeting, Dalton would score some major points.

"That would be ... awesome." Dalton stared at Rhino, Elle completely forgotten.

Behind his serious nerd glasses was a boy-band cute face. So cute that in another dimension he might be some A-list hottie type. Then Elle touched his arm and the illusion shattered. It was just one finger, but that was enough to make Dalton jump. His *Star Wars* case slipped, and pens and pencils rained across the floor.

I helped Dalton chase after all his Sharpies and mechanical pencils, but by the time I grabbed the last highlighter, he had already given up and was trudging down the hall.

Rhino stepped in front of Elle then, a shield between her and Dalton. Why? I wondered. In case he decided to come back for another dose of mortification? The two of them stood there, face to face, even after Dalton had disappeared up the stairs. A few seconds of staring in silence went by, then Rhino turned his back on Elle.

"Cams," he said. "Did you figure out that calc problem yet?"

The one we'd spent zero seconds working on? Right. I rolled my eyes.

Elle tapped Rhino's shoulder, but he didn't respond.

"Ben?" she said.

That worked. Rhino spun around. He stepped far enough back that she couldn't reach him.

"It's Rhino," he said.

Elle made her hair do this swaying-to-one-side thing. She peeked up at him through her eyelashes after that—a look that probably turned ordinary boys into liquid.

"I like the name Ben better," she said.

"I don't."

I think I've said it before: Rhino is no ordinary boy.

Elle might be the queen of ultra-cool at Olympia High, but Rhino was the king of anti-cool. Really, if you combined the two of them in chem lab, you'd probably blow up the entire school. Here in the lobby, it was just awkward and kind of weird for everyone.

Okay, I lie. The truth is, it was only awkward and weird for me. Rhino and Elle seemed perfectly fine with the whole deal. He wouldn't break his death stare. She refused to stop smiling. It was almost as if they were enjoying the challenge. The three of us stood in suspended animation until the bell rang. Then I raced for my locker, leaving both of them behind.

♡ ♡ ♡

In homeroom, Mr. Moore held up a stack of papers. When the bell rang, he said, "Ladies and gentlemen, you are now entrusted with the first important decision of your senior experience. It will, in fact, set the tone for the entire year."

I should probably tell you that Mr. Moore teaches Drama. He directs all the school plays. He's an actor in the Olympia Community Theater Group too. So he never actually hands stuff out. Instead, he walks up and down the aisles and plunks things on desks with a flourish.

"It's a tremendous responsibility," he continued. Flourish, plunk, flourish, plunk. "You need to choose." Flourish, plunk. "But remember, choose wisely."

The name of every single girl in the senior class was on the paper. All of us, alphabetically. At the top of the page, the instructions stated: Circle ten.

Jason Abernathy raised his hand. "Mr. Moore?"

"Ah, Mr. Abernathy. Is there a problem?"

"Am I supposed to circle all the girls who are in love with me? 'Cause that's way more than ten."

"Why, Jason, I'm so glad to hear you can count that high," Mr. Moore said.

Ouch. But The Ab only grinned.

"For those of you who prefer not to read the full instructions, you are supposed to cast your vote for—" Mr. Moore stopped talking in the middle of his sentence. He walked around his desk and pulled up the screen that covered the white board. In big block letters it said:

Homecoming Queen Candidate Vote Today!

Every year, two weeks before the homecoming game, Olympia High kicked off activities that were far more important than a mere sporting event: the OHS Homecoming Court Competition, otherwise known as (drum roll, please) The Trojan Wars.

"Like I said," Mr. Moore added. "Choose wisely."

Over the years the rules of the competition had morphed into a complicated set of regulations that I'm pretty sure no one understood completely any more. Mostly, though, it worked like this: Each member of the senior class nominated ten girls. The five girls who got the most votes became the contestants for homecoming queen. But once those five were chosen, it was the entire town of Olympia that had the final vote. Each girl chosen was required to come up with at least one campaign container and place it (them) in a public location. Then everyone in town dropped their votes inside the canisters.

The thing was, those votes weren't ballots on flimsy slips of paper. No. In Olympia, Minnesota, we did our voting with cold, hard cash. Every penny counted as one vote, although crisp bills and checks were happily accepted too. One day soon, someone would probably figure out how to attach a debit card reader to the canisters.

The money raised in the contest was used for the annual senior trip at the end of the school year. Forget bake sales and car washes; the cash we collected during those two weeks made up eighty percent of our travel budget. That's why it was important to choose the right candidates. Critical, even. All we had to do was pick the perfect combination of girls. Then, when May finally arrived, we'd roll out in luxury motor coaches, the kind with air conditioning, bathrooms and TV/DVD combos, for a week-long, all-expenses-paid trip to Washington, D.C.

But if we picked the wrong set of girls? We'd be eating stale bologna sandwiches on a sweltering school bus before geo-caching at Bear Head Lake.

For a minute or more, most of us in homeroom just sat there. A few people bent their heads and started circling names. Everyone else glanced around. Guys studied girls. Girls studied other girls.

A creepy feeling crawled up the back of my neck. I ran my fingers over the skin there to wipe it away. I thought about who Rhino might circle. Then I gave that up and started selecting the girls I thought should represent Olympia High. You know the type—the ones no one really noticed.

I circled Tara Tanaka. She was Dalton's co-leader in the chess club and she could kick his ass at timed games. I marked Alicia Weingeld next, the president of the French and Spanish clubs. I couldn't leave off Prudence Laramie. She played first violin and was concertmaster for the school orchestra. Some people might call her a "big girl" but I'd never seen her hide her figure.

I'd circled nine girls with a minute to go. That creepy feeling returned. I looked up and found Jason Abernathy staring at me. I said a silent prayer of thanks to the seating chart gods that this year his desk was three rows away from mine. I *so* didn't need to be sniffed at the moment.

He gave me a quirky half smile. If I'd been the kind of girl to crush on The Ab, it might have made me melt across my desk. But I wasn't that kind of girl. I watched while he circled one last name on his list, one that was near the start of the alphabet. Then he slapped his desk and gave me a thumbs up.

I had no idea what that meant in Ab language.

I tapped my pen against the paper and tried to decide: To Elle or not to Elle? She'd end up as homecoming queen anyway. The whole school—no, the whole town—knew that, so it didn't matter if I voted for her or not. On the other hand, who else was there? I'd already picked all the girls who really deserved it.

No, I thought. There was one more. The bell rang and I pulled my pen from the Es of Emerson fame, closer to the bottom of the list. I circled one final name: Sophie Vega.

♡ ♡ ♡

By second block that day, news of the mass breakups had spread through the school. The boy boycott was going viral. Groups of scowling jocks prowled the halls between classes, searching for someone, anyone, to shove.

Clarissa Delacroix led the dance team down the hallway with their heads high, looking straight ahead. When Aiden Tuttle stepped into their path, they fanned out around him, like a stream around a rock. The move looked so choreographed it was like they'd practiced it for months.

My knee still ached from jogging with Dad so I took the steps to the tutoring room one at a time after school that day. I teetered a little on the third floor landing. My eyes were on my shoes, so I barely noticed the shadow at the top of the stairs. And I definitely didn't notice the person attached to it. When I looked up, I found Gavin Madison standing between the tutoring room door and me.

As usual, the sight of him took my breath away. There was something special about him and it didn't have anything to do with looks. Okay, it didn't have *much* to do with looks. I'm not sure, but I don't think I ever heard anyone call him cute. He had these amber-colored, tractor beam eyes, though. They could stare right through you. And his hands. I had them memorized. Even with my eyes shut, I could still see the way they held a football, or a pencil. The way they had once (only once) held my own hand.

Gavin blocked my way, and I was still too breathless to ask him to move. I looked from his eyes to his hands to his mouth. It was like there was no safe place to stare.

I could hear the sound of the football team warming up through the open door and windows behind him. The sound was hushed today. All I caught was an O, an M and an IA.

"Shouldn't you be at practice?" I regretted the words as soon as I'd said them. What if he'd been benched because of Friday's game?

"Coach gave me a pass."

I nodded, even though I wasn't sure what a pass had to do with the tutoring room or me. Gavin was still blocking my way, and it felt like I had to say something more.

"Do you miss it? Practice, I mean?"

He grinned. "I'm missing it right now."

I shook my head, hoping to shake the right words into it. "No, like, when you're not down there on the field. Do you miss it?"

"Do you?"

Part of me wanted to release the answer and let it come rushing out. *Yes. I miss it. Why do you think I come to every single football game?* But I didn't say that. I didn't say anything else, either. Things got so quiet that I thought I could hear the rattle of shoulder pads from the football field.

"You have a customer," Gavin said at last.

"What?"

He nodded toward the tutoring room. "I think someone needs help in there. Is it your first one of the season?"

Oh. Tutoring. Of course. "Yeah. I guess so."

Gavin stepped to the side and headed for the stairs. "I'll get out of your way, then."

He was halfway down the flight of stairs before I found the nerve to say, "Gavin?"

He stopped and turned. He rested his elbow on the railing and stared through me with those eyes again.

"C-can I," I stuttered. "I mean, did you need something?"

"It can wait." He took the stairs like he was running a speed drill. I listened to the echo of his footsteps until I couldn't hear them any more. I turned toward the tutoring room then, wondering who, or what, was waiting inside for me.

A boy was sitting at a desk near the back of the room, staring out the window. He had the round cheeks of a freshman and that white blond hair you see a lot of in Minnesota. I didn't know him.

"Can I help you?"

He jumped a lot like Jason had. Maybe it was a guy thing. Then he stared at me, all huge eyes like a rabbit.

"I'm the peer tutor," I said. "Do you need help?"

He let out a breath, then spoke so softly that I almost couldn't hear him. "My mom says I have to get tutoring or else."

"Or else what?"

"I can't play video games if I don't get at least a C in math."

At least he was motivated. And math? I didn't love it, but I could do it; most of it, anyway. I could probably get this kid to do it too.

"What are you working on?" I pulled up a chair across from him. "I'm Camy, by the way."

"Byron." He pulled his math book out of his bag and opened it to a page near the beginning.

"Ah, please excuse my dear Aunt Sally."

"Huh?" Byron said.

"You're working on order of operations. Parenthesis, exponents, multiplication and division, then addition and subtraction, right?"

He nodded at me but I could tell that he thought I was crazy.

"Please. Excuse. My Dear. Aunt Sally. It's just an easier way to remember it. Get it?"

"Cool."

He smiled and we both relaxed. For the next few minutes there was no Gavin, no wiki, no Hotties of Troy to worry about, no boy boycott, and no pervy Greek play either. Just me, a little math, and a slightly confused freshman. Right *now*, I thought. *This* was the official start of the school year.

Three minutes later, the door to the tutoring room burst open. Pom-pom fringe exploded everywhere. And the official start of the school year came crashing to a halt.

I wasn't sure how many girls were on the pom squad. When I looked at the amount of fringe being tossed around, I decided to go with the estimate of: a lot. They looked so much alike, too. All of them in ponytails, yoga shorts, and matching tops. They filled the room, sitting on the desks and tables.

"Oh, look!" one of the girls by the windows squealed. "You can see football practice from here!"

Great. Now I'd never get rid of them.

Their leader was a girl named Lexy. When she leaned in close and gave Byron a big smile, I thought the poor kid was going to faint. Seriously.

"What are you guys doing here?" I asked.

Lexy crossed the room and pulled her legs up on the windowsill. "Elle sent us," she said.

Of course she had.

"How long did she tell you to stay?"

"I forget." Lexy glanced out the window, and her eyes got all wide. "Ohmigosh, everyone, it's Gavin! Come see Gavin!"

All the girls rushed forward and smashed themselves against the glass. Really, it was like someone took a gigantic vacuum cleaner, attached it to the tutoring room windows, and turned the setting to *pom squad.*

No wonder Elle had sent them up here. Their usual hangout (the chain link fence around the football field) was within flirting range. Although I wasn't sure how long the barrier of glass would last. I couldn't tutor like this.

"Excuse me," I said to Byron, although I don't think he heard me. "I'll be back in a few minutes."

I took the stairs and walked outside as fast as my knee would let me. On the track that surrounded the football field, the cheerleaders were running through their routines. Mercedes waved at me, then she flipped herself over backward. I waved back and waited for Elle to come to her "office." When she did, I climbed the bleachers and plopped down on the row beneath her.

"Why is the entire pom squad in my tutoring room?" I asked.

Elle checked her phone and grumbled to herself. She tapped a response before she looked at me. "Yeah?"

"Pom squad. My tutoring room."

"If somebody isn't watching those girls, they'll hang off the fence and slobber all over the boys out here. That would *not* be good for our plan. Like it says in the Bible, their spirit is willing, but their flesh is weak." She shook her head. "Very, very weak. And really, their spirit isn't all that willing, either."

"I'm trying to tutor someone," I said.

Elle looked bored.

"He's a freshman. I'm not sure he'll survive."

She snorted. "I thought about locking them in the batting cages, but that's probably against the law."

I looked back at the school, my gaze drawn to the third floor and the tutoring room's long bank of windows. Pressed up against the panes were various faces. I couldn't tell who was who, not at this distance, but a slow, sinking feeling filled me. How many times had I stood in that very spot? How many hours had I spent staring out the window, gazing at Gavin?

I glanced from the window to the football field and back again. Had Gavin seen me there, watching him? Today's lunch rose up in my throat and my earlier conversation with Gavin rang in my head:

"When you're not practicing, not on the field. Do you miss it?"

"Do you?"

Maybe he already knew the answer to that.

I turned back to Elle. "The pom squad?"

She stared past me at the boys on the football field. "Get me something on Lexy," she said. "Something from the wiki that will prove to her that we're not just being 'big ole meany pants.'"

"She was in the meeting on Friday, wasn't she?"

Elle cast me a world-weary look. "I swear, some of these girls lack a grasp of the obvious."

"'To see what is in front of one's nose needs a constant struggle,'" I quoted.

"Churchill?"

"Orwell."

"Quote me something from The Ab, and we'll talk pom squad." Elle turned back to her phone. "Until then, they're all yours."

Dismissed, I trudged back up to the tutoring room, hoping the pom squad had decided to defy Elle and leave.

They hadn't. I found three of the girls sharing a table with Byron.

"Still need help with math?" Without waiting for an answer, I squeezed a chair between him and the girls. "You know what?" I said to them. "Next time, why don't you guys bring your assignments? That way you can get them done before you go home."

"You want us to do homework instead of watching football practice?" Lexy said from her spot on the windowsill.

She was right. What kind of suggestion was that? "You can still watch practice," I said.

The girl on my left clapped her hands together. "Isn't Gavin just the best?" she said, and her expression went all dreamy. If she were a cartoon character, little hearts would've shot from her eyes.

"Yeah," I said. We both looked toward the window. "He is."

Chapter Six

♡

ON TUESDAY, the wiki was wild with speculation about the girls' newfound reserve, and Byron brought three friends with him to the tutoring room. The boys shuffled in with the hoods of their hoodies pulled over their heads. They hadn't been there very long when one of them said, "I don't believe you, man."

"They *are* going to be here, right?" Byron whispered to me.

"I don't know." I shrugged. "I guess."

He looked like he might vomit. "I mean, yesterday really did happen, right? I didn't just dream it."

It'd been more of a nightmare, I thought, but all I said was, "Math?"

He huffed and shrugged.

"What about you guys?" I asked his friends.

"They suck at math worse than I do," Byron said.

Somehow, I convinced all four of them to stay. For ten minutes, I was pretty sure no boy was even thinking of the pom squad. I'd almost forgotten all about them when they burst through the door again. The only difference was that today they were carrying their book bags.

The pom-poms still went everywhere, but in between, there were notebooks, pencils, and calculators filling the tables too. I dug out the kitchen timer I used for practice tests and set it. That way I could send a fresh batch of girls to a study break at the windows every ten minutes.

When I started helping the boys with simple equations, even the pom squad girls listened in.

"Gosh, Camy," Lexy said. "You make it sound so simple." She was actually taking calculus like me this year, but I guess she liked the review.

"'If people do not believe that mathematics is simple, it is only because they do not realize how complicated life is,'" I said.

All of the girls and most of the boys looked at me like the *dork* sign on my forehead had just switched on again. Byron was the only one who smiled.

"That's … John von Neumann, isn't it?" he said.

"How do you know that?" I was shocked … and a little impressed.

"My mom," he said, and made a face. "She teaches math at Olympia Community College."

Okay, so that explained why she was making him get the C.

"I have this friend named Rhino. It's one of his favorite quotes, but math is actually my worst subject," I said.

"No way!" both Lexy and Byron said.

I grinned. "Way." But I don't think either of them believed it.

Change was definitely in the air. By Thursday, the guys on the wiki were openly questioning the silent treatment they were receiving in the halls, and my tutoring room had never been so busy. Byron brought more boys with him each day. That many boys in one spot attracted a few more girls. I still set the timer for ten minutes, but sometimes the pom squad ignored the beeps. They were too busy working on their projects.

Lexy lugged a big folder of clothing designs with her that day. I hadn't taken a Family and Consumer Sciences class since the required one two years ago. They taught fashion design at our school? Really?

I stood near the windows, stealing looks at the football field while watching Lexy sketch.

"Oh, Camy," she said. "Stay just like that, with your arm right there. You can be my model."

I was flattered. Plus, I had an awesome view of practice.

"I'm designing a 1920s flapper dress," Lexy explained. "They look best on girls with flat chests. You're perfect."

At least I still had football.

Later, I stood by the tutoring room door and just watched everyone work. It was almost as good as watching the guys on the field.

"What have you done here, Ladybug?" I turned to find Rhino leaning against the doorframe. "This is some kind of miracle."

I'd always loved the tutoring room with its bank of windows that let in the sunshine, even during the long Minnesota winters. But now it had become some kind of nerd heaven. Classical music was playing from somebody's iPhone and that math quote was taped to the wall above the white board. Lexy had brought it in the day before. She'd done it all up in fancy letters and glitter glue. It was beautiful, even if she'd given credit for the quote to Rhino instead of von Neumann.

Rhino pointed at the quote. "I know I'm good, but I don't remember ever being *that* good." He took another step into the room. "You've done something pretty amazing here," he said, and the corners of his eyes crinkled.

I shook my head. "Nah, it was Elle. She's the one who sent them." I pointed to a few girls from the pom squad. "I just gave them stuff to do."

"Do you see Elle here? Is she hiding in the storage closet or something? Elle dumps her problems on you and you make … I don't even know what to call this. It's like scholastic Shangri-La."

It felt good to hear Rhino praising me. I would've liked for it to go on forever. But, just then, Ms. Pendergast and Elle appeared behind him. Ms. P blinked, like finding actual students in the tutoring room was some kind of freak accident.

She turned to Elle. "Did you say there was a problem?"

Elle stared into the room. She looked a little shocked too, but she shook her head. "No, no problem. I just wanted you to see all the great work Camy's doing." She perked up and gave the teacher a giant smile.

Ms. Pendergast smiled back. "Oh, Elle. You're such a positive influence on everyone."

Barf.

A clomp, clomp, clomp on the stairs got everyone's attention. We turned all at once, and there was Sophie Vega. She barreled forward with her head down, all skinny jeans and scary boots. She was three feet from the tutoring room when she finally looked up and skidded to a stop.

"Holy sh—" she said.

Ms. Pendergast stiffened from the top of her head all the way down to her toes. She gave Sophie a look that was so cold, I had to blink to make sure actual icicles weren't forming on her eyelashes.

"I'll leave you to it, then, Camy." Ms. Pendergast headed for the stairs. She turned back and aimed another frosty look at Sophie. "You seem to have your hands full."

"Screw this," Sophie said. She bolted down the hall, away from the stairs and Ms. Pendergast.

"Wait!" I shouted. I ran after her, putting all my weight on my right leg.

Halfway down the hall, I felt a twinge zing through my knee. Then it gave out completely. I fell and smacked against the tile floor.

"What the—?" Sophie screeched to a stop. A second later, she was kneeling beside me. "Are you okay?"

"Yeah." I pulled myself up, then sat on the floor. My right knee was throbbing, but I was more embarrassed than anything. "It's just … I hurt it playing football."

"Playing what? You know, you're the weirdest girl I know."

From anyone else, that would've felt like an insult, but Sophie sounded sincere. I started to explain, but just then Rhino landed next to us.

"Jeez, Cams," he said.

"I'm fine," I told him. "Remember when I said I was going jogging with my dad? I forgot my knee support and I'm paying for it now."

"And you." Rhino ignored me and turned on Sophie.

Sophie raised her hands. "How was I supposed to know there was something wrong with her leg? I'm sorry, okay? I wasn't expecting the Pender-witch to be here. She still hates me because she couldn't flunk my ass last year." Sophie held out her hand to help me up. "Actually, she should hate *you*. You're the reason I managed to get a B."

"You got a B *plus*," I said. I remembered how happy Sophie had been when it happened. I'd been pretty happy about it too. It had taken two weeks of hard work (and swallowing back my fear of her) to get Sophie to write an extra-credit book report.

I limped back down the hall. When we got to the tutoring room, I turned to Sophie. "Come on in," I said.

Sophie stood on her toes to look past me into the room. Her gaze landed on the pom squad first, then Elle. "I-I don't think so," she said. "It's just not my thing."

"What's not your thing? Tutoring?"

"Them." When she clomped off down the stairs, her boots hit the floor so hard I thought they'd leave dents in the linoleum.

I sank back against the door, taking the weight off my leg. "Damn."

"You can't save everyone, Ladybug."

"What good is this?" I pointed to the tutoring room. "If it can't help people like her?"

Rhino raised an eyebrow. "She doesn't want your pity, you know."

"It isn't pity." I pressed my palms against my eyes until I saw stars. "The whole time I was working with her last year, I wanted to shake her. She's so smart. She could be anything she wanted. She just doesn't see it."

"If you did shake her, she'd probably beat you up."

"True."

Rhino laughed. "Speaking of people who could be anything they wanted, have you looked in a mirror lately?"

"Huh?"

"Think about it, Ladybug." Rhino headed for the stairs. "See you later?"

I nodded and he took off. I considered heading to the bathroom and its mirror right then. Instead, I stared at the glittery quote above the white board.

If people do not believe that mathematics is simple, it is only because they do not realize how complicated life is.

As much as I struggled with calculus, one thing was for sure. Math might hurt my head, but it had never hurt my heart.

♡ ♡ ♡

Friday morning, I followed Rhino up the bleachers, past rows of whispering girls and boys who looked like they wanted to kick puppies. The wiki had exploded with conjecture all week until they'd finally come to a consensus: Something was definitely up with the girls. When they found out what it was and who had started it, well, payback was going to be a "mutha."

I took slow steps since I still wasn't sure my knee would hold me. Why Rhino was insisting on a specific spot for the pep rally escaped me. It wasn't like he cared that our football team wouldn't play a home game for two weeks. He wouldn't care if they never played another game. Ever. But today, he didn't plop down in the lower section. Instead, he picked a seat near the top of the bleachers, right in front of Sophie Vega and her group of slackers and dregs.

"Ms. Vega," Rhino said, nodding at her.

Sophie rolled her eyes. "Mr. Rhinoceros."

Rhino turned to me. "Have you thought about how sexist this thing is?"

"What thing?"

"This." He spread his arms wide.

"Which way?" I asked. "I mean, the list is really pretty endless."

"For one, did we vote on any guys?"

I was the Tutor Girl, right? It wasn't like I was stupid. Plus, my mom was one of those "I am womyn, hear me rawr" kind of feminists. I knew what he meant, but I made a joke about it anyway.

"Poor Rhino. Why didn't you tell me you wanted to be homecoming queen?"

Sophie snorted and leaned forward. "You have such pretty eyes, too."

The band started up and the pom squad ran in holding their humongous pom-poms above their heads. They lined up to make an archway, which the cheerleaders burst through. Mercedes came through last with so many back handsprings that it made me dizzy.

"Girl's got some moves," Sophie said.

The cheerleaders held up a paper banner that said *Go, Trojans, Go!* Gavin Madison and the football team tore through that. For the next few minutes, there was a lot of running around. No one seemed to know where to sit or stand or what came next.

"Fascinating," Rhino said.

I poked him in the ribs. "Quiet. Elle's going to talk."

Elle stepped away from the rest of the cheerleading squad and took a cordless microphone from one of the techies. In half head cheerleader, half student council president mode, she stood in the center of the gym.

"Good morning, Olympia High Trojan Warriors!" she cried.

I think her voice could have filled the gym even without the microphone. With it, her words ricocheted off the high ceiling. She jogged to each set of bleachers and held the mic toward the stands, commanding us to show our school spirit. She kept that up, zigzagging from one side of the gym to the other until she deemed us sufficiently spirited. Back at center court, Elle stood, legs braced as if against a storm.

"Let's give our guys a big Trojan sendoff!"

On her command, the entire gym went wild. Well, almost. I glanced at Rhino, who was now feigning sleep, complete with fake snoring.

When the noise died down, Elle passed the mic to Aiden, since the presumptive homecoming queen couldn't exactly announce her own candidacy. He held something above his head.

"Inside this envelope are the names of the five most beautiful and accomplished senior girls at Olympia High School."

It was kind of hard to tell from where I was sitting, but I think even Elle rolled her eyes at that one. While Aiden walked around, waving the envelope like a flag, this year's royal escorts made their way to the center of the gym. Gavin and Lukas stepped forward from the group of football players. Jason stomped down the bleachers next. Kyle Monroe, the swim team captain, followed him.

Back at center court, Aiden tore open the envelope and pulled out a slip of paper. "Our first candidate needs no introduction. You know her from cheerleading, the girls' gymnastics team, and from the way she brought home the girls' state tennis championship last year. Give it up for the most flexible girl in school ... Mercedes Washington!"

Mercedes shot up three feet off the floor. She bounced when she landed, and both hands were clamped over her mouth. Her escort, Kyle, stepped forward and she dashed to meet him. He took her arm and led her to a spot in the middle of the gym.

When the applause slowed down, Aiden reached into the envelope again. He pretended to tug, as if the envelope wouldn't give up the next name.

"Lame," Rhino said.

"Aha!" Aiden finally pulled the slip of paper free. "The dance team and the drama club won't be the same when our next candidate moves on to college next year. Let's hear it for the girl most likely to hear the phrase 'and the Oscar goes to'—Clarissa Delacroix!"

Applause rocked the bleachers. The dance team leaped to their feet. Clarissa rose and picked her way down the stands, pausing briefly for quick hugs and congratulations. It was like she was already practicing for that Oscar walk. Lukas met her, but Aiden stared after them. Despite all the words on the wiki, despite the deep freeze she'd given him all week, his expression was almost wistful. After a second, he turned back to his envelope and slipped the third piece of paper free.

Rhino yawned. "How many more?"

"Our next candidate really shows what it means to be a Trojan warrior." Aiden glanced from the slip of paper to the crowd. "I think we can say that she's touched all of our lives one way or another. I know for sure," he continued, "the school couldn't run without her. Give it up for true Trojan royalty..."

"Elle Emerson," Rhino said a split second before Aiden did.

The school went wild. Even Rhino applauded. Okay, so he did it with long pauses between each clap. Still, he did it. It was impossible not to. This was Elle Emerson. And this was her school.

Aiden himself walked over to the cheerleading squad and linked arms with Elle. They glided back to the others. Elle managed to look both surprised and not surprised at the same time. I still don't know how she did that. Aiden left her standing in the middle, between the other two couples, waving at the crowd. It looked like she'd been crowned queen already.

Aiden pulled the fourth slip from the envelope. For a few long seconds, he stared at the name in front of him. He blinked a few times.

"I knew it," Rhino said. "He's finally run out of ridiculous things to say."

A thought came to me as I watched Aiden wipe beads of sweat off his forehead. This hadn't been rehearsed. Whatever was on that slip of paper was a Big Surprise. I turned to Rhino, but he was busy chewing a cuticle.

"Our next candidate." Aiden cleared his throat. "She's touched ... um, I mean, she's ... well, she definitely gives new meaning to the Trojan Warrior name." He glanced up at the ceiling like the words he was looking for might show up there. I guess they did because, after another awkward moment, he went on to say, "She's ... unique. Yeah. So let's, uh, let's hear it for ... Sophie Vega."

No one clapped at first, not even that polite kind of applause people use in those extra-special moments of humiliation. Sophie jerked forward, but she didn't stand. Her eyes grew wide.

Then one of her friends shouted, "Dude! You're in the homecoming court. Get! Out! There!" With both hands, she shoved Sophie in the back, forcing her to rise.

Sophie wobbled. She swayed forward, then back. I thought she might fall. Or faint. I even held up a hand to steady her. Then Jason Abernathy did something I'll never forget. He left his spot on the gym floor and crashed through the crowd, taking the bleacher steps two at a time. He landed next to us and the planks thundered under his weight. Without a word, he scooped Sophie into his arms.

"What the—" Sophie began.

A few people started clapping then. But when Jason carried Sophie down the bleachers, everyone went crazy. Okay, so everyone who wasn't really anyone went crazy—the misfits, the loners, the losers. But it wasn't just them. The geeks and the gamers, the skaters, and the kids who were usually invisible at school jumped to their feet. I stood along with them. Then I tugged Rhino by his shirt until he got up too.

Jason wouldn't put Sophie down until he was standing next to the other couples. She smacked his arm, but he just laughed. Her cheeks were bright red, and she scanned the crowd like a kitten in a cage, like she wanted to trust us, but didn't dare.

"Explain that," I said to Rhino when the cheers faded and we sat back down.

"Well, I do have a theory. But it's sexist ... and crude." He eyed me. "Incredibly crude."

"Spare me, then."

"Already planned on it."

"There is one more candidate," Aiden said. He felt around in the envelope, making a huge show of digging out that last slip of paper.

"What do you think?" Rhino said. "Another cheerleader? I mean, we have the queen bee, the athlete, the drama queen, the school sl—"

"Don't even say it," I growled.

"Well, how would you describe Sophie, then?"

"Misunderstood."

Rhino snorted. "The 'misunderstood.'" And he drew those little quotation marks in the air. "Who's left?"

"You," I told him. "I added your name as a write-in candidate."

Finally, Aiden drew the last name from the envelope. He stared again, a lot like he had after pulling out Sophie's name.

"Well." He gave the paper a shake and held it away from him. "No one can say the Olympia homecoming court isn't well-rounded. I'm pretty sure half of the senior class will graduate because of this next girl. Our fifth and final homecoming candidate has beauty *and* brains. So let's hear it for good grades and … Camy Cavanaugh!"

Rhino's jaw dropped open. "It *worked*," he said. "It actually worked."

"What worked?" I asked. Then I looked around for some other girl to stand up and head to the middle of the gym, some other Camy Cavanaugh. People started clapping. Kids started turning in my direction. It felt just like that time when I wasn't paying attention in class and the teacher called on me. I had no idea what I was supposed to do. This insane urge to apologize came over me. *I'm sorry!* I wanted to shout. *It isn't my fault. I'll do better next time.*

Rhino nudged me. "Go on," he said.

Gavin, the last royal escort—*my* escort—crossed the gym floor and stood at the bottom of the bleachers. He propped one foot on the lowest seat and held out his hand. It was a very Prince Charming kind of move.

I studied the amount of space between us. It was a long way to go on a knee that had refused to hold me up just the day before. It was a *really* long way to go with everybody in the school watching. Forget making it all the way down to the gym floor; I wasn't sure I'd even get to the next row. But there didn't seem to be any other option.

Come on, I told myself. *You can do this.* And I did.

Just as I stepped off the last row of bleachers and onto the gym floor, I felt my knee start to buckle. Gavin caught me by the elbow and held me up.

"You okay?" he whispered.

I inhaled, one long breath. "Sort of. I'm a little shocked, I guess."

He smiled. "I'm not."

I stood in the middle of the gym with Gavin's arm locked around mine. If you'd asked me ahead of time, I would have told you that things like pep rallies and queen contests were just silly rituals that grownups forced young people to do. If you asked my mom, she would have told you it was something a whole lot worse.

But when I looked up into the stands and thought about stuff like traditions, I wondered: Do we do these things because they really mean something? Not in the whole big picture of things but, like, in the here and now? Is it like holding a snowflake on the tip of your finger, and seeing its beauty before it melts away?

Maybe, I thought. And maybe, having that in the here and now was enough.

Chapter Seven

I N THE FINAL PART of the ceremony, each homecoming queen candidate received a single red rose, which we were required (more or
less) to tote with us for the rest of the day. Why, I couldn't say. In case
someone forgot we were candidates? In case we forgot?

I lost Rhino in the crowd leaving the gym and only saw him again
at lunch, leaning against my locker.

"I'll buy you an ice cream sandwich," he said the second he saw me.

Rhino knew all my weaknesses. I could walk away from cake and
chips, even chocolate, but wave a can of Cherry Coke or an ice cream
sandwich in front of me, and I lost all control.

"I'll trade you that ice cream sandwich if you tell me what you
meant at the pep rally," I said.

Rhino looked at me like he didn't know what I was asking. Of
course he knew. He just wanted me to say it out loud.

So I did. "When you said 'it worked,' what, exactly, did you mean?"

"In the caf." He crooked a finger at me and started slouching down
the hall. I didn't have any choice but to follow.

At the cafeteria doorway I skidded to a halt, wondering if everyone still had their rose or if I was the only one obeying the rule. Mercedes had the stem of hers threaded through the rings of a spiral notebook. Elle was wearing hers in her hair. Sophie's rose was peeking out from her cleavage. Clarissa was waving hers around like a wand, or maybe like a sword. Either way, a flower had never looked so much like a deadly weapon.

I just carried mine like a dork, but that didn't seem to matter to anyone.

Our table in the cafeteria was usually pretty quiet. Today it looked like Geek Central Station. All the honor roll kids, the math and science freaks, and the book nerds were there. But other people crowded the space too. Kids I'd tutored over the years. There were some from the arty clique, a few semi-slackers, even some of the girl jocks who needed to keep their grades up to compete. I hadn't realized there had been so many.

All of them had the same thing to say: "I voted for you, but I still can't believe it."

Seriously? Neither could I.

Dalton from the chess team managed to squeeze in next to me. He picked my rose up from the table and sniffed it. "It's real," he said. "But a silk one would last longer."

True. My rose was already drooping. I hoped it would last until I got home. I wanted to show it to Dad.

"You should tie a string to the stem and hang it upside down. That way it'll dry and keep its shape," Dalton said. When everyone at the table looked at him like he was some kind of alien, he added, "My mom. She likes horticulture."

"What kind of culture?" Sophie pressed herself between us. "Hey, Dalton, want to smell mine?" she said. "It's real, too."

And yes, the rose was still stuck between her breasts.

Dalton went redder than any of the roses we were carrying. He pushed back his chair, grabbed his books, and stumbled away.

Rhino scowled as Sophie slipped into Dalton's empty seat. "So. What's up with all this?" she said to me.

"All what?"

She picked up my rose and bopped me on the head with it. "You're the big brain. I was hoping you'd figured it out."

"You're smart, too," I said. If I could get her to believe that, she might out-brilliant Rhino one day.

Sophie went on as if she hadn't heard me. "I'm thinking maybe it was backlash from that thing Elle started."

I cast Rhino a quick look, trying to gauge if he was listening or not. We were edging close to wiki talk, but with his face down, he appeared more interested in the goulash than in anything Sophie and I were saying.

Still, I whispered when I said, "Elle's on the homecoming court too. How much payback is that?"

"Everyone else voted for her."

"I didn't," I said. "I voted for you."

"Shut up." She glanced away for a second. When she turned back she pointed at me with my rose. "The way I see things is: you and me, we get voted in because guys like The Ab and Aiden think it would be funny. How else do you explain the school brain and the school slut?"

Was that what she thought? That we were a joke? It wasn't too hard to believe about myself, but I hated that Sophie felt that way. I started to say something, but she shut me up with one of those sharp-as-broken-glass looks.

"Anyway, about that Lysis-what's-its thing," Sophie said under her breath. "Is it one of those plays where everybody dies at the end?"

"Actually, *Lysistrata* is a comedy."

"But who wins?" she asked. "The guys or the girls?"

"The women." I hadn't read the play before Elle brought it up, but I'd found a copy online and scrolled through it one night while making backup copies of the wiki.

Sophie tilted her head toward the center of the cafeteria, where Elle was sitting with the rest of the A-list girls. "You really think her plan will work?"

Rhino was staring right at me by then. I waited until he looked away and said, "It all depends on which side can go the longest without … you know."

Oh, mature, Camy. Try a real word next time. Heat prickled my cheeks.

Sophie leaned forward like what I was saying riveted her. "Without?" she said.

"Each other." I cleared my throat. "Near the end of the play, the men walk out on stage with huge—"

"Swords?" she suggested.

I don't know when he'd clued into the conversation, but Rhino laughed and said, "Yes, swords. That's it exactly."

That he'd read *Lysistrata* at some point didn't surprise me, but Sophie turned toward him.

"You've read this thing?" She waved a hand, immediately dismissing him. "What am I saying? You've read everything." She turned her attention to me. "No swords, then. No bloodshed? I was really kind of hoping someone dies."

"It's a comedy," I said again, if only to stall. "The men … actually … well … when they walk on stage they…" What was I? Twelve? Why couldn't I force a simple clinical term from my mouth? It wasn't a bad word, not really. "The men have great…"

Rhino came to my rescue. "Excitement."

It wasn't the E-word I was thinking of, but it would do, especially since a knowing look settled on Sophie's face. "No way! In some crusty old play? Boners?"

"Giant ones. You might be surprised how much sex there is in those crusty old plays," Rhino said.

"Wait." Sophie held up her hands, stopping us both. "I have to struggle through *The Grapes of Wrath* while all the smart kids get to read porn? That is so freaking unfair."

Just then, Rhino stood and slouched over to the vending machines. When he returned, he was holding two ice cream sandwiches. He held one in front of me, and the other in front of Sophie.

"Who wants one?" he said.

Both of us reached and grabbed air at the same time. Rhino held the sandwiches just out of our reach. I looked up at him and he stared back for half a second.

"I win," he said flatly. Then he grinned, dropped the sandwiches into our hands, and turned toward the cafeteria doors.

♡ ♡ ♡

I got a message during last block. All it said was: *Report to the office after school.*

No explanation. Even though I knew I hadn't done anything wrong, my heart pounded harder with each step I took toward the school's administrative offices.

When Elle and Mercedes streamed in alongside me, my heart rate, oddly enough, didn't slow. We stood in front of the reception desk. Clarissa strolled in next, looking unconcerned. Only Sophie, who skidded in last, looked as flustered as I felt.

"Girls," Ms. Pendergast greeted us. The look on her face made it clear that this was the last place she wanted to be on a Friday afternoon. I was pretty sure that went double for the rest of us. She herded us into a tiny conference room. There weren't enough chairs, so I ended up perched on the radiator.

"I'm sure you're all aware of the guidelines for homecoming court," she said.

Well, I wasn't. Judging by the look on Sophie's face, she wasn't either.

Ms. P pulled a stack of papers from her tote bag. "Even so, take one of these. It details the code of conduct, the dress expectations, and the rules for campaigning. This will be your lifeline for the next two weeks."

She handed the stack to Elle, who passed them on. A few sets were still left by the time they got to my spot on the radiator. I waved the stack at Pendergast. When that didn't work, I leaned forward and slipped them onto the table. Why did I always pick the spot where leftover handouts came to die?

"As for the dresses," Ms. P was saying, "you're responsible for buying those and the shoes. The school will provide the gloves, tiaras, and fur stoles."

I hoped those hideous fur things were as fake as they looked from a distance. In Minnesota, late September could be almost any temperature. Last year it had been a summery seventy-five degrees. But the year before that, it had snowed all through the homecoming parade and game. The girls wore their winter coats *and* the fur stoles, and they still had to huddle next to their escorts the whole time just to keep from freezing to death. I didn't care how cold it got, I was not spending an entire evening with a dead animal slung across my shoulders.

I was still considering the horror of it when Ms. Pendergast spoke again. "This year, we're going to shake things up a bit. Instead of the usual white dresses, everyone thought it would be a nice change to go with Trojan blue."

Clarissa's head jerked up. Elle's eyes went wide.

"Actually, any shade of dark blue will work fine. Tillie's Bridal and Formalwear has several, ahem, age-appropriate dresses set aside for you girls."

I saw it then. The half-panicked, half-ticked-off look that passed between Elle and Clarissa. Had they bought their dresses already?

I pressed my fingers over my lips to keep my mouth from falling open. Who did that? How did anyone develop the kind of massive self-confidence that told them they were a sure thing? Was it something hardcoded in your DNA, a gene that determined whether you occupied prime real estate in the cafeteria, or whether you ended up wedged onto a radiator with the leftover handouts that not even the teachers wanted?

Ms. Pendergast went over the rest of the rules. "For the next two weeks, until one of you is crowned queen, all eyes will be on you," she said. There would be no keggers, no smoking, no inappropriate behavior. We were to "conduct ourselves with a modicum of decorum" at all times, whatever that meant.

Next she skimmed through what we could, and couldn't, do to campaign. Finally, she went through the schedule of events, times for the photo shoot, the rehearsal, the parade, the coronation, the game, the dance.

"Anyway," Ms. P said, "it's all there on your information sheets." And she shooed us out of the conference room and into the hall.

As soon as we were out of sight of the office, Clarissa threw herself against a locker. "Well, isn't that just shit on a stick?" she said.

"You might as well chill. There's nothing we can do about it," Elle said.

"But blue? It's alllll-ways been white." Clarissa pulled out her phone and checked the screen. "Wait. I know. I'll wear the blue one for the ceremony and I'll change into the white one for the dance."

Sophie rolled her eyes.

"When are you guys going shopping?" Mercedes asked, then her eyes got all bright. "No. Wait. Together. We should totally all go together."

Sophie took a step away from us. Clarissa and Elle didn't look too thrilled about it either.

And me? Shopping with Clarissa Delacroix? No, thank you. I'd tried it before and had no desire to repeat that particular form of torture.

"Well?" Mercedes said. Her gaze flitted back and forth amongst the four of us.

Sophie shook her head. "I'm outta here." She looked at Mercedes, then added, "Gotta work."

"Oh." Some of the excitement left Mercedes' face. "Maybe the rest of us could go?"

"We'll have to invite Rhino too." Clarissa wrinkled her nose. "You know, since Camy can't make any kind of decision on her own."

Camy can't ... *what*?

She stepped in front of me and put a hand on each of my shoulders. Her voice was full of fake concern when she said, "It's okay, Camy. Elle will be there with us. She'll order you ar—I mean, she'll tell you what to do."

"Seriously, you guys, that's a great idea!" Mercedes clapped her hands. "We should totally ask Rhino. He can give us a guy's opinion. It'll be great!"

My cheeks burned and I felt the sting of tears in my eyes. Without a word, I turned away from them. I was five feet down the hallway when Mercedes called out, "Did I say something wrong?"

Elle was next. "Hey, Camy. Come on. It'll be fun."

I turned back to them. Mercedes looked confused. Clarissa looked triumphant. And Elle? Like everything else in her wardrobe, she wore pity well.

"I'll go some other time," I said. "Besides, I need to..." What? I searched my brain for an excuse. What did I have to do, besides tell Dad I was now a candidate for homecoming queen? *Dad*. That could work.

"It's my night to cook dinner," I said, and headed down the hallway as fast as my knee would allow.

I tried to load up my book bag when I got to my locker, but the day had left me rattled. I couldn't remember what assignments were due, so I tossed in everything. Better safe than a sinking GPA.

I closed the locker door gently. I didn't have enough energy left to slam it. I thought about trudging back to the office to ask Ms. Pendergast if I had really, truly made the homecoming court, or if it was all some big mistake. But that would mean walking past Clarissa again, and I didn't have the energy for that either. Instead, I rested my forehead against the locker door and let the metal cool my skin.

"So. Did Cinderella and the evil stepsisters go shopping?"

I jerked back. My book bag slipped off my shoulder and crashed to the floor. Sophie was standing at the end of the hallway. Had she been there the whole time?

When she reached me, she lifted my bag off the floor. "Holy shit." She let the bag fall again. "Are you taking everything home?"

"Pretty much."

"Hey, you wouldn't want to ... forget it."

"What?" I said.

"To … shop." She said the word like it burned her lips. "For dresses. I work again tomorrow and you're probably, uh, studying or something." She rolled her eyes. "But Tillie's opens at noon on Sundays."

"How do you even know that?" I asked. I was trying to connect this dress-shop-hour-knowing alien with the Sophie Vega I thought I knew.

"Shut up," she said. "I just do."

I shrugged then. I didn't want to scare her off, but I hadn't been shopping with another girl in a long time. I wasn't really sure how I felt about it.

"Come on. Who else can you trust to make sure you don't end up looking like a second grader?" she added.

Like I said.

She leaned against the lockers and checked me out. "You know, in the right dress, you might be able to flush out the guy who thinks you smell fantastic."

"But he'll be on the anti-hit list," I countered.

Sophie raised an eyebrow. "For the right boy? You could break a few rules."

I picked up my bag. Would I make an exception for the right guy? I let myself think about it for a second. About dancing to a slow song in the dark gym, about Gavin pulling me closer to him …

And then I imagined what Elle would do to me when she found out.

"Nah," I said. "Not worth it." Besides, the Gavin thing? Never gonna happen. I mean, he'd barely spoken to me in three years.

Sophie and I started toward the side door. We fell into step, like we did this every day after school.

"Hey, want a ride home?" she asked.

No nearly left my mouth, but I swallowed it back.

Most days I still walked to school. We only had one car, which Dad needed for work, and I still hadn't taken the test to convert my learner's permit to a permanent license. Rhino said I was afraid of taking one of the final steps to independence. I said I'd just been busy and walking was good for your health. Plus, I was conserving the Earth's resources.

But the sad thing? I wasn't independent or resourceful at all. Not when it came to homecoming, anyway. I had planned on consulting Rhino about the dress—right up until the second Clarissa had predicted I would. Now I felt lost. I could use someone to help me figure it all out.

So when Sophie asked about the ride a second time I said, "Sure. This homecoming stuff." I waved the rose, indicating the school. "It's exhausting."

She drove the long way around, avoiding Rhino's street, and I was too embarrassed to thank her for it. Her car grumbled, like it resented the extra passenger, but it was more than clean. It was impeccable. The dashboard gleamed; the seats were worn, but spotless. She let it idle in the driveway while I got out.

"Sunday. Tillie's. Noon," she said before I could close the door. "If you're late, I'll kick your ass."

I laughed, but really? I was pretty sure she *would* kick my butt if I didn't show up. Still, after she'd pulled out of the drive and disappeared around the corner, I felt … alone. I thought about how I might tell Dad the news. Then I thought about telling my mom, the feminist, and I cringed.

I thought about all the things I wanted to talk to Rhino about too. But with Elle's not-so-hidden threats and Clarissa's definitely-not-hidden shaming hanging over me, I wondered if I ever would.

Even though my excuse to get out of shopping had felt like a lie, it really wasn't. I usually cooked dinner a couple of nights a week.

Sometimes all I did was order pizza online, but other nights, I'd throw something together. Breakfast for dinner was Dad's favorite. When he arrived home, I was cracking eggs for a cheese omelet while slices of Spam (yes, *Spam*) sizzled in the frying pan.

His laptop case landed with a thud on one of the kitchen chairs. He looked at the crushed eggshells and the empty can of Spam. "Thank you," he said. He shut his eyes and sighed.

"Bad day?" I pushed the Spam to one side and added the eggs to the pan.

"Something like that," he said. He crossed the kitchen and planted a kiss on my forehead. "And how was your day? Any tests?"

"Just a quiz in French," I said.

Dad's gaze stopped on the rose in a vase on the table. I'd trimmed the end and added an aspirin to revive it. The flower did look perkier. If I leaned in close enough, I could still smell it a little, too, even through the thick odor of processed meat.

"And since you already have enough As, they gave you a flower instead?"

All of a sudden, my mouth felt weird, like there were words I couldn't say. I was pretty sure those words were *homecoming* and *court* and *queen* and *contest*. This was stupid, I thought. What was I afraid of?

"And I'm in the homecoming court," I blurted.

He blinked a couple of times.

"It's why I have the flower," I said.

"You're going to homecoming?" he asked. "With Rhino?"

"No, Dad." And I swear, he looked relieved. "I was voted into the homecoming court. You know, the five girls who—"

Dad let out a whoop. He picked me up and spun me around. "So, my little girl is going to be princess?"

My face burned so hot I could've cooked the eggs on my cheeks. "It's *queen*, Dad, not princess, and there are four other girls who are a lot more …" *Popular.* I couldn't get the word to leave my mouth. "I'm not going to be queen."

"But you're a candidate, so statistically, it's possible."

Statistically? Yes. In real life? Come. On.

But Dad looked so happy. I didn't want to ruin his mood. I went back to the eggs, which were starting to stick to the pan.

Dad leaned against the counter next to the stove. "You know, when you were really little, I used to walk you down to Rhino's to watch the parade. Remember that, Camy? You loved the girls in their long dresses and those little—" He made a motion like he was placing a crown on his head.

"Tiaras."

"Oh, and your mom." He shook his head and smiled. "I got in trouble for doing that every single year. You know how she feels about all that stuff. She'd go on and on about gender expectations and exploitation and … she'll probably blame me for this too." But he didn't sound all that upset about it. In fact, he almost looked like he couldn't wait to tell her.

I concentrated on getting the eggs and Spam onto plates. I didn't want to think about Mom's reaction. Maybe Dad really *should* be the one to tell her. If I couldn't make that happen, email might be the best plan. Or maybe I'd pull a Mercedes and message her on Facebook. I could say something like:

Oh hai, mom. In h-coming ct. Kthnxbye.

"We'll worry about your mom later," Dad said, as if he'd just read my mind. "I'll help you get your campaign canisters together. We should use that picture of you in that paper crown when you were … what? Six? Seven?" He looked like he was far away for a minute, like he was watching some old movie in his head. I had to reel him back in.

"Dad. Don't go all crazy about this thing. Besides, I'm pretty sure the rules say parents aren't allowed to help."

Actually, I was *exactly* sure of that. I'd already read through Ms. Pendergast's handout three times. I was also sure that most candidates didn't follow any of those rules, but I wasn't telling my dad that. Besides, maybe I was wrong. Maybe last year's winner really had paid for that enormous campaign ad in the *Olympia Times* all by herself. And maybe that anonymous thousand-dollar "vote" came from a random citizen of our town too.

It could happen.

I guess.

We weren't poor, but we didn't have that kind of money to throw around, either. No way was I winning this thing. No way would I even come close. The most I could hope for was that Dad's friends at work, and my grandparents, and maybe some of my neighbors would put a few pennies in a can so I wouldn't be flat-out disgraced.

Now I was the one who was far away. I was trapped so deep inside my own lack of expectations that I didn't hear Dad when he started to say, "… must be a ceremony or something? I'll take off work and—"

"You would?" I asked, but I already knew the answer. Of course he would take off work to see me in the coronation ceremony. He'd gone to every single football game I'd ever played in. But once my time in sports was over? Well, getting your name on the honor roll isn't exactly a spectator event.

But the homecoming ceremony—he could go to that. I could see it: Dad, with his geeked-out digital camera, taking about a thousand pictures. It was pretty mortifying to imagine. It was also kind of cool.

"Are you kidding?" he said. "I wouldn't miss it."

I handed him a plate of eggs and Spam. Then I focused on buttering the toast so I wouldn't have to look at him. "Just don't be disappointed when they don't crown me queen, okay?"

He put his plate on the table, then took the butter knife from my hand and set it on the counter. "Right here," he said. He held my hand in his and tapped the spot over his heart. "In there you've always been queen."

Chapter Eight

♡

I WOKE UP EARLY the next morning with one thought in my head—I *still* hadn't found out what Rhino had meant at the pep rally. *What had worked?* We'd hung out online for a while last night. We'd texted back and forth too. But every time I'd brought up the pep rally, Rhino had changed the subject.

I turned on my computer and checked to see if he was connected, but his avatar was grayed out. I decided to give him a little more time while I started the wiki backup. Catching him while he was groggy might be a good idea, but waking a sleeping rhinoceros? Not so much. Instead, I logged in to *The Hotties of Troy*.

And nearly threw up.

My name was all over the wiki, in the recently-updated list, the recently-accessed list, and even the Hottest of the Hot list. I pushed back from the desk and headed downstairs. I needed coffee.

We were out of cream but I drank a full cup in the kitchen anyway. Then I poured a second cup and carried it upstairs. I swallowed down a large gulp and clicked on my name.

Not only were there new comments on my page, but comments about the comments went on forever. There was a new link for photos too. I clicked on that to discover a shaky cell phone pic of Sophie and me in the school parking lot. *What the hell?* That creepy sensation crawled up my neck.

I clicked back to my main page. Words. So many of them. Even the nice ones left me feeling violated:

kylem: I never noticed how pretty she is.

Kyle Monroe, the swim team captain. Part of me wanted to scream: *Really, Kyle? How many years have our lockers been across the hall from each other? And you never noticed me?*

And then there was this:

aident: She's got a pretty face, sure. Maybe we can take up a collection for implants—or at least a new wardrobe. She dresses like my little brother.
lukasn: True. Would it kill her to wear a skirt?
jasona: Yeah. One of those short ones. I bet she's got cute legs.
mchottie: I bet she's got better legs than Aiden's little brother.
adm*n: That's enough, gentlemen.

I looked down at the Vikings football jersey and Pokemon shorts that I'd slept in the night before. Okay, so maybe they had a point. I still resented the comment. To tell the truth, I resented *all* of the comments. I resented all of the guys, too. Even the nice ones like Adm*n. Maybe he was trying to control the boys on the wiki, but it was like trying to put out a fire with a squirt gun.

My phone vibrated against the desk, and I whacked it with my hand. "Yeah?" I said, not bothering to look at the number on the display.

"It's me." Elle's voice was quiet.

"Oh."

"You saw it already, didn't you?" She sounded sad.

"Yeah," I said again.

"I'm sorry. I should've known those wankers would do something like this. I was trying to catch you before you logged on this morning."

"I don't think it would've mattered," I said. "But thanks."

"If it makes you feel any better, all of us are getting the same treatment."

It didn't. *None of us* should be getting that kind of treatment. I clicked on the home page and realized that the five girls on the homecoming court were listed in all three categories. At the moment, Sophie was topping Elle in the Hottest of the Hot list. I went to Sophie's page and read a comment or two. Then I clicked the whole thing closed in disgust.

"How were the dresses at Tillie's?" I asked, just to change the subject.

Elle laughed. "Not bad, but we didn't have much time to look. Clarissa had auditions for the fall play and Mercedes and I had to get on the bus for the football game."

The game. I wondered, "How did it—?"

"We lost again. Big time. I should've stayed in town and shopped."

"Maybe you could just dye the dress you already have." I had no reason to be mean to Elle. None of this was her fault.

Elle laughed again. I was starting to suspect that she actually liked the bitchy side of everyone's personality. "I can't believe I let Clarissa talk me into that," she said. "Maybe I'll wear it to the holiday dance or save it for prom."

There it was again: the difference between us. For Elle, every dance was a sure thing. She could buy a dress for any of them, any time she wanted. Me? I hadn't been able to bring myself to even *think* about a dress for homecoming yet. I was scared I might jinx it.

"What about you?" Elle asked. "When are you going shopping?"

"Not until Sunday," I said. On my laptop, I clicked the icon for the wiki and logged back in. There hadn't been any new comments in the past few minutes, but anger brewed up in me anyway. It tasted bitter and dark, like this morning's coffee.

"No," I said.

"No what?"

"Just … no. What these boys are doing is disgusting. We can't let them get away with it."

"Hello. Isn't that what I've been saying?"

"I mean, I'm going to figure out who's behind this thing. I want to know who started it. And whoever it is, when we get to him—"

"We can kick him in the nuts?" Elle suggested.

"We can finally make it stop," I said.

"Um, this won't involve a certain rhinoceros, will it?"

"No. For one, I'm not sure we can solve it with technology. And two." I paused before admitting, "I really don't want him to see my page."

"Your page and what's on it are not your fault. You know that, right?"

"I know. It's just..." I couldn't find the right word. Embarrassing? It wasn't like Rhino hadn't seen me humiliated before. *The Hotties of Troy* shouldn't be any different. But this felt worse, more personal, like one of those parasites that worms its way through your system and leaves your heart full of holes.

"It sucks," Elle said. "These guys are like Dysons on overdrive."

"What?"

"Dysons. You know, the vacuum cleaners?"

I couldn't help it. I laughed.

"Look," she continued. "I have a debate tourney again today. But you can call me later … if it's getting to you, or whatever."

"Thanks. And, Elle?"

"Yeah?"

"You can call me too," I said. "If it's getting to you. Or if you get nervous about the tournament or anything."

"Oh, I already know we're going to win."

I wasn't sure whether she was talking about the tournament or the wiki. Either way, when she hung up, I had a smile on my face.

I spent the rest of the morning up in my room, on the computer, looking for sites that might help me hack into the wiki better. I tried to find a way to link ISPs with locations and then those to the user IDs. If I could get a handle on who posted what and where, I'd be one step closer to discovering who was behind the wiki.

I didn't have much luck, so, after lunch, I decided to look at the problem in a different way. What would a tutor do? What would I tell Byron, or Sophie, or one of my other students working on a math problem?

I knew the first step was to ask, "What is the question?" Okay. That was easy. The question I wanted answered was: *Who started the wiki?* Since the problem had to do with people, I knew I'd have to concentrate on the human aspect too. And I'd have to choose variables that involved things that I could measure, like time. I picked up a pencil and bit the eraser. *If I use T for time...*

I looked for patterns that might reveal clues. I diagrammed the timing of threads, too; who usually commented when. I also studied *how* they commented and linked that information to other threads. Two of these boys were the admins. There had to be some way to figure out who they were.

By four in the afternoon, I had a pretty good idea which boy posted when, and where he posted from. It was simple once I added in things like television schedules and sports practices. Like, I could tell every time the Twins had played, because the number of postings Jason made equaled zero. I was feeling kind of Nancy Drew-ish. It was really kind of amazing.

I was about to start checking the times of the postings against the admin user names when my phone rang. This time, I glanced at the screen. Oh! Rhino! I remembered my earlier goal to find out what he'd meant at the pep rally.

"Hey," I said. I'd have to find a way to ease into the question. If Rhino knew how badly I wanted to know, he'd make things difficult.

"Hey yourself, Ladybug. Where've you been all day?"

"Right here. I'm ... working on a project."

"Well," he said, "I'd say drop the project and come over, but we're going out to eat at OCD."

Actually, he meant OCC, the place everyone else called the Olympia Country Club. According to Rhino, everyone there was *Obsessive* about money and *Compulsive* about status symbols, and all of that equaled a *Disorder*.

"I'd invite you along, but Jason's family is coming. Unless you have some secret crush on The Ab?"

"Shut up," I said. As much as I liked Rhino, the idea of spending an entire evening with Jason had disaster written all over it. After his latest comments on the wiki, I'd probably go super-bitch on him and drench him with my drink. Then I'd have to explain why I'd doused Olympia High baseball's only hope with Cherry Coke.

"I think I'll pass," I said.

"How about tomorrow? Brunch at Rolly's?"

I loved the pie at Rolly's, the coffee shop and café downtown. But I had already promised to meet Sophie at noon.

"You mean, like, ten?" I said.

A heavy sigh filled my ear. "I was thinking more like twelve."

There was no way around this. I took in a deep breath, exhaled and said, "Um, sorry. I can't. I'm shopping for dresses tomorrow."

Rhino responded with ... nothing.

"At Tillie's," I added.

Still nothing.

"With Sophie."

I thought I heard a dog bark at the other end of the line. It was my only clue that Rhino hadn't hung up.

"Oh, come on," I said. "It's for homecoming. I have to buy a dress. It's in the rules somewhere. A blue one."

"Why not wear one of your *Doctor Who* shirts? They're blue. Then you could staple a matching ruffle to the bottom of your jeans and *voilà*! Formal wear a la Camy. "

"Very funny," I said, but it wasn't really funny at all. In fact, it was probably what those guys on the wiki expected me to do.

"I'm kidding," Rhino said. "We'll get you a dress that will have Gavin groveling at your feet."

I didn't know which bomb in this minefield of a conversation was more dangerous. The one where "we" got a dress together? Or the one where Rhino had Gavin groveling at my feet? I hoped he couldn't hear the way my heart was pounding.

If Rhino could take one comment about a cute baseball player and torture me with it for months, what would he do if he knew I had a head-over-heels crush on a real live boy?

I. Could. Not. Talk. To. Rhino. About. Gavin.

"That's okay." I tried for calm. "I don't need your help to buy a dress."

"What?"

"You don't have to come."

"But I want to be there."

"You really don't."

"You know what?" he said. "I do. I think it'll be the highlight of my high school experience. Next to seeing you nominated, I mean."

Ooh! My way into the subject of the pep rally. I tried to sound uninterested. "By the way, what did you mean Friday, about something that worked?"

"Let me come dress shopping and I'll tell you."

There was no winning with him.

Dad called up the stairs. "Cams? You're doing that freaky hermit girl thing again."

I was. I really was. I looked down at my laptop and realized I'd spent the whole day on a bunch of jerks who didn't deserve my time.

"My dad wants something," I told Rhino.

"Nice excuse."

"Don't you have to go put on a suit coat with a little gold crest on the pocket, or whatever it is you people wear to the country club?"

The quiet at his end of the line felt different this time. "Wait," I said. "Do you really have to wear a suit?"

"I barely escaped a haircut."

Actually, he could use a trim, but I didn't say so.

"Plus," he added, "I may have to dance."

I snorted. The thing was, Rhino could dance. He could really, really dance. His mom had forced him to take lessons back when we were little kids, so Rhino could do a bunch of dances that went way beyond what we'd learned in eighth grade social dance. That was the year Mrs. Holleman, the PE teacher, had made him demonstrate each step with her.

No one had been brave enough to tease him on the gym floor. But once they got to the locker room, I guess things had turned brutal. Poor Rhino. Remembering what he'd gone through made me feel sorry for him.

"I ... I could pull out a skirt and go with you," I told him. "I do have one somewhere. I think."

"Nah, Ladybug. I'll be all right. But I *will* see you tomorrow." And with that promise, or threat, he hung up.

"Hey, Camy?" Dad's voice came from downstairs.

I opened my bedroom door. Dad was standing at the bottom of the stairs. He was decked out in running pants, trail shoes, and his Code Monkey t-shirt.

"How about a walk?" he asked. "Maybe to DQ?"

"It's dinnertime," I pointed out.

"That's why they invented Grill and Chills."

Dad food was great, but a girl's got to have a vegetable every now and then. "Rolly's has salads," I said. "And those bread bowl things you like."

Dad looked like a five-year-old who'd been denied his ice cream, so I added, "DQ for dessert? Just let me change clothes, okay?"

I pushed back my chair and walked to my closet. I flipped past a couple dozen t-shirts and jerseys. Was that really all I owned? Where was that shiny gray blouse, the one I'd worn to my aunt's wedding last year? My fingers grazed a sage green sweater with tiny black rosebuds that felt satiny when you rubbed them. A layer of dust covered the top of it, and a crease now ran from one shoulder to the other. I tried not to think about the skirt that matched it, although sometimes I still wondered what Clarissa had done with it.

I remember the exact moment I pulled that skirt from the rack at Macy's and held it up to my waist. It was eighth grade and I was shopping with Clarissa Delacroix. We were best friends.

The material felt incredible, silky and soft. The rules for Spring Fling said no floor-length dresses. (The note home started with: *This is not prom!*) No dresses shorter than three inches above the knee were allowed either.

I'd only been off crutches from my football injury for a couple of months and the surgery scars on my leg were still raw and angry looking. I wasn't planning to show *any* knee. I took the skirt over to the mirrors and held it against my waist. The hem skimmed just below the scars. It was perfect.

"What do you think?" I asked Clarissa.

"I think you should try it on."

She shoved me toward the dressing rooms. Once I had the skirt on, I didn't want to take it off. I'd never been much of a girly girl. My mom hadn't allowed Barbies in the house. And the only time I remember playing princess was when I had Rhino's paper crown on my head. But as soon as I fastened the clasp on that skirt … I got it.

I finally understood the whole *great dress, right pair of shoes* thing and what they could do for a girl. In that skirt, I felt like I couldn't lose. In that skirt, I'd get Gavin to speak to me again.

He'd stopped showing up for tutoring the week before. And the few times I'd tried to ask him about it, he'd spun away from me. It was almost like the sight of me burned him. I'd tried to ask the tutoring advisor about it, but she'd just mumbled something about "private in-struction." Then she'd run away from me too.

But in that skirt? I could fix it. All of it.

I used all of the money Mom had given me for shopping to buy it.

Clarissa tried on a two-piece outfit that dipped low on top and ended way more than three inches above her knees. I thought she was joking when she walked out of the dressing room.

"Where's the rest of it?" I said.

She waved a handful of lace at me that turned out to be a shrug with rhinestone buttons. When she put that on, the top looked mostly decent. But still …

"It's way too short. They'll never let you into the dance like that," I said.

"They just don't want anyone treating this like prom. They won't make anyone leave just for showing a few extra inches of skin. That would be cruel."

The next Saturday night we discovered just how cruel the school could be.

"I'm sorry, but there's a dress code for the dance," Vice Principal Tanner said. We both heard the echo behind his words: *And you know it.*

Clarissa's lip quivered and I pulled her into the girls' bathroom.

"Now what?" She leaned close to the mirror and pushed tears away from her mascara. "This is so not fair. Did you see Elle, in her freaking almost down to the floor dress? How does she get in and I don't?"

I shrugged. "Maybe you can call your mom?"

Clarissa rolled her eyes. "Right." Her gaze in the mirror's reflection flickered, not to my eyes, but to my skirt. "Hey, I know! We'll use yours."

"We'll use my what?"

"Your skirt. We can take turns. I'll wear it for twenty minutes, then come back here and we'll switch." She crouched so her waist lined up with mine. "It kind of matches and it'll be long enough, see?"

"I don't know." This was my magic skirt, the one I planned on having an honest-to-goodness princess moment in. I wasn't sure there was room for two princesses in one skirt.

"Oh, please, Camy, please." She gave me an all-out dazzling smile, the kind that took your breath away, the kind that said *you know I'd do this for you.*

I laughed. "Okay."

"Me first," she said.

Which was how I ended up in a bathroom stall, stepping out of the skirt and handing it over the top of the door. Clarissa changed, right there in the middle of the bathroom. If I'd been thinking, I would have suggested we swap entire outfits, but the thought didn't cross my mind until the bathroom door had already whooshed open and closed.

Her skirt would be too big. Clarissa was already five foot eight. On me, the skirt might skim my knees. I could sneak into the dance and stand along the bleachers. I could at least check things out. I could at least not be stuck in the bathroom wearing nothing but a sweater and pantyhose.

For twenty minutes, I lived on hope. Every time the screen on my phone went dim, I refreshed it. I counted the minutes and wondered at the wisdom of handing over a magical skirt to a girl I'd only known for five months. Clarissa had moved to Olympia that winter. She'd started at Olympia Middle School after the holiday break.

Rhino had tried to warn me. There was something about Clarissa that he didn't like. But then, there was something about him that Clarissa didn't like either.

"He's so nosy," she'd say. Then she'd laugh and point to her own nose. "Get it? He's got a big nose and he's nosy too?"

And yeah, your new best friend making fun of your old BFF? Kind of uncomfortable. But I couldn't gush about Gavin to Rhino like I could with Clarissa. She wanted to know everything. So I told her how smart he was. How it didn't matter that he was flunking every subject. He was just bad at test taking; a lot of smart people were. Wait until football season, I said. She'd see how amazing he was then. We made plans to go to every single game. I told her everything I knew about him, especially about the time he'd held my hand when we left the tutoring room.

There were girl things and guy things, I'd decided. And finally I had a friend for both.

I started to worry after twenty-five minutes had passed. I called her cell phone, but she didn't answer. She was dancing with someone, I told myself. If I'd been dancing with Gavin, she'd want me to keep on doing that.

Wouldn't she?

After thirty minutes, I cracked open the bathroom door. Vice Principal Tanner, standing nearby, looked bored. Two girls burst from the gym and headed straight for the restroom. I ran back to my stall.

"Did you see Clarissa's skirt?" the first girl was saying as the door swung open.

"I am, like, so jealous," the second girl said.

"It doesn't fit her right, though. I mean, come on, try a bigger size."

"Wonder where her shadow is tonight?" girl number two added.

I held my breath.

"Probably couldn't get in because of the dress code," girl one said.

"Huh?"

"I don't think they allow those football shoulder pad things at Spring Fling."

Girl two laughed. Then, a second later, she asked, "Do you think she's ... *you know?*"

"Who, Camy? Nah. I think it's more like she's desperate. How else would she get boys to pay attention to her? I mean, besides Rhino."

They both laughed at that.

"And those crutches. I bet she wasn't even really hurt. She was just trying to get sympathy from Gavin. You know she's in love with him, right?"

"Puh-leaze. Could she be any more obvious about it?"

The clatter of their shoes echoed against the tile, and the bathroom door opened, letting in a hint of music from the dance. And then they were gone. I gripped my phone so tightly that, for a second, I thought I'd broken it.

I tried calling Clarissa again. Forget about the skirt. I needed *her.* I needed her to tell me everyone wasn't laughing at me behind my back. I needed her to tell me that there was nothing wrong with a girl playing football. I needed her to tell me Gavin wasn't embarrassed to be seen with me, that there was some other reason he was suddenly pretending I didn't exist.

But she didn't answer.

I pecked out a text message to Rhino. He was there in less than five minutes, tossing his backpack into the restroom. He'd stuffed his mom's neon orange skirt inside of it. And no, he hadn't done that to be mean. Rhino is many things. Color blind is one of them.

I pulled on the skirt and tugged the belt as tight as I could. I tried to ignore the clashing image my beautiful sage top made with the pumpkin of a skirt below it. Rhino stopped me at the gym door.

"Camy. Cam-ster, don't," he said.

But I gave his hand a quick squeeze and raced into the dance anyway. The scent of Axe cologne was floating in the air, along with something sweet, like fruit punch or bubblegum. A slow song was pouring from the speakers. It took forever for my eyes to adjust. Once my vision improved, I could tell no one was putting their social dancing skills to use; it was all zombie-shuffle with some swaying back and forth.

About what happened next: The betrayal turned out to be epic. But if they did it on purpose, it sure didn't look like it. If Clarissa really had orchestrated the whole thing, she should have gotten some kind of award. Just as I could start to pick out couples in the crowd, she danced into view.

I want to say that she was clutching her partner in a death grip. Or that he was letting his hands hang loose at her waist. I'd like to believe that dancing with Clarissa was an obligation. That it was like homework, maybe, or like eating Mystery Hot Dish in the cafeteria. Something you did because you had to. But that might not be true.

What I do know is this: Light from the glitter ball hit their faces. And then it hit mine. They saw me. I saw them. Clarissa, dancing with Gavin. They both smiled.

And I ran from the gym.

Clarissa never talked to me after that. At least she never said anything nice.

One dance with Gavin was all it took to launch her into Elle's crowd. One dance in a magical princess skirt ... and she didn't need me anymore.

Two weeks later, after the last week of school, my parents sat with me at the kitchen table and told me they were separating. My world tilted again. If not for Rhino, I would have fallen through the hole in what used to be my life. If not for Rhino, I would've crashed at the bottom.

I shoved the sweater to the back of my closet and pulled out my old youth football jersey instead. I sat at my desk to tie my shoes. I resisted the temptation to turn on my laptop and do a quick wiki check. I knew what I'd find there: some pretty awful guys.

I thought about Dad instead, ready to eat ice cream for dinner. Then I thought about Rhino. He might dread it, but he was still willing to put on a suit coat and dance with his mom at the country club. Even though he knew better, he would always come to my rescue. Despite anything I might read on the wiki, I had undeniable proof that living, breathing decent guys really did exist.

Chapter Nine

♡

DAD SURPRISED ME when we pulled up in front of Tillie's the next day. I'd already jumped out, slammed the door and was starting to wave goodbye. Then I realized he had turned off the engine and was opening his own door. Of course. He wanted to shop for homecoming dresses too.

I told him I'd be okay. Then I pointed out that the Vikings were playing at noon. When that didn't work, I walked around the car and gave him a hug.

"It's kind of a girl thing," I said.

He looked embarrassed. And maybe a little hurt too. I felt like a bad daughter but, really, I was desperate. The idea of both Rhino *and* Dad helping me buy a dress? I figured Sophie would take one look at the three of us and never speak to me again.

So, at five minutes before noon, I was standing outside Tillie's Bridal and Formalwear alone. Actually, I didn't just stand. I walked past the display window once, twice, ten times. I had to work up the courage to try the door, even though the sign told me: *Yes, We're Open!*

Before Olympia turned into a faraway suburb of Minneapolis, it had been its own little city. We still have a real downtown here, where people come to shop and eat. We still have a glockenspiel. And kitty-corner from that glockenspiel, we still have Tillie's. It's kind of a tradition. Shopping for a formal dress somewhere else, like the Mall of America? That's considered a form of treason.

I'd never been inside the store, but I knew my mom had bought her wedding dress there. (Apparently, even ultra-feminists have their girly-girl days.) And every time I'd been in the car with Rhino and his mom, if we even got close to the place, Mrs. Reinhold would slow down.

"One of these days you'll buy *your* dresses there, Camy," she'd say. Then she'd get a goofy look on her face. I could never figure out if she was remembering old times or if she just really wished she had a daughter.

The glockenspiel chimed twelve times. I pulled out my phone and checked for messages. No Rhino. No Sophie. Just the formalwear and me.

I held a hand over my eyes and looked through the window. Near the back of the store, a giant HOMECOMING! banner was hanging on the wall. Below it, two huge racks threatened to burst with formal dresses, an explosion of sapphire, azure, and navy.

The glockenspiel had just finished its song when Sophie's car roared down Main Street and rocked to a stop in front of me. She leaped out of it. "Hey," she said, but her eyes were fixed on the window just over my shoulder. "This is going to be so much fun."

"Sort of like playing dress-up." The second the words had left my mouth, I wanted to shove them back in. I was such a dork sometimes.

Sophie raised her eyebrows. "Whatever."

Inside the store, the satin, the tulle and the silk took over. Both Tillie and the salesclerk hovered over us as we eased the dresses aside on one of the racks.

Tillie pulled out a sleek gown and held it up so Sophie could see. "Honey, try this one. It's a little too sophisticated for most girls, but I think you could really pull it off."

"Thanks," Sophie mumbled.

I could see it in the way she barely glanced at Tillie and the dress. I could see it in the way she held her shoulders too. Even though she'd been the one to set up this shopping trip, and even though she'd been the one to say this was going to be fun, something had changed. As tough as Sophie could be, it was like the dresses *scared* her. She wasn't going to try anything on.

So I did the only thing I could do. I picked the most ridiculous item from the rack and headed for the dressing room. I came out a few minutes later in a dress with a hoop so huge, I had to tip it sideways to get through the door.

"You're freakin' kidding me," Sophie said. "Go try on something real."

"Not until you do." I pulled out the dress Tillie had suggested.

She rolled her eyes. "Only if you take that hideous thing off," Sophie said, but she grabbed the dress and vanished into a dressing room.

I wasn't about to duck back into my own room to change. I didn't want to miss seeing Sophie in the dress. I was still waiting five minutes later. Tillie smiled at me, then crossed the room. She knocked once on the dressing room door. "How are you doing, sweetie?" she asked, but before Sophie could answer, Tillie pulled open the door and stepped inside.

Sophie yelped.

"Oh, don't you just look lovely?" Tillie said. "A vision. An absolute vision. Now get out there and show your little friend how it's done." A second later, she was shooing Sophie out onto the sales floor.

The dress was strapless, with crystals that spilled across the bodice and a split up the leg. It was just the right shade of blue, too. The color looked amazing on her. It made her hazel eyes shine, her hair appear blonder. She looked older, but in a good way. Grown-up, sophisticated, just like Tillie had predicted.

"You could be a model," I said. "They should take your picture and use it in the catalogue."

"Shut up." She sliced me with a cut-you glance, but her expression softened as she viewed herself in one of the three-way mirrors.

Tillie bustled over. "Oh, I knew it. That dress is simply stunning on you," she said. "Of course, you're free to try on the others, but would you like me to hold this one for you?"

Sophie turned again in the mirror. "Maybe."

"What, maybe?" I started to say, but the bell above the front door chimed.

In walked Elle, Mercedes, and Clarissa.

"Convenient how they just happen to show up."

I turned to find Sophie behind me. Her eyes were locked on the newcomers.

"Well," I said, "I did mention to Elle that I'd be shopping today." As soon as the words had left my mouth, I knew how they sounded, like I was either incredibly stupid or intentionally cruel.

"You know, for a smart girl, sometimes you really don't get it." Sophie spun away from me. She hiked the dress above her knees and marched toward the dressing room.

She was right. I didn't get it. I didn't understand why Elle was here. And I definitely didn't understand why she'd brought Clarissa along. *I thought we were friends.* Something cold and tight squeezed my heart and I froze. Right there, in that huge and hideous hoop skirt. If my phone hadn't started chirping from the dressing room, I might have stood there all day.

I swooshed into the stall, knelt by my bag, and was completely swallowed in an avalanche of ruffles. Everywhere I looked, all I could see was scratchy blue eyelet lace. I felt the floor for my bag, then dug for the phone.

Someone laughed. I craned my neck and squinted through the lace in time to see long legs and several blue dresses float by. Clarissa. A second later, Mercedes bounced past with an armload of satin and silk.

"Wow, Camy!" she said, glancing into the room. "Totally radical choice."

Three things happened all at once. I grabbed the phone, pushed the icon to talk, and landed on my butt.

It was Rhino. I felt relieved for a millisecond. Maybe he planned on shopping with me via cell phone? If he did, I was all for it.

"You have no idea what I'm going through," I said.

"I'm pretty sure I do."

"Unless you've been trapped inside a giant blue puff pastry with lace frosting, then trust me, you don't." I crawled to the doorway and searched the store for Sophie. Tillie had one hand on Elle's shoulder. With the other, she pointed to a pedestal across the room.

I pushed aside another handful of lace and scanned the store again. Sophie was standing with her back to me. She was halfway between the dressing rooms and the register. She was holding the dress in her arms. Even though I couldn't see her face, I could feel the indecision roll off her.

"You do look uncomfortable," Rhino said.

"I ... look?"

"And no offense, but the Antebellum South just isn't your era."

I jerked my head toward the front of the store. Outside, on the sidewalk, Rhino's big nose was pressed against the window.

I hung up the phone, stood, and took a few steps from the dressing room, the skirt tilting wildly as I squeezed through the door. I pulled at the hoop to clear a three-way mirror. I darted another look at the dressing room doors. Could I get rid of Rhino before Clarissa saw him?

And what would Elle think about his arrival? She had already slipped on a dress and taken her spot on the pedestal. Tillie was hovering near her while the salesclerk placed pins in random spots on the gown. Elle looked beautiful, of course. Regal, even. All she needed was the crown.

The bell over the door jingled and Rhino marched through the store. Elle swiveled on her pedestal so fast that her skirt swirled. The salesgirl went down on all fours to collect the pins that popped off as a result. Rhino nodded to Sophie, then stopped as close to me as the hoop skirt would allow.

"This." Rhino plucked at a ruffle with a finger and thumb. "This is why I'm needed here today."

I rolled my eyes. "Shhhh. I just tried it on to make Sophie laugh."

"You're going to make me cry if you don't take that thing off," Sophie said.

"I'm not changing until you buy your dress."

She glanced away. "I'm still thinking about it."

"What's there to think about?" I looked to Rhino for support, but what did he know? "You should've seen her," I told him before turning back to her. "It's perfect and so pretty."

"It's also pretty expensive."

I'd been trying my hardest not to look at price tags. I knew from experience that dressing like royalty didn't come cheap. But now I forced myself to search for the tag on the hoop skirt from hell. Not that I planned to buy it. I found it in my left armpit and had to hold my elbow above my head to read it (backwards) in the mirror.

"Four hundred and seventy dollars?" I felt my eyes widen, and the words came out much louder than I'd meant them to.

Elle shot a look at me from her pedestal. She pulled her eyebrows in close and gave her head a quick shake.

"You're kidding," Rhino said. He hefted up my left arm, inspecting the tag (and my armpit) himself. "Holy … granola." He turned back to Sophie. "She's not kidding."

"Guess mine's a bargain, then."

"How much?" I held my arms out from my sides, afraid I'd have to pay for the thing if I sweated on it.

"Two eighty, but I only have one fifty for shoes and everything."

I heard the rustle of silk and satin behind me. Mercedes and Clarissa emerged from their dressing rooms and took spots in front of the three-way mirrors.

"Oh!" Clarissa said. "Now I see it." She pivoted and planted herself in front of Sophie. "Having trouble deciding?" Her voice oozed out, honey sweet. "Tell you what I'm going to do. I'll go ahead and buy that dress for myself. Then you won't have to worry your *poor* little head about it."

The way Clarissa emphasized the word *poor* made my mouth go dry. It wasn't right; we all knew that. Even so, we all just stood there.

Clarissa held out a hand, like she expected Sophie's dress to magically appear there. No one moved. Elle glared at us from on high. I think we all held our breaths, waiting for the epic homecoming court smackdown that was sure to come.

Except it didn't go like that. Sophie swiped at a few strands of hair that had fallen into her eyes.

"This is stupid," she said. "I didn't want to be on the effing homecoming court anyway, and I don't want this dress." She shoved the mass of satin at Clarissa and spun to leave.

Surprise lit Clarissa's eyes, then that triumphant smile appeared on her lips. I tugged the hoop skirt and myself forward, nearly knocking

CHARITY TAHMASEB AND DARCY VANCE

Rhino off balance in the process. Taking someone's, anyone's, dress was something you only got to do once in a lifetime. Clarissa had already cashed in that token.

"It's not even your size," I told her as the chime over the door jangled.

"Of course it is."

Maybe Clarissa didn't expect someone to snatch the dress away from her. Maybe she didn't expect *me* to. Maybe that was why the satin slid through her grip so easily. I was halfway to the cash register before she called out, "Hey!"

"I'd like to buy this dress," I said.

I shoved the blob of blue satin at the girl behind the register. Her eyes got huge. Not that I blamed her. I was still wearing the blue cream puff, after all. And I was trying to buy a dress I hadn't even tried on with … my cell phone. My bag and my wallet were back in the dressing room.

"It's mine." Clarissa's fingers crumpled a handful of dress, but I held on tight.

"You can't have this dress," I said. "You already did that."

From across the room, Tillie's voice sang out, "Lovely to look at, delightful to hold, but if you rip it, consider it sold."

For a second, my gaze locked with Clarissa's, and for a second, I thought we both might roll our eyes at that.

"Oh, please." Clarissa's tone went nasty. "You know you're a joke, right? It's the only reason you were even voted in. Just so people will have something to laugh about. So why don't you make it a little less embarrassing for yourself? Give it up. Quit the court, just like your skanky friend."

"I guess there's only room on the court for one skank," Rhino said. "What was it Aiden said? Something about the girl most likely to …?"

At that moment, Mercedes burst onto the sales floor. She was holding my wallet in her hand. "Rhino said you were going to buy the hoop! Wow, Camy, you really are radical!"

Clarissa shot both Mercedes and Rhino a death glare. I shoved my credit card at the poor girl behind the register, then turned to look for Sophie.

She was gone.

The moment the charge went through, I gathered the dress in my arms, tore off the price tag, and threw the whole thing over Rhino's shoulder.

"Run. Find her. Please? I would." I glanced down at the hoop. "But I'm not getting very far in this."

He took forever picking his way through the bridesmaid dresses, but the second his feet hit the sidewalk, Rhino broke into a sprint and vanished from sight.

The girl at the register pushed a slip of paper toward me. "You need to sign," she said. Then she took a step back, like she was afraid I might bite her. So I took the pen and signed. I had bought a dress that wasn't mine, and it sure as hell wasn't going to be Clarissa's. If Rhino couldn't catch Sophie, the dress might not belong to anyone.

"I can't believe you did that," Clarissa said.

Neither could I. Neither, I was betting, would Dad when I had to tell him I'd bought a dress with the emergency credit card, and it wasn't *my* dress. Instead of answering Clarissa, I turned to Mercedes.

"Thanks," I told her, "but I'm not buying the hoop. I'm not that radical."

"Yeah, thanks, Mercedes," Clarissa added loudly. She crossed her arms over her chest. "You know what?" She spat the words at the salesgirl. "Thank *you* too. Thank you for reminding me that I didn't want to shop in this stupid store in this stupid town anyway."

A loud "shhh" came from Elle's corner. She twisted around, hitting Clarissa with a look sharp enough to shred satin.

Clarissa continued in a singsong voice. "I'm driving over to the Mall of America. Who's with me?"

Elle's hands flew to her hips. She scowled at Clarissa, then turned her back on her. Mercedes took her cue from Elle. She turned away too, although not as deliberately. I found myself holding my breath and waiting for Clarissa to look at me next. She didn't bother.

Instead, she marched back to the dressing room alone. A few minutes later she marched out of Tillie's, also alone. Something pulled me toward the front window to watch her. It was like there was an invisible thread connected to my bellybutton. I resisted it. I didn't want to press my cheek against the glass and peer down the street after either Clarissa or Sophie. Not in front of Mercedes and Elle.

I glanced at the salesclerk. She looked away. I was about to head for the dressing rooms to escape the hoop when Rhino blasted back through the door. He took a few steps inside the shop and bent over at the waist. His hands were on his knees, and he panted hard.

He didn't have the dress.

"I ran," he said between breaths.

"I guessed." I stared past him at the door. It was like waiting for a text to show up on your phone. "Where's Sophie?" I asked when I couldn't wait any longer.

"Somewhere ... behind ...me."

"You know, the best way to recover from a run is to stand up straight and—"

Still hunched over, he shot me a glare.

Sophie appeared in the doorway behind him. She studied the dress in her hands, then looked at me. "I can't believe you did this."

I shrugged. "It's a killer dress."

"It's got a killer price tag too." She turned toward the register. "I hope Tillie's has a layaway plan."

"It doesn't matter," I said, "because I do."

"Huh?"

"No interest," I added.

"I don't like this," she said. "I don't like … owing people stuff."

"Could you ask your mom?" I asked.

"My mom? Yeah. Right."

"Or your dad?" I suggested. After all, Dad always came to my rescue.

"Oh, sure. My dad. He'll fix everything." The words coming from her mouth didn't match the sadness on her face.

My own face burned. Stupid, stupid, stupid. I knew from tutoring her last year that Sophie lived with her mom. I knew her dad wasn't around.

"This whole thing is ridiculous, anyway," she said. "It's not like either one of us has a real chance." She nodded toward Elle.

That was when I realized we'd lost Rhino and Mercedes. They were both standing below Elle on her pedestal. While I couldn't hear their words, it looked like Elle and Rhino were trading insults. Well, at least they were happy.

"I mean," Sophie said, "The Ab is probably collecting pig's blood as we speak."

"What?"

"Come on, it's in a book." She looked surprised that there might be a piece of literature I didn't recognize immediately. "By that guy, Stephen King. It's the one where this weird girl gets voted prom queen?"

I drew a blank.

"And then the popular guys throw blood on her at the dance?" Sophie held out the hand that wasn't holding the dress and let her mouth fall open. "You have to know this. It's a classic."

CHARITY TAHMASEB AND DARCY VANCE

I shrugged. "Is it one of those stories where everybody dies at the end?"

For a moment, Sophie was like stone. Then she burst out laughing. Peals of it bounced off the walls, filling the store. Everyone stopped what they were doing and turned toward her. Tillie smiled. Up on her pedestal, Elle beamed. Mercedes giggled. The clerk with the pins, the girl behind the register, even Rhino grinned. Because Sophie's laugh?

It sounded happy.

"Okay," she said after calming down. "Now let's get you something real to wear. I'm thinking..." And she examined me again, the look pointed and unforgiving. "Something retro."

Fifteen minutes later, I was standing in front of the three-way mirrors, my expression stunned. The dress looked like vintage 1950s. The neckline went straight across, showing off my collarbone and shoulders, but not much else. It nipped in at the waist, then exploded into a full skirt that didn't quite reach the floor. Tillie called it tea length. I'd need shoes, really nice shoes.

Tillie sent one of her minions to search for a pair in my size. "I haven't had a waist like that since I was ten." She sighed and pinched the extra material along the sides of the dress. "We could have this taken in."

I shook my head. The dress fit fine as far as I was concerned. Plus, tailoring cost extra and my credit card had a limit.

Sophie stared at me with one eye closed. "You *are* going to get the dress," she said. "Right?"

"It's not floor-length."

"I don't think there's a rule about that."

I glanced toward Elle.

"She doesn't make the rules, either," Sophie added. "Come on, try to tell me you hate it."

I couldn't. "Well," I said. "It *is* long enough." I bent down and raised the hem, revealing the scars along my knee.

"What the ... What did you do?"

"I should probably do a chair test, too," I said, ignoring her question. I found a seat not far from the mirrors and plopped down. If I sat just right, the dress still touched the bottom of the lowest scar. It would do.

Sophie stood above me. "Jeez, what's wrong with your leg?"

"I told you before," I said. "It's a football injury."

"I thought you meant, like, tossing a football around in your backyard."

"Well, you know, my dad says Walter Payton once—"

"Walter who?" Sophie interrupted.

"Payton. Sweetness? Greatest running back of all time?"

Sophie stared at me like I was a refugee from the planet Weird.

"So, yeah," I said. "I used to play in the Olympia Youth Football League."

She crossed her arms over her chest. My answer still wasn't good enough.

"There isn't a rule against girls playing, you know," I added.

"You mean, you played with Gavin and Lukas and all of them?"

I nodded.

"You." She picked up my wrist and circled it with her finger and thumb. "You have, like, bird bones or something."

I did. But I had never played the line, and I'd been fast enough that I never ended up at the bottom of a pile. *Almost* never. "For a while in grade school, I was taller than a lot of the boys. I even outweighed some of them."

Sophie leaned against the mirror. "That's right. Gavin was a shrimp, wasn't he?"

"It's like I turned around one day and he was." I stood and waved my hand about six inches above my head. Then I shook out the skirt of my dress. Yeah, *my* dress. I'd decided. For the second time in my life, I felt like what I wore could really make a difference. This time, I wouldn't let anyone take that away from me.

From out of nowhere, Sophie laughed.

"What?" I said.

"These." Sophie grabbed my wrist again, this time by one of my string bracelets. "You're going to have to lose these, at least for one night."

I'd never been all that into crafts, but I'd started on the bracelets down in Iowa that summer. My mom's roommate had given me the kit as a welcome present.

I pulled the prettiest one from my wrist. A midnight blue and silver one. "Here." I held out my hand, the bracelet dangling from my fingers.

"I can't. I've already taken enough," she said.

"It's *string.*"

She mumbled a few words, but then she slipped the bracelet onto her wrist. We were saved from having to actually say something about this by Rhino.

"Whoa," he said.

"What do you think?" Not that I really needed Rhino's approval. After all, this was the boy who thought dressing up meant pulling something flannel over a chicken butt tee.

The crinkles around his eyes deepened. "Perfect." Then, without another word, his hands went to my waist. He plucked the price tag from the dress, taking me a few steps with him.

"Hey!" I said, but Rhino ignored me.

He crouched, scooped up the shoebox, and headed for the cash register. By the time I caught up to him, he'd pulled out his wallet and was handing the salesgirl a big stack of bills.

"What are you doing?"

Rhino nudged the shoebox my way, then the tag he'd taken from my dress. He tapped the price of each of them. The numbers swirled for a moment, then jumped out at me. My dress? Two hundred and twenty-five dollars. The shoes? Another seventy-five. I added in the two hundred and eighty I'd spent on Sophie's dress and felt sick. I didn't need Rhino's mathematical genius to figure this one out. I wasn't sure what my credit card limit was, but I'd probably burst through it and gone soaring into the stratosphere.

He handed the receipt to me. "You'd better hang on to that, just in case."

The piece of paper felt flimsy between my fingers. My dress. My shoes. Paid in full. In cash.

"What ... what have you done?" I asked.

"Well, yesterday I sold two really sweet custom computer systems. Made 'em out of parts I got off of craigslist." Rhino shook his head. "The things most people think are worthless ... So, anyway, I felt like donating to a worthy cause."

The salesgirl took the shoes and placed them in one of Tillie's signature pink-and-white striped bags. The rustle of it filled my ears. I had no words for what Rhino had just done. Except, in a way, it seemed inevitable.

Didn't he always ride to my rescue, whether it was with an ugly neon orange skirt or the cash for the perfect homecoming dress?

"Thank you," I said. Sure, I knew I'd be paying him back. But I also knew that *when* and *how* wasn't important to him.

He waved away my words. "Totally worth it. Besides, I figured there'd been enough dress drama for one day."

Rhino glanced over his shoulder toward Sophie. I followed his gaze, relieved to see that she was busy with Mercedes. That feeling lasted only a second, until a pinprick sensation ran down my spine.

I turned to see Elle staring at the mirror. It wasn't me she was looking at. Not herself, either. It was Rhino. And, no matter how hard I tried, I couldn't tell what her expression meant.

♡ ♡ ♡

Dad had another surprise waiting when he picked me up from the dress shop. "Take a look." He pointed to the backseat of our car. Nestled beside a stack of RedBox returns sat the most nerdalicious collection of homecoming campaign canisters in Olympia High School history.

I should have known this might happen. Dad had spotted contest containers for Clarissa and Elle while we were eating at Rolly's the night before. A corner of the cash register desk had featured a gallon-sized blue plastic water bottle. A 5x7 glossy photo of Clarissa was splashed across it, along with inch-high Trojan blue letters that spelled out VOTE 4 CLARISSA!

Beside it, less than half the size and looking almost modest and oh-so-elegant, sat a tall white cylinder with one word spelled out in blue sequins: Elle.

What? I'd thought as my salad threatened to make a return appearance. *When did they have time to …?* And then I realized, *of course,* just like the white dresses, the campaign canisters had been ready in advance. They'd probably made them months ago. Years, maybe. That's how sure these girls had been that one day they would be nominated to the homecoming court. That's how sure I was that I didn't stand a chance.

When we walked to DQ for dessert, Dad spied a canister for Mercedes too. At least hers looked like it had been made at home and not produced by a big-city advertising agency. A coffee can, some spray paint, puffy foam letters in bright colors spelling out her name, and a few cottony pom-poms scattered around. The effect was as fun as Mercedes herself. I couldn't resist dropping in a few coins for her.

Peering at the canisters on the car seat made me sigh. My dad has so many talents. Subtlety is not one of them.

"They're so … shiny," I said.

"I know. I had trouble getting the aluminum foil to stick at first, but then I remembered that can of spray adhesive in the garage. How do you like the label?"

Which part, I wondered? The photo of me in pigtails and football pads, taken when I was five? Or the part where he'd turned my name into a bright blue acrostic that read:

Clever

Attractive

Mighty

Your best choice for queen!

He looked so proud.

I hid my face behind a canister, pretending to be captivated by what I saw there. "These are … great, Dad. Just great." And really, they were very sweet. Up close, I could make out a faded caption beneath the picture: *Daddy's little girl*, it said in my father's familiar scrawl.

"Think I could take a couple to work with me?" he asked. "And your grandma, I know she'll want one for her knitting club, and one for the senior center where she does her line dancing."

Oh! I perked up. If I could figure out how to control the distribution so Dad's canisters were seen exclusively by people who were either old or related to me, this might not be so bad. "What about Grandpa?" I said. "Does he still volunteer at the genealogy center? And how about Aunt Abby? And …"

"Whoa, there. If you give them all out to family, you won't have any left to take to Rolly's," Dad said.

Was he reading my mind?

"Now that you've shown me how to do it, I can make more later. And, Dad? Thanks."

"Anything for you, princess. Anything for you."

Chapter Ten

♡

DIDN'T KNOW WHAT to expect on Monday. Would people still stop me in the halls to congratulate me or would I already be old news?

In case I was in for extra attention, I took a little more time getting ready for the day. And by that, I mean I chose a T-shirt that didn't feature a sports team or a cartoon character. I tugged on my favorite jeans and coordinated the entire outfit with my green Chuck Taylors. I even spent five extra minutes trying to tame my hair before I gave up in disgust. I didn't care what anybody said, though; I still wasn't going to wear a skirt.

Despite my best efforts to prepare, I was startled when Rhino and I walked into school that day. Shocked even.

Nearly every surface of the building was covered with posters and banners. Flyers had been stuck into locker vents too. And on all of those posters, banners, and flyers? Clarissa Delacroix in one pose after another. A sassy over-the-shoulder look here, a straight-on at the camera look there, a third one where she appeared surprised—yet very, very glad—to see us all.

Again, the thought struck me: *How did she know?* Did a girl like

Clarissa get professional photographs taken because she knew she'd be a homecoming queen candidate, or was she a candidate because she was the kind of girl who got a bunch of pictures taken? Which came first, the chicken or the tiara?

A few oh-so-tasteful campaign posters for Elle were scattered here and there too. As for Mercedes and Sophie? Well, even if they'd managed to throw a few things together, all the prime real estate had already been scooped up.

Rhino blinked a few times, then turned in a slow circle. "Do you have a strategy to counter all this?" he asked.

A girl from the dance team sashayed past. Her eyes caught mine and she smiled. "Isn't it awesome?" she said, pointing to the wall behind Rhino.

"Well, it certainly is something," Rhino muttered. "Although I'm not sure 'awesome' is the first word that comes to mind."

I nudged him in the ribs.

"Here." The girl pressed buttons into my hand, then Rhino's. Then she continued down the hall, stopping everyone she met to offer them a button too.

I looked at my palm. Staring up at me was Clarissa's smiling face with the message *CD 4 HQ* above her head. Apparently, the girl who'd handed it to me had forgotten that I was also a queen candidate. Or maybe she knew and just didn't care. I thought about pinning the button to my shirt. But first I'd have to find a marker. Clarissa would look so much more realistic if I drew a witch's hat on her head.

"Again," Rhino said. "Strategy? You have one?"

Did I want to traipse down the hall every day with my face plastered everywhere, looking down on every move I made? The notion was kind of unsettling. Really, I just wasn't that into me.

"I-I'm not sure I want one," I said.

Rhino sighed. "Don't say that. After everything I—"

"After everything you what?" I leaped on the statement. "What did you do? Come on, Rhino. You promised to tell me."

"Technically, I didn't do anything." His voice trailed off and his eyes lost their focus on me. I followed his line of sight, turning to glance over my shoulder.

Elle was standing near the cafeteria door. The second she started toward us, Rhino retreated.

"I feel electronically deprived this morning," Rhino said. "Think I'll stop in the computer lab before first bell. Later, Ladybug."

For someone who made it a point never to hurry, Rhino sure managed to vanish up the stairs pretty quick.

"What is wrong with that boy?" Elle said the moment she landed at my side. "It's like he's afraid I'll give him cooties or something."

I snorted.

"I'm serious, Camy. I sent him at least twelve texts yesterday, and nothing. He didn't answer a single one."

Twelve text messages? To Rhino?

Elle tugged me by the arm until we ended up against a bank of lockers.

"The two of you don't have anything going on, do you?"

"Like what?" I asked.

"Something like … you know." She placed her hand over her heart and made a fluttery motion with her fingers.

"What? No! We're just friends."

"Then what does he have against me?"

She hadn't lost her cool, not really. I was pretty sure Elle Emerson *never* lost her cool. But she did bite her lower lip, her eyebrows drawn together.

"It's not you," I said, feeling around for the right words. "It's…" I glanced at the students crowding the hallway, at Clarissa's and Elle's faces smiling down at the masses. I pointed to her poster on the wall. "Okay. It is you. But *that* version of you. Elle Emerson, head cheerleader, student council president, and all the rest. It's like you're the anti-Rhino."

She laughed, but hurt flashed in her eyes. "Well, here's the thing," she said. "Did you know I've been to every single dance since fifth grade?"

Fifth grade? *Did we even have a dance in fifth grade?*

"And I've always had a date. I'm not so sure I want that to change this year."

"What about the boycott? Are we going to bend the rules?"

"And give these fecal faces the satisfaction?" Elle shook her head. "There are other boys in this school, you know." She waved a hand at the hallway and the students walking down it. "I mean, there's lots of guys who are not actually asshats."

True, there were. Most days, I ate lunch with a bunch of them.

"And for the boys in this school who think they're something special, it would send a message. You want to dance with a girl? Then act like a decent human being." Elle sank back against the lockers, her binder clutched to her chest like a shield. "But I need your help." She gave me a little smile. "Again."

I nodded, even though I had no clue what Elle wanted or how I could be of assistance.

"I want to go to homecoming with Rhino."

She wanted ... *what?*

"It's why I asked about you two." She unclenched a hand from her notebook and pointed at me. "I don't poach, okay? So, if you guys are really ... you know ... just tell me, and I'll totally forget Rhino's name."

"I'm not. We aren't." I started, but then I was hit with a fit of laughter. I had to bend over from it, it struck me so hard. Tears filled my eyes. I couldn't catch my breath. People were starting to stare.

Could I set up Elle with Rhino? The idea of Rhino attending home-coming with *anyone* seemed ridiculous. But the queen of the school with the king of anti-cool? And even if I could get them together, one freaking huge IF … should I?

"I don't know," I said, and another snicker escaped me. "I mean, you're so *you*, and he's so *not*. I don't see any way that I can—"

"You just need to get him talking to me. He won't even do that at this point."

I looked at the stairwell where Rhino had disappeared. I shook my head. "I still don't see how."

"Easy," she said. "That boy does everything you tell him to."

"What?" I laughed again, because that was the most absurd thing I'd ever heard. "Rhino does whatever *he* wants, when he wants to. Trust me."

"So when he paid for your dress yesterday?"

"I didn't ask him to do that. Besides, it's just a loan."

Elle waved her hand. "Whatever. If you can get us talking, I'll do the rest."

"I have no idea how to do that."

"You'll think of something. Meet you at the bleachers after cheer practice." She pushed away from the lockers and glided into the crowd heading for the cafeteria.

"You mean after tutoring," I called, but I don't think she heard me.

♡ ♡ ♡

Elle and Clarissa campaign canisters had magically bloomed on my homeroom teacher's desk over the weekend, and in every other classroom I entered that day. By lunch, Water Bottle Blue had become my least favorite color. Even Rhino's promise of a Cherry Coke couldn't tempt me to stay in the cafeteria, not after I discovered mini Clarissa containers on all of the tables. I grabbed a sandwich and hid out in the Earth Sciences lab for the rest of the period.

The end of the school day couldn't come fast enough. I craved the moment when I could climb the stairs to the tutoring room, a Clarissa-free zone. Finally, it arrived. But if I'd had to write out some sort of equation to describe the effect my homecoming status would have on tutoring, I would've gotten it all wrong. A round of applause broke out when I walked into the room. Byron and his friends were wearing huge silly grins. The pom squad performed some sort of can-can tribute dance. I was flustered and embarrassed. But to be totally honest, it also felt kind of nice.

Once everyone got busy with their individual projects, the only thing left for me to do was to stand by the windows and send waves of support down to the football team. Even that was going pretty well. Gavin had just thrown a long pass, right on target. The receiver pulled the ball in over his shoulder and raced for the goal line.

I was congratulating myself on my superior ESP skills when I heard a voice behind me. "Hey, Camy, where do you want this?"

I turned to find Lexy standing in the doorway. She was holding a blue bottle. A *big* blue bottle, the size used in offices to refill the water cooler. And plastered across the front of it? Clarissa Delacroix's smiling face. I thought my head might explode.

"I ran into Clarissa downstairs," Lexy said. "She told me you wanted a special campaign canister to go in this room. You are *so* cool. I mean, if I was a candidate, I don't think I could be such a good sport. So. Where do you want me to stick it?"

I had a few ideas. But they were All. So. Inappropriate.

She ended up placing the container on a stand under the white board. I looked at the bottle, then at the quote above it: "If people do not believe that mathematics is simple, it is only because they do not realize how complicated life is."

When Byron walked up to the canister, dug deep into the pocket of his pants, and dropped a few pennies in the jar, I knew for sure: Life = Complicated. At least that much was true.

♡ ♡ ♡

I was out of breath when I got to the bleachers that afternoon. I stayed that way while I watched Gavin fade back to throw a forward pass. The spin, the trajectory, the perfect placement. He made it look easy. Except I knew how hard he worked at it. I squinted down the field, my eyes following the ball. Then I felt him looking at me.

I turned away from the catch and toward the boy who'd thrown the football. Gavin was still wearing the helmet. It hid his expression. I couldn't tell what he was thinking, but something was different.

A poke in my back sent my heart racing. I spun around to find Elle.

"They're pretty," she said, nodding toward the field, "but don't forget, they're also total butt nuggets."

Not all of them, I wanted to say.

"So, I assume you've come up with some sort of plan?" she asked.

Actually, I hadn't. Judging by the look on Elle's face, that was a mistake. I took a step toward the field. I wanted to walk the fifty-yard line for luck, but the team was setting up for another scrimmage. Instead, I headed toward the gate near the end zone.

"We should probably meet Rhino on his own territory," I said.

"You think he'd be more comfortable that way?" she asked, following me.

I thought he couldn't escape that way.

The walk to Rhino's went by too quickly. He spotted us when we were halfway up his driveway. Or, at least, he spotted me. He raised his hand to wave, then froze. He held his arm in that awkward half-salute until I stepped up to him and pulled it back down to his side. Then he spun around without a word and retreated into the garage.

I nodded to Elle. "Come on."

"Wait." She grabbed my arm. "His parents make him live out here?"

"No. I mean, well … it's complicated. But he could live in the house if he wanted to." I crept a few feet forward, taking Elle with me.

Rhino was sitting at a computer with his back to us. His fingers were clacking against the keys like whatever he typed there might make us disappear. When that didn't work, he stood, planted his hands on his hips, and glared at both Elle and me. I was the only one who seemed to notice. Elle was checking out the garage. She smiled. Then she trained her eyes on Rhino.

He stood there without flinching. The sweatpants he was wearing hung loose at his hips. The plaid of his boxers was peeking over the top. He was wearing the chicken butt T-shirt I'd bought him for Christmas and the hem hit just below his bellybutton.

But here's the thing. The green stripe in his boxers? It matched the green of his eyes exactly. And that little strip of skin that showed between his shirt and pants? It highlighted some fairly excellent abs. Add in the mussed up but clean and shiny hair and …

Oh. My. God.

When did Rhino get hot?

Okay, I'll admit it. For a second I thought about marching Elle out of there and keeping this upgraded version of Rhino for myself. But when I tried to imagine slow dancing with him in a dark gym (and I tried; believe me, *I tried*) all I felt was … nothing. Nothing like what I imagined with Gavin, anyway.

I don't know what Elle and Rhino were imagining as they gave each other the laser eyes, but no one spoke. No one would, either, unless I did. I said the first thing that popped into my brain.

"Remember way back in the dark ages of last Friday," I said, "after they called my name for homecoming candidate? And you said something 'worked'?"

Rhino jerked his head toward me. He pursed his lips and narrowed his eyes. He threw a glance at Elle next, and his whole face brightened, but not in a good way. It was more of a *don't get mad, get even* kind of look.

"Well," he said, and slouched his way over to the couch. "Have you ever heard of grassroots campaigning?"

Elle and I both nodded.

"I just went around to everyone I knew—the chess club, the math league, all the usual suspects. And I suggested that it might be nice to see someone like you in the homecoming court for a change."

"Someone like me," I repeated. "Did you use my actual name?"

"I did. I said, 'someone like Camy.'"

"That's awesome." Admiration filled Elle's voice. "I've always wanted to try something like that at school," she said. "You have to tell me the details of how you did it."

A scary twinkle appeared in Rhino's eyes. "You don't know enough people to pull it off," he said. Ouch.

But instead of acting offended, Elle just snorted. "Please. I know everyone at OHS."

"No, you don't. You don't *know* them."

"I've memorized the names and faces of every incoming freshman. Have you?"

Rhino waved his hand like he was dismissing her and turned to me. "What I realized was, there are more of *us* than there are of *them*." He nodded toward Elle. "But honestly? I never guessed it would be so easy to storm the Bastille."

Elle stepped forward. "What do you mean, us and them?"

"I'm just stating the obvious. There's your group of ... whatever." He held up his hands like he was trying to shake off something sticky. "And then there's everybody else."

"That's not fair." Elle folded her arms across her chest. "I treat everyone the same, and you know it."

"Yeah? Well, maybe that's the problem," Rhino said. "I mean, just because you lower your standards long enough to give us the royal wave, that doesn't mean you think we really *are* the same as you. Nobody wants your pity."

Elle opened her mouth, but only a small squeak came out.

Rhino sat back. He had the start of a smirk on his face.

But that wasn't fair. Elle really *was* nice to everyone. Well, everyone who didn't qualify as an asshat, anyway. "Can *you* name all the freshmen?" I asked Rhino.

"Do I need to?"

"Know what I think?" I didn't give him time to answer. "I think you're a reverse snob."

He sputtered a few words, but nothing that made sense. For once in my life, I'd managed to make Rhino speechless.

"Have you even given Elle a chance?" I went on, puffed up by my small victory. "Have you really gotten to *know* her? Because I have."

"And the convenient timing of this friendship doesn't make you a little suspicious?" Rhino said. "I thought you'd learned your lesson about her kind of people already. Clarissa Delacroix? Eighth grade? Does that even tickle your memory?"

I hadn't seen that coming, and the blow landed hard as a slap.

"And if you think the fabulous Elle is any different, then—"

"You both know that I'm standing here. Right?" Elle said.

Of course we did, but we were also locked into something that neither of us could stop.

"Ladybug, can't you see it? I don't like Elle and her kind because of what they *do*, not who they are. I am *not* a reverse snob. I'm just a guy who's in touch with reality."

"Prove it." Elle pounced a step closer to Rhino. Her feet landed slightly apart and her hands locked into fists at her hips. She looked like she was about to lead a cheer. Either that or set phasers to stun. It was pretty intimidating.

But if Rhino felt threatened, he didn't show it. "Sure," he said. "How?"

I saw my chance. "You could go with one of 'them' to homecoming."

"Right," he said. The edges of his lips turned up in a sneer. "Just for the sake of argument, which of the crème de la crème of Olympia High's finer young ladies do you propose I ask?"

"Me," Elle said.

He sputtered at that.

"Yeah, I'm willing to 'lower my standards.' What about you? Are you too good to be seen with someone like me?"

Rhino shut his eyes "You're kidding, right?" When he opened them again, he turned to me. "You really think I'm a reverse snob?"

"Uh, let's see," I said. "I remember you saying something about us and them? *Her* kind of people? Storming the Bastille. Sure sounds like it."

A muscle twitched in his jaw. He took in a breath and let it out slowly.

"I guess I don't have a choice." He stomped over to a computer and started typing furiously.

And somewhere in the Amazon, a butterfly the size of a truck flapped its wings.

Chapter Eleven

TUESDAY AT LUNCH, Mercedes cornered me at my locker. "I heard about Elle and Rhino," she said. "Can you do that for me?"

"Do what for you?"

"Set me up with someone. I was supposed to go with Lukas, but Elle won't let that happen. So, I was thinking ... maybe you could help me date on the dork side?"

"On the what?"

"You know, get me hooked up with one of those nice guys you know. All the boys in my classes are either jocks or jerks. And they're all on the list." She rolled her eyes. "So, will you?"

I wasn't sure what to say. On one hand, Mercedes Washington was the real deal, a true Hottie of Troy. She didn't need my help to get a boy. But on the other hand ... the girl standing next to me was bouncing on the balls of her feet like she could barely contain her enthusiasm. And, underneath all that energy, she was really very sweet. I couldn't tell if she didn't see the difference between us or if she was just pretending it didn't exist.

Someone like Mercedes deserved a boy who would treat her with the respect she deserved.

"Do you like *Star Wars*?" I asked. It was an impulse question and a long shot.

"Which ones? The first ones? Oh, yeah! Some of the newer ones?" She waved her hand. "Not so much. But Han Solo?" She fanned herself. "Talk about fine. Sure, he's old enough to be my grandpa, but you know what I mean." She fell back against the lockers, and the beads in her braids clicked against the metal.

"Yeah." I smiled. Mercedes Washington, closet *Star Wars* geek. Who knew?

"So, you got someone for me?" she asked.

"I think I might." Okay, so it wasn't a sure thing, but I had a pretty good feeling about it. "Meet me at the tutoring room after cheer practice."

♡ ♡ ♡

Mercedes poked her head into the tutoring room after school. "So, where's my guy?" she said. Her gaze darted around the classroom like I might have one stashed under a desk or something.

"Downstairs, but—"

"Let's go get him." She pivoted back toward the stairway.

I hurried to turn off the lights and shut the door behind me. "About that," I was saying, but Mercedes was already on the landing beneath me. "Hey! Slow down," I called.

Even though she stopped, it was like her body was still buzzing with energy. She pushed a couple of braids behind her ear and fidgeted with the zipper on her jacket while she waited. "Sorry. Sometimes I get a little ahead of myself," she said when I caught up to her. "So, this boy, what did he say when you—"

"Actually, I haven't talked to him yet. The thing is, he's kind of shy. Okay, that's not true. He's *really* shy, especially with girls. So, even if he likes you, he … what I'm saying is, you might have to be the one to ask him to the dance."

"Sure. No problem," she said. She started down the stairs again, then stopped and looked back at me. "Sorry," she said. "Are you ready?"

Ready as I'd ever be.

We made it to the second floor and came to a stop in front of one of the science labs. Inside, long black tables filled the room. Pairs of students were sitting across from each other with their heads bent as if in prayer. No one glanced up, not even when someone hit the timer alongside their chessboard.

"Over there," I whispered, "by the teacher's desk. Dalton Reese. He's the president of the chess club."

Her eyes got huge. "Oh, I'm going to homecoming with the president!" She looked at Dalton, then back at me. "And he's cute too. Oh, thanks, Camy."

"Don't thank me yet," I told her.

By then, we'd attracted some attention. Tara Tanaka glanced up.

That caused her opponent, Dalton, to do the same. He dropped his chess piece when he saw us. He picked it up, placed it on a new square, then his hand came down on the timer. Tara grinned and I got the feeling Dalton had just made a mistake.

I waved at him to come over, but for a moment I thought he wouldn't. He turned back to the chessboard and his face crumpled.

"Ooh, that wasn't a good move, was it?" Mercedes whispered.

I shook my head. "It's okay," I said. "It's just a game."

"Right. So is tennis."

Dalton pushed back his chair and headed our way. "Uh, hey, Camy," he said when he reached us. "Are y-you here to join the team?"

"Not exactly." I could play chess but I didn't love the game. Not like Dalton did, anyway.

Mercedes bounced forward. "Actually, I am. Hi. I'm Mercedes Washington."

"I know," Dalton said. Only it came out more: I! KNOW! He took his glasses off, then put them back on. A bead of sweat popped up on his forehead.

"I want to," Mercedes began. "Well, see, I play tennis. And everyone's going to be gunning for me this spring, since I won state last year. So I thought I should—"

"Work on strategy and mental toughness?" Dalton suggested.

Mercedes' face lit up. She nodded and I just stood there, a little amazed that she'd managed to get him to speak, and that he'd managed to produce six words that contained most of the parts of a sentence.

"But I don't know anything about chess," Mercedes said.

"You don't have to," he said. "We're not that kind of club. Anyone can join."

"And will *you* teach me how to play?"

Dalton blinked in surprise. So did I. Because, here's the thing: It wasn't so much what Mercedes said, but how she said it. If you could do a rewind, you wouldn't see anything obvious. It's not like she batted her eyelashes at him or anything. Still, she'd clearly just made Dalton an offer he couldn't refuse.

Maybe flirting was another one of those genetic things; either you had it or you didn't. Whatever. Dalton blushed and led Mercedes to a table in a far corner of the room.

He did that even after Tara Tanaka stood up, cleared her throat loudly, and pointed at their unfinished game. It wasn't so much that Dalton ignored Tara on purpose. It was more like all of Mercedes' energy had trapped him and pulled him helplessly along.

Tara threw me a glare as if this was my fault. And all right, in a way, it was. I backed out of the room, hoping whatever it was I'd just done wasn't a huge mistake.

♡ ♡ ♡

I didn't see Mercedes or Dalton in the halls before school on Wednesday. I saw no sign of Rhino or Elle, either. The only presence I couldn't escape was Clarissa. With her smile pasted all over the walls of the school, she was pretty hard to miss. But that afternoon, in the tutoring room, Lexy pulled me aside.

"Camy, I have to go to the bathroom," she said.

"Yeah?" I said, because here's another thing about having a guy as a best friend: You miss out on learning a lot of social cues that every other girl seems to know.

I'd gone back to explaining negative integers to Byron when another pom squad girl whispered in my ear. "That means she needs to talk to you."

So I followed Lexy to the girls' restroom. As soon as we got there she flung each of the stall doors open, checking to see if they were occupied. Then she turned to face me.

"Can you hook me up like you did for Elle and Mercedes?"

"Like I—"

"Here's the deal," she said. "My mom doesn't usually let me date, but since this is my senior year and it's homecoming, she's making an exception. Only with Elle's stupid boy boycott, I'm stuck."

Lexy didn't date? That explained the lack of comments about her on the wiki.

"And I was thinking ... maybe one of those guys from the chess club?" She looked at me with puppy-dog eyes. "That way, Mercedes and I could double date and that would keep my mom from freaking out so much about the whole thing."

"I guess," I said, "but I'm not even sure Mercedes and Dalton are going to homecoming."

"Oh, yeah, they are. He asked her yesterday."

"He ... what?" I shook my head, trying to wrap my brain around the idea. "How did that happen? They just started talking after school."

Lexy laughed. "That girl works fast. All she had to do was convince him that no one else in the school would ask her."

I stared, totally speechless. *Damn*, Mercedes was good. But I wondered, had I just unleashed something on our school that no one was ready for?

"So can you?" Lexy asked, "I *really* want to go to the dance."

I sighed. Who was I to crush dreams?

Mentally, I reviewed the chess club roster until I got to Tim Lansing. He was cute and shy, and he also had an artistic streak. That might make a nice match with Lexy's talent for fashion design.

Chess club didn't officially meet on Wednesday, but a bunch of them usually showed up anyway. Official or not, if another A-list hottie disrupted everyone's game, I was certain Tara Tanaka would leap across the desks and strangle me. She'd already thrown me dirty looks all during earth science.

"Meet me at the caf tomorrow morning," I told Lexy. "I'll introduce you to someone I know."

"Is he cute?"

"Very."

She clapped her hands together. For a moment, I thought she might jump up and down. Instead, Lexy threw her arms around me.

"Thank you," she said. "Thank you so much!"

♡ ♡ ♡

When Lexy arrived in the cafeteria the next morning she was accompanied by several members of the pom squad and a few girls from the dance team. I panicked until Tim arrived with a posse of chess club members and mathletes in tow.

Then I did the only sensible thing: I skipped the introductions and ran.

All through the day I saw evidence of what I'd done. Mercedes bounced down the halls, her arm linked with Dalton's. They looked like they were having an actual conversation. Tim and Lexy stood side by side in front of one of the school's display cases. Rhino even graced Elle's table in the cafeteria for a whole five minutes. Apparently he said something funny too, something that sent the entire cheerleading squad into peals of laughter.

That night, when I logged in to the wiki, the proof was all over the place.

> **jasona: wtf is going on? i've asked 18 girls to h-coming—and nothing. wud go to prairie stone, but cant. this sux.**

Unlike winter semi-formal and prom, the Olympia High homecoming dance was in-school-only. I guess that was supposed to encourage all of us to bond under the guise of school spirit or something.

> **aident: She's already gotten to everyone, so don't bother trying.**
> **jasona: beenthere/donethat. how do you think I asked 18 girls? she's ruining everything.**
> **aident: The whole dance team has dates and Clarissa won't talk to me.**
> **jasona: even lexy's got a date—and she NEVER goes to the dances. but some guy from the chess team asks her and now she's all "leave me alone" to ne1 else.**
> **mchottie: THE CHESS TEAM?**
> **jasona: 4 reel**
> **Lukasn: There's got to be a way to stop her.**

randallb: She has a weak spot. Everybody on the football team knows that. Gotta play a little offense here. It's not that hard.
adm*n: If this turns into any kind of threat, I'm shutting down the thread. Got it?
jasona: o0o, tough guy. Say what, bro. Why don't *you* do sumthin about it?

The conversation (if you could call it that) cut off there. I went looking for other threads, but all I found were the usual suspects making the usual comments on the usual pages. I paid extra attention to Elle's page, since I guessed she was the "her" they wanted to stop, but I got nothing there either. The wiki only let us see so much. If the guys ever took things offline, we'd never know.

Chapter Twelve

ON FRIDAY AFTERNOON, I stood at my locker way past last bell. The empty halls made Clarissa Delacroix watching my every move from the posters above me even freakier. In less than a week, one of us would be crowned homecoming queen. I still hadn't campaigned in any way. Sophie hadn't done much that I could see. And Mercedes was so into Dalton that I wasn't sure she'd thought about the contest at all.

That left a runoff between Elle and Clarissa. The only question left was whether Clarissa could buy enough votes to beat Elle. Today, I'd added a custom-wrapped cookie and a package of licorice whips to my *CD 4 HQ* swag. It was all sitting on the top shelf of my locker.

I was still staring at the pile of Clarissa loot when Sophie slumped against the locker next to mine. "I hear you're the person to see if a girl needs a hookup," she said.

I laughed. Sort of. "Where did you hear that?"

"Where didn't I?" She smacked my arm just hard enough that I felt it. "It's all over," she continued. "Come on, a lot of these boys were dateless wonders before you came along. Now they're the hottest guys in school? Who else even knew they existed besides you?"

"I didn't really do anything," I said. But I didn't believe my own words. From the look on her face, neither did Sophie.

"I mean, I didn't plan any of this," I amended.

"Who needs a plan? Especially when I need a homecoming date. So. Got a guy for me?"

I flipped through my mental roster of boys at school. I was too consumed with the weight of what I was doing to consider the words I said next. "I'm not sure. It's … I'm just not that experienced."

I didn't notice her silence until I shut my locker door. Then I caught her expression. She looked cold, hard, and maybe a little hurt. I didn't know how, but I'd managed to screw things up.

"Whatever I said, I didn't mean anything bad by it."

"Sure you didn't."

"No, really," I said.

"It's not like I'm the last to know or anything," Sophie said as she leaned forward, focusing her whole attention on me. It was like she wanted to make sure I didn't miss a single word. "Sophie Vega isn't good enough. She's a skank. A slut. Nothing but stupid trailer trash. I get it."

"I didn't say that."

"You didn't have to."

When she spun around on one of those serious boot heels, I grabbed for her arm. She pulled it back with such force that I was sure she was prepping for a punch. I cringed and closed my eyes, bracing for a hit that didn't come. When I opened them again Sophie was still standing there, lip quivering, eyes filling with tears. Frantically, I hit the rewind button on our conversation until I got to a certain word. *Experienced?* Was that it?

"Listen. When I said … what I meant was … I didn't think you were … I was talking about me."

"What? You mean you don't have any *experienced* guys on your list?" she said.

"Sophie, I have *Rhino* on my list. I'm just making the rest of it up as I go along." A thought struck me then. "And you know what? I think I *do* have a guy for you, and I'm pretty sure he already likes you."

"Never mind. I don't need your pity." She dug through the pocket of her oh-so-tight jeans and pushed a crumpled twenty-dollar bill at me, so hard I didn't have a choice but to take it.

"My first payment on the loan," she said. "I might be trailer trash, but I keep my promises." Sophie stormed off, her heels hitting the floor with such force, I expected to see holes in the tile.

God, every conversation with her was like walking through a minefield. I sagged against my locker and contemplated the money in my hand. For a few moments, I willed myself not to think of anything. For a few moments, I simply stood in the hallway and smoothed every last crinkle from that twenty-dollar bill.

♡ ♡ ♡

Even though it was a Friday, and one of those perfect autumn days, I trudged up to the tutoring room anyway. Not that I could see anything inside the room when I got there, since Gavin Madison was standing in front of the door, blocking my way. Again.

I might have been clueless about what I'd said to piss Sophie off, but that didn't mean I was stupid enough to think Gavin was there by accident. A lot had happened since that first time he stood between me and that room. And the way he was staring at me made me feel like he was sizing up an opponent.

I decided to play offense. "Coach give you another pass from practice?"

"Nope."

"Oh." So much for offense.

"We need to talk, but not here," he said. He brushed past me on his way to the stairs. "Come on."

I followed him to the second floor hallway, where he disappeared into the boys' bathroom. I froze at the entrance.

He reappeared with an OUT OF ORDER sign in his hand and stuck it to the door. "Don't worry," he said. "It's all clear." The door swung shut behind him.

Did he expect me to go inside? Really? I waited a beat, then another. The door opened a crack. I didn't see Gavin, but I heard his voice.

"Come on, Camy. It's fine." A pause. "Trust me?"

I'm not sure what I expected, but the boys' bathroom was a lot like the girls'. We didn't have urinals, and our walls looked cleaner and less, er, sticky. But everything else about the place was so ... normal.

It was kind of disappointing.

"What do you think of the office?" Gavin asked. "We should really redecorate, but Jason wants stripes and Aiden has his heart set on floral."

Part of me wanted to laugh at the idea of Jason and Aiden going all death match over wallpaper. But there was another part of me that was way too nervous to make a sound. It won out.

"Note to self," Gavin said. "Redecorating jokes? Not so funny."

"It was funny," I managed.

"Thanks. My ego needed that." He grinned at me. Then he unslung his backpack and pulled out a paperback book. I recognized the cover immediately. Two women in togas, a Greek temple behind them. *Lysistrata*. My throat got so tight I couldn't swallow.

"A lot of the guys are wondering why a bunch of girls in this school are suddenly interested in ancient Greece." He studied the book, then looked at me. "It wouldn't seem weird to see you reading a book like this," he said. "But Lexy had it in Goals Lab. Then Aiden heard Sophie asking for a copy of it in the library. Come on, Sophie? She's not exactly genius material, if you know what I mean."

I had decided to keep my mouth shut. Okay, "decided" might not be true. It was more like I had been stunned into silence so far. After all, this was Gavin. And he was *talking* to me. How long had I wished this would happen?

Only, the words he was saying were all wrong.

"You do know that some people used to say the same thing about you, right?" I said. "Once upon a time there was this boy who couldn't pass a test. Do you even remember him?"

Gavin winced, but it only took a second for him to recover.

"Here's the thing," he said. "None of the guys in school can get dates to homecoming."

"That's not what I hear," I said. "The chess club is very popular these days."

"Yeah, well, the football team isn't doing so great."

"On or off the field?" I asked. He cringed again.

Oh. My. God. What am I doing? At this point, Gavin wouldn't speak to me again for another three years, if ever. Still, I couldn't stop myself.

"Maybe if the football team would stop underestimating the girls in this school, they'd do a little better in the dating department. I mean, just because a girl can shake a pom-pom, that doesn't mean she can't do anything else. And just because someone doesn't have very much money, or is a little, uh ..." I stopped to grope for the right word. It didn't come. "Anyway, that doesn't mean she can't be smart."

"Nobody's saying that."

"Yes, they are, Gavin. And they're saying a whole lot of other things, too. Butterface? Sasquatch? Furnipple? Any of those sound familiar?" I was about to mention something about girls who dress like someone's little brother when I glanced down at my Teenage Mutant Ninja Turtles shirt and scuffed-up Chuck Taylors and changed my mind. It was just too embarrassing. Instead, I clamped my mouth shut and stared at him.

And there it was. That look. The one that said: *Gotcha!*

Gavin Madison was quarterback of our football team for a lot of reasons. He had a good arm, sure. But he also had the ability to sniff out the other team's weakness and use it against them. Until that moment, I'd guessed the weak link in Elle's plan would be Lexy, or Mercedes. Maybe one of the girls from the dance squad. I was horrified to discover … it was me.

At least he wasn't cruel about it. He didn't shout, "I knew it!" or perform some sort of touchdown victory dance. He just quietly said, "Okay."

I knew I should spin around then. I knew I should push through the door and sprint for the safety of the tutoring room before I did any more damage. But I couldn't. It was like the sticky stuff on the walls had transferred to the floor. My feet felt glued in place.

"So, here's my idea." Gavin rummaged in his backpack again. This time he pulled out a handful of spreadsheet printouts. He held up the first one. "These are the guys who need dates," he said.

The list read like a who's who of the wiki commenters: Jason, Aiden, Randall Benson—all of them, minus Gavin. Obviously, Elle's strategy was working.

Gavin flipped the page to a second sheet. "And here's all the …" He paused, the start of a small smile tugging the corners of his mouth. "All the smart girls in school."

Every girl on his list had been on the honor roll since elementary school. Tara Tanaka, Prudence Laramie, Babette Riley. The only girl missing?

Me.

"And here." Gavin flipped the page again. "I've made kind of a matrix. Some guys have certain preferences and some would date the flagpole if you could get it to wear a dress and teach it how to slow dance."

I couldn't help it. I snorted. Gavin's grin grew wider.

"So, what do you think?"

"You really want to know? I think you're going to have a hard time getting any of these girls to go to a dance with the Neanderthals who've been ignoring them since fourth grade."

"That's where you come in."

I shook my head. "Oh, no."

"This isn't any different than the chess club and the pom squad. You didn't have a problem with that, did you? It's just one date. One night. Nothing goes too far. No one gets hurt."

"You can't guarantee that," I said.

"And neither can you. What happens when this is all over and the guys on the chess team go back to being untouchable?"

I hadn't thought of that, and the realization now made my lunch rise in my throat. "I can't do this," I said.

"You *can* do this," Gavin said, "and I think you *will*."

"Or else?"

"Or else I let everyone know who's behind this whole … what are you calling it?"

"Boy boycott," I whispered.

"Cute."

His fake approval didn't make me feel any better. I felt even worse when he said, "I'll tell Elle how I found out and …"

Did he need to say anything more?

"I'll cut off your access," he added.

My access? Did he mean to the wiki? "You can do that?"

"I can do that." He glanced at the papers in his hand and held them out to me. "But I won't."

My head spun, a thousand thoughts crashing together. This wasn't something that had popped up on the spur of the moment; it was a trap. Somehow, Gavin had known I was involved in the boycott. He knew Elle was involved too. Had he tracked us by our IP addresses when we logged on as Jason? Some other way?

And then it struck me. If Gavin could cut off my access, did that mean ... "Were you the one who started the site?"

"I can't say who started it. But it wasn't supposed to be—"

"Wait a minute," I interrupted. "You can't say who started it, or you won't?"

"What does it matter?" Gavin said.

"It matters to me."

He took a few seconds to weigh the options, then he closed his lips tight, like there was a string of words he was trying to hold inside. "I ... I can't."

The realization that Gavin was involved with the wiki intimately enough that he could affect my access sent a jolt through my body. But when I looked up into those amber eyes I was willing to bet that someone else had started it, that someone else was the mastermind.

Not that Gavin wasn't smart enough. I glanced at the dating spreadsheets. Clearly he'd developed some mad geek skills in the past three years. But the Gavin I knew just wasn't the kind of guy who would do something so ... cruel. Well, unless you wanted to count holding a girl's hand one day, then denying her existence the next. But I didn't have time to think all of that through.

Gavin held the papers out until they fluttered just inches from my fingertips. He was waiting for an answer.

What if I took those papers? What if I worked with Gavin?

If I refused, he would cut off access to the wiki and tell Elle it was all my fault. But if I did it, if I betrayed Elle and went double agent, maybe I could figure out who was really behind the thing. I looked up at Gavin again. Maybe I could figure *him* out too.

I reached out and slipped the papers from his hand. Taking them didn't mean I was agreeing to anything, I told myself.

I scanned the list of preferences some of the guys had. Hair color and length, height, weight, and more. I peered at him over the top of the spreadsheets. "Have you ever heard the phrase 'beggars can't be choosers'?"

He laughed. "Some of these guys have never had to beg before."

I rolled my eyes. "If I do this, you can't tell anyone I was involved," I said.

"Same here."

I smiled at Gavin and he smiled back. In that moment, we were in this together. I thought he might even reach out to take my hand, but he only pointed toward the door.

Three steps into the hallway, I halted. Gavin unstuck the OUT OF ORDER sign and returned it to the bathroom. The door whooshed closed, and he stopped behind me. He stood so close that the warmth of our bodies seemed to combine. And then all that warmth drained from both of us.

Because standing in front of us, flanked by two of her dance team minions, was Clarissa Delacroix.

I ran for the stairs. With each step up, I couldn't help but think: *Stupid, stupid, stupid.* I was stupid to make a deal with Gavin. Stupid to let Clarissa catch me.

The tutoring room was empty, but instead of relief, a wave of loneliness washed over me. I'd been looking forward to losing myself in explaining the same equation over and over again or detailing the symbolism in *The Grapes of Wrath*. Instead, I had what I'd always thought I wanted: an empty tutoring room, on a beautiful fall day, with the sounds of football floating in through the open windows. The team was running through an informal practice on the field below.

Ten minutes had passed when Gavin Madison walked across the track toward the field, his helmet tucked under one arm. Before I had time to duck, he looked over his shoulder, straight at the tutoring room window.

I sank to the floor, my back against the wall beneath the sill. I took one deep breath and then another. What I needed was something safe, something predictable, a slice of the ordinary.

I needed Rhino.

Chapter Thirteen

RHINO'S GARAGE DOOR was shut tight. I probably should have taken that as a warning. Instead, I went in through the mud room. It always felt rude and a little weird to walk through the house without saying anything, so I poked my head into the kitchen. "Hey, Mrs. R," I called.

She turned toward me and smiled. "Oh, Camy, there you are! We haven't seen you in a while."

"School," I said. "Busy."

"I know. Ben told us about the homecoming court. How exciting for you! Wait. Hang on. Here," she said, handing me a plate of warm chocolate chip cookies. "Can you take that out to Ben and his ..." She paused and tucked a strand of hair behind her ear. "His friend."

I nodded.

"Oh, and be sure to tell your dad to come over this weekend. Darren will be home, and we're having a cookout. Besides, we don't see enough of him since he and your mom—" She re-tucked the strand of hair. "We just don't see enough of him."

I stood there for a second, not sure what to say. Dad wasn't much on socializing. And the Rineholds were ... okay. I guess they meant well.

The oven timer went off and I was saved by the bell. Or the beep. Whatever.

The smell of warm chocolate mixed with a hint of cement as I stepped down the few stairs to the garage. Maybe I should've thought more about who Rhino's "friend" might be. His list of them wasn't huge, but it did exist. He had a way of drawing people to him. They were geeks, mostly, but he attracted his share of nerds and hopeless dorks too. Padawan learners to his Jedi Master.

I shoved open the door to the garage with my hip and stopped. Because sitting on Rhino's couch was no dork. Not unless the new nerd uniform included short shorts with the word CHEER! printed across the butt. I was willing to bet that most geeks were never student council president, head cheerleader, or co-captain of the debate team either. (All right, so maybe that last one.) I pulled the door closed quietly behind me.

Rhino flipped his hair in my direction and his eyes crinkled. "Let me rewind and I'll show you," he was saying.

"I see enough of Todd the Toad already." Elle glanced over her shoulder at me. "He's my cousin, you know." She rolled her eyes and shook her head.

"And he's going to beat you tomorrow if you don't pay attention," Rhino added.

It was like they noticed me without actually noticing me. I don't know why that surprised me. It wasn't like either of them ever missed a thing. Together they could probably take over the world. Or at least beat Prairie Stone High at debate, which looked to be their current objective.

Rhino pressed a button on the remote. On the screen, a boy with dark hair, smart-looking glasses and a *Star Wars* tie moved backwards, as if retracting the point he'd just made. Debate in reverse, a politician's dream.

"Right ... there," Rhino said. "When he's not sure what he's talking about, he touches his index cards, see? When he's confident, it's like the cards don't exist."

Elle let out a breath. "You are a freaking genius."

Rhino patted her knee, then raised his hands in mock modesty. "That goes without saying." Which meant, of course, that Rhino had to say it. "Want to take a break?"

He stood and turned toward me. He blinked once or twice, and it was like his eyes were adjusting from the dazzling colors of the TV screen and Elle to plain old, real life, black and white me. I raised the plate of cookies, but he focused on my face. "You okay?"

"Fine." I wondered if he could hear the lie in my voice.

"You look dehydrated or something."

I sighed. Or *something*. "Maybe I am."

"Grab a Coke from the fridge." Rhino scooted past me and went to check one of the computers on the far wall of the garage.

I think it was what was in the fridge that did me in. I opened the door. For a second, I shut my eyes and let the cool air hit my face. When I opened them, row after row of Diet Coke greeted me. At first I thought it was only the ones in front. I pushed a few cans aside. Then a few more until, at last, I'd checked every can of soda in the mini-fridge.

All Diet Coke. Not a single can of Cherry. Damn.

I shut the door. Not a slam; I wasn't in that kind of mood. I wasn't upset about Elle's takeover of Rhino's garage. I wasn't jealous. But I felt the last strands holding my day together fray and I sighed.

"I thought you were okay with this," Elle said.

"Okay with what?" I worked on feigning innocence, but Elle crossed her arms over her chest and tapped a foot.

"It's ... different, okay?" I glanced to where Rhino was fiddling with one of his computers.

"Got it!" he called across the room. "Want to see what he did at last week's Edina Invitational?"

"The Invitational?" Elle said. "How did you ...?"

"I have some excellent AV techie connections. A friend of a friend of a friend." He waved a hand in the air. "That kind of thing."

"You're amazing," she said.

He spread his hands, his grin equally wide. "Again, goes without saying."

Ha, I thought.

Out loud I said, "Are you supposed to be doing this?"

They both gave me the exact same look, a *Why are you pestering us with mundane and inconsequential details?* sort of stare. They both, I suddenly realized, had that same streak of ruthless ambition, a "win at all costs" mindset. And combining these two? They were either perfect for each other, or whatever I'd started on Monday would surely rock the school before the year was out.

Rhino had planted himself on the couch next to Elle again and was firing up the new recording.

"I think I'll go home," I said.

"Stay, Ladybug." Rhino waved at the screen. "You can help psychoanalyze poor Todd the Toad. He won't know what hit him tomorrow."

"That's okay," I said. "You guys are doing fine on your own."

That was it, of course. They were fine. Without me. It wasn't that I wanted Rhino to pat my knee. Not at all. But overnight, he'd let Elle into his bubble of personal space. The one he had, until now, reserved completely for me. When he pointed at the screen, he leaned toward her. And if a strand of her hair graced his shoulder? He ran it through his fingers as if gauging its silkiness.

I left without saying goodbye.

I felt a twinge at the edge of the drive, the tiniest bit of regret fueling my doubt. But I reminded myself again: I didn't like Rhino *that* way. We'd tried it, of course. On more than one rainy afternoon back in ninth grade, when there wasn't anything better to do, we'd danced around the edges of making out. But even though Rhino might be as naturally talented at kissing as he was at math or dancing … something was missing.

Standing in his driveway now, I knew that this feeling was loneliness, not doubt, not true regret. I was rudderless without Rhino's ever-present company.

I left his driveway in increments, one step backward at a time. Maybe, I thought at the last second, the garage door would rumble open and he'd insist I come back inside. But it didn't, and he didn't. I turned toward home, knowing I'd feel just as lonely there.

♡ ♡ ♡

I caught Dad on the phone that night, talking quietly with my mom.

"I'm telling you, Olivia, it's different," he said. "She's distant and kind of jumpy." After a pause he said, "No, I don't think it's the college thing. Maybe it's the pressure of the homecoming competition?" Followed by a quick, "What? She didn't tell you?"

Great. Until that second, homecoming had felt like the least of my problems. I had a dress and a ride in a convertible. I was leaving the rest of it up to the universe, fate, karma, or whatever. Now I'd have to explain the whole thing to my mom. And to keep Dad from worrying

CHARITY TAHMASEB AND DARCY VANCE

I'd have to make sure the phrase "freaky hermit girl" would not leave his mouth all weekend long.

I did my homework downstairs at the kitchen table. I raked up a big pile of leaves in the yard. When it came to the wiki, I vowed not to get sucked in—too much. A few times a day, I looked through the new comments. I added a few notes to my tracking spreadsheet before I studied the ones Gavin had given me in the boys' bathroom. I had a feeling I was missing something and it bothered me.

On Sunday afternoon I decided to take one last peek at the wiki before the Vikings game. I was upstairs, fingers on my laptop, when the doorbell rang.

"Camy, someone's here to see you," Dad called.

I was halfway down the stairs when I stopped to think: *Who?* Dad would've said if it was Rhino. I slowed my steps. Elle, maybe? But then I had another thought, and my heart sped up. Maybe it was Gavin. I gripped the handrail and forced myself down the last few stairs.

I found them in the kitchen. Dad … and Sophie.

"Oh, hey," I said, hoping I didn't sound too disappointed. I wasn't, not really.

Sophie looked at her shoes. Not those serious boots today, but a beat-up pair of knockoff Chucks. Then she glanced up at me. "You wouldn't know anything about *Grapes of Wrath*, would you?" she said.

"I know everything about it."

Dad laughed and grabbed a beer from the fridge. "Well, ladies, if you get bored with great literature, there's always the Vikings at three."

"Football," I said to Sophie. "It's kind of a tradition around here." She looked confused, her gaze going from me to where Dad had vanished into our living room.

"I thought…" she began. "I mean, I didn't know you lived with your dad."

"My mom lives in Iowa. She teaches Women's Studies there."

"Oh."

Yeah. That was most people's reaction.

"So," I said, trying to break through Sophie's odd politeness. "*Grapes of Wrath*?"

"Actually, I was wondering." She picked at the label on the bottle of water Dad had handed her. "Do you really have a guy for me?"

"Yep."

"And does he really like me, or does he just think he can get laid?"

I fought off a blush and thought about Kevin Orrs, former stoner, former slacker supreme, mysteriously turned AV tech geek. I thought about how, whenever he took video footage of an assembly or pep rally, he always let the camera stop on Sophie a few moments longer than anyone else. It wasn't something obvious. If you weren't looking for it, you'd probably miss it.

"I'm pretty sure he likes you just to like you," I whispered, peeking into the living room. Dad seemed engrossed in football. Still, there was no sense in taking any chances. "Let's go upstairs," I said.

Sophie stopped at the door to my bedroom. "Whoa," she said. "Sweet. Is this all yours?"

I nodded.

"I gotta share with my sisters. It sucks." She shook her head. Then she pierced me with a look. "So this not-wanting-to-get-laid boy. Who is he?"

"Kevin Orrs?" I said it like that too. Like it was a question, not a fact. Like Kevin could become someone else, depending on Sophie's reaction.

"Are you kidding me? Kevin Orrs does not like me."

"Ever watch the videos of assemblies?"

"Nobody watches those." She hesitated for a moment, then said, "Don't tell me. You watch them?"

"Sometimes."

"You are the weirdest girl I know."

If that was enough to qualify me as weird, what would Sophie think if she learned the whole truth? That I'd strung together a series of clips that featured Gavin, and even synced them to music?

Weird or not, something in the way she'd said it made things okay between us. She pushed the hair away from her face, and I caught a flash of blue and silver circling her wrist, the bracelet I'd given her.

I sat at my desk, opened my laptop and brought up the school website. I scrolled through the archives for Video Fridays until I found the one marked "Homecoming Court." I'd already watched it. Dad had wanted to see the candidate announcement, which he'd then played about a thousand times.

Unlike Dad, Sophie watched the video in mock horror. "When aliens take over the world, they'll probably use this video to prove that humans have no higher brain function," she said.

I snorted. She was so funny, and so smart. And she *so* didn't realize it.

I muted the volume. "It's easier to see with the sound off."

"What? The 'no brain' part?"

I snorted again.

Even before Aiden pulled the first slip of paper from the envelope, Kevin's camera had zoomed in on Sophie. He'd made sure all the important stuff was captured, sure, but Sophie was obviously the star of the show. At least the way he saw things.

When the video ended, Sophie exhaled, then sat on my bed. "I don't know if I should think it's cool or be creeped out."

"Cool. Definitely," I said. "For one thing, Kevin is not on the wiki. Plus, he's..."

I wanted to say something about the way he had transformed himself from slacker into ... I didn't know what to call him. I still saw him

196

skateboarding in town sometimes. And most days, he still dressed like he did his shopping from the Goodwill store's throw-away pile. But sometime last spring he'd started sitting with the techies at lunch, instead of the dregs. And when his name was called over the intercom, it was more likely that he was on the honor roll than the detention list these days.

I thought I'd caught a glimpse of something similar when Sophie had first slipped on her dress at Tillie's last week. When she'd looked in that three-way mirror, it was like she saw a whole different girl in there.

But I couldn't tell her any of that. "He's cute," I said instead.

"Whatever." Sophie shrugged. "Sure. Set me up with my own geek love connection."

I thought she might leave then, but she scooted back on my bed and crossed her legs at the ankles. I smelled cooking oil downstairs and a faint pop reached my ears. Dad was getting ready for the Vikings game.

"Speaking of love connections," she said. "What's up with you and Gavin in the boys' bathroom?"

My stomach iced over. The feeling spread until most of my body was freezing. At the same time, my cheeks started to burn. I pressed my fingers against them to cool my face and warm my hands.

"It's all over school. The dregs know, anyway." Sophie pointed to herself. "So I figure everybody else does too."

"What about Elle? Do you think she knows?" I asked.

"Probably."

"What am I going to do?" Even though I said the words to Sophie, I was really asking for help from the universe, or karma, or that great whatever. I was probably screwed on all accounts.

"You're gonna tell me, that's what."

I shook my head. "It's ... complicated."

CHARITY TAHMASEB AND DARCY VANCE

"When is there ever anything between guys and girls that's *not* complicated?" Sophie sighed. "Does this have anything to do with the boycott? If so, forget Elle and her stupid rules. Gavin Madison is a fine reason to break *any* rule."

"He is, isn't he?" I barely whispered the words, but Sophie's eyes lit up.

She grinned. "Tell me what's so complicated about Mad Dog, anyway."

I looked at Sophie Vega sitting on my bed. I watched her fingers twist the blue and silver string bracelet, and I made a decision. I'd tell her. Everything. I'd even show her Gavin's spreadsheet if she needed proof.

"Holy shit," she said, her eyes scanning Gavin's matrix. "What are you going to do?"

"I don't know. If I help him and Elle finds out…" I shook my head, not sure what would happen, only that it would be unspeakably awful.

"Or Clarissa," Sophie said.

"Or Clarissa," I echoed.

"That girl has got it in for both of us."

Dad chose that moment to clomp up the stairs. Sophie's eyes got all big and I stashed the spreadsheets under my calculus homework. He knocked, then opened the door. A wave of warm, buttery air came in with him. The rituals of Sundays: popcorn, football, and rooting for the underdog.

"Here you go, ladies." Dad set the bowl on my desk with two bottles of water and some extra paper towels. "Vikings play at three," he added on the way out.

Sophie frowned after he'd left. "Does that mean he wants me to leave?"

I wondered what part of on-the-stove homemade popcorn she didn't understand and reached for a handful. "You mean the Vikings thing?" I asked. "He's trying to convert you."

"Convert me? Into what?"

"A fan. He believes everyone should share in the misery."

Sophie didn't move. She didn't reach for the popcorn, either. I moved to the bed, bringing the popcorn bowl with me and setting it between us.

Sophie shook her head. "Sorry. I'm still trying to wrap my brain around you living with your dad," she said, staring out the window. "See, 'dad' is kind of a ... an ambiguous term at my house. There's the 'dad' we lost our food stamps for, but he was gone after Mom caught him with the babysitter. Then there's the guy before him, the one who spent our rent money on an Xbox system. Or the 'dad' to my little sister, or my other little sister."

Sophie exhaled. "Then there's my real dad, but he disappeared before I was even born." She squeezed her eyes shut, and when she opened them again, she turned to stare straight at me. "My mom got kicked out of the house when my grandma found out she was pregnant. She had no place to stay. And he left her. All alone. She was seventeen."

The minutes stretched between us. I knew I should say something. *I'm sorry? Can I do anything to help?* I was pretty sure Sophie didn't want to hear either of those.

"So," she said finally. "You can stop pretending that I'm some kind of princess. I'm nobody's Cinderella. There's no such thing as Prince Charming, either. At least not in my world."

I was still trying to figure out what to say when Dad called up the stairs again.

"Vikings in five!"

I shut my eyes and sank against the wall next to my bed.

"We can go somewhere else if it makes you uncomfortable," I said.

"And waste all this amazing popcorn?" Sophie tossed a piece in the air and caught it in her mouth. "How about this? If you explain football to me, I'll keep Clarissa off your back this week. I mean, if you"—she nodded at the spot where I'd stashed the spreadsheets—"decide to help Gavin."

"Would *you* help him?"

"You mean if Mad Dog looked at me the way he looks at you?" Sophie smiled. "Elle would have to call out the Army to keep me away from him."

"It's not like that," I said.

"Sure it isn't."

We made it downstairs in time for the kickoff. Dad and I took turns explaining the rules to Sophie until she had to leave for work. I waited until I was sure the Vikings would break Dad's heart (again) and used that as an excuse to take a walk.

"I know how this ends," I told him on my way out.

"Traitor!" he called after me.

I laughed and stepped outside. Maybe I couldn't change the whole world, or even make the Vikings win. Could I change things for one person? I stood on the porch and took in a deep breath. In that moment, the world smelled like dry leaves and fresh-cut grass, like warm sunshine, like … possibilities. I headed down the stairs and my feet automatically turned toward Rhino's.

Changing the world would take a little help.

Chapter Fourteen

"ARE YOU SURE THIS WILL WORK?" I asked Rhino on Monday morning as we walked into school.

"Ladybug, please." He placed a hand on each of my shoulders and forced me to stop. We'd gone over the plan last night, and again this morning. But there were new and improved displays touting *CD 4 HQ* and they made me feel a new and improved kind of panic.

"A grassroots campaign isn't going to be obvious." Rhino frowned at the posters all around us. "And it might not work. The only way to guarantee it would be to manipulate the data, but the tallying is all done on paper. I can't hack into that kind of system." He rolled his eyes in contempt.

"That's not how I want her to win, anyway."

Rhino shrugged. "Then you'll just have to trust me."

I nodded, but I wasn't totally convinced.

"You don't feel weird about this, do you?" I'd asked Rhino the night before, while we were poring over the queen contestant rules in his garage. It was just after he'd yelled "Aha!" and given me his best evil genius look.

"I thought I remembered my mom saying something about this," he'd said.

Apparently, sometime back in the 1970s or 80s the whole beauty pageant thing had taken on a negative vibe. Somebody then had an idea to make our homecoming queen contest mean something more than a straight-up competition to see who was the prettiest. That's when the whole deal about funding the senior class trip came in. With it came a mechanism to increase the amount of money raised. "The Silver Clause" had never really caught on, but it was never actually removed from the rules, either.

According to Section C, Paragraph 2: Every *penny* collected in the contest counted as one vote for a candidate. Dollars counted as 100 votes. But if someone slipped *other* coins into a campaign canister, they counted as *negative* votes. So, if Rhino were to persuade a member of the chess team to drop a quarter into one of Clarissa's containers, or Elle's, or anybody's, then twenty-five votes would be taken away from her total, instead of added to it.

It was complicated. It was also perfect!

"Is there something I *should* feel weird about?" Rhino said, once his eyes had stopped glowing from the possibility of gaming the system.

Was he waiting for me to spell it out? "Do you feel weird about helping Sophie when you're … you know … with Elle?"

"Nah, not really. I'm always up for a little social manipulation," he said. Then he rubbed his hands together and twirled the ends of his invisible villain mustache. "It's … my hobby. The real question is, are *you* sure?"

"About what?"

Rhino shrugged. "I thought maybe you'd like to be queen."

I thought about it for a second, really thought about it, then I shook my head. "All I ever really wanted was to be in the parade, and wear the dress, and—"

"Sit next to a certain football player?"

I felt a blush coming on and looked down at my shoes. "Shut up."

"Okay, I'll quit," Rhino said. Then he added, "You know, you worry about things too much." He'd put his hands on my shoulders again. It wasn't quite a hug, but it wasn't exactly *not* a hug either. It was Rhino, sharing his space.

I'd known I could count on him then. But standing in the school hallway the next morning, everything seemed a little less certain.

Just then, Gavin walked past me, coming from behind. I couldn't stop myself from staring after him. Rhino took a step back. Gavin turned and winked. Then he kept walking like nothing had happened.

Rhino's face crinkled into a squint. "You know, Ladybug, there are some people who will vote for you no matter what I do."

♡ ♡ ♡

I saw Gavin two more times that day. Before lunch, when he gave me a questioning look. Then, as I was running to French class. That time, the look felt like he was accusing me of something. I dreaded climbing the stairs to the tutoring room after school. Would he block me again on the third floor landing? Would he insist on another not-so-secret meeting in the boys' bathroom?

The landing was empty but the tutoring room was full. From the windows, I spotted Gavin in full practice uniform, warming up his arm. I guess not even Mad Dog Madison could sneak out of practice the Monday before a homecoming game.

That night, just before I backed up the wiki, my Facebook page showed a new friend request. Gavin Madison. Before I'd thought things all the way through, I confirmed the request and he sent a message to me.

Gavin: So, how's it going?
Camy: Ummm…

I touched the folder that I'd stuffed Gavin's spreadsheets into. I'd looked at them, sure, but so far I hadn't done anything to start Operation Hookup.

Gavin: I've given you some kind of impossible mission, haven't I?
Gavin: Ha. Mission Impossible.
Gavin: 6 impossible missions.
Camy: 6 impossible jocks.
Gavin: Got anyone for them?
Camy: Not yet.

I hadn't even tried. I guessed I should probably explain why.

Camy: The Ab = bad reputation
Camy: Aiden? He's -

I let the cursor blink and tried to figure out the right word to describe Aiden. At least Jason had that goofy charm going for him. But Aiden? His preference list was longer than any of the other boys'. From what I could tell, what he really wanted was a clone of Clarissa. Only three inches shorter. Picky, much?

Gavin: Aiden's an @ss

I laughed. Gavin had a way with words. Or non-words. I flipped from the message session back to the wiki, then back again a couple of times. *No way*, I thought. *It can't be.* But as much as I wanted to deny it, the evidence was right there in front of me.

Gavin was Adm*n.

The second I thought it, I knew it was true. I also knew that accusing him of it might cause even more trouble. Maybe, *maybe*, I needed to keep this to myself, for now. I took in a deep breath and let it out slowly, trying to maintain control as I typed my response.

Camy: The problem with Aiden is we all know him.

Of all the wiki boys, Aiden was the one guy that every "smart girl" on my list knew. We'd all shared honors classes with him. We'd all listened to him endlessly talk about, well, everything, but his favorite subject was always himself.

Gavin: How 'bout Randall. He's cool.

I knew Randall from my football days. We'd been on the same youth league team. There was only one problem with him.

Camy: He's a player.

Gavin: Yeah. He's a great linebacker.

Camy: You know what I mean.

Gavin: He really likes this one girl

Camy: What if she doesn't like him?

Gavin: That would be a problem.

Randall had started "dating" in the fourth grade. By the time we hit middle school he'd already been through all of the popular girls in our class, plus the ones in the class ahead of us, and behind us. Twice. But even though his relationships never lasted very long, I'd never heard anyone complain about having him as a boyfriend. And the things he'd said on the wiki weren't too horrid. I guessed that counted for something.

Camy: He really likes her? For real?

Gavin: I know. It's weird. But yeah.

I flipped through the spreadsheet and studied Randall's entry. He hadn't listed any preferences or types. Just the name of one girl, a girl who wasn't his type at all. I was pretty sure he wasn't her type either. Still…

Camy: Okay. I'll do it. Have R meet me at his locker 20 minutes before first bell.

I thought that would end our conversation. I pushed away the spreadsheet and pulled out earth science. All my new extracurriculars (double agent, homecoming candidate, private eye) were ruining my grades. I worked for a while and was about to shut down my laptop when the message window pinged me again.

Gavin: You still there?

My heart did this crazy beating thing. My fingers trembled on the keyboard.

Camy: Yes.

Gavin: Can I call you sometime?

My hands shook, but I pulled myself together long enough to type back:

Camy: Sure. Fine.

As soon as I sent my phone number to him, he signed off. I still wasn't sure what had just happened, or if he would ever really call. It was enough to think he might, though. I danced through getting my pajamas on. And even after I'd climbed into bed, I still had a smile on my face.

I jumped when my phone chirped on the nightstand. I jumped again when I checked the display screen and found an unknown number there.

"Hello?"

"I hope it's not too late." It was Gavin. It was really, truly him. Unless I'd already fallen asleep and was dreaming. A definite possibility.

"Late? Not too," I said. Awesome. I was talking like Yoda.

"You're sleepy. I'll let you go. I just wanted to say 'sweet dreams.'"

"Thanks. You too."

Then he was gone.

♡ ♡ ♡

I needed to make a stop at the AV Tech room the next morning. It was early, but I only had fifteen minutes before I had to tackle the Randall issue. Accomplishing two impossible things before first bell was about all I could handle.

I pushed open the door and was relieved to see Kevin Orrs at one of the computer stations. I wouldn't say we were close friends, but I knew him well enough that my showing up in the tech room wasn't all that weird.

"Hey," he said when he saw me. "What's up?"

I almost said, "The best thing that's ever happened to you!" But I thought that might be overselling it. Instead, I went with, "Nothing much."

He nodded. Kevin was totally attractive, with brown hair and sleepy blue eyes. He was a flannel shirt and ripped-up jeans kind of guy, the kind of boy you could relax around, and just be yourself. He'd be good for Sophie.

I dropped into the chair next to his and watched him work for a few seconds. I leaned closer while Kevin spliced video of various homecoming activities into some sort of slideshow.

"Are you doing video for the ceremony on Friday?" I asked.

"Yeah. Somebody's got to." He gave me a grin. "By the way, I never said congratulations. I hope you win," he added.

"No, you don't."

He blinked and looked away, but he didn't deny it.

"And speaking of that, she needs a date for the dance."

"I don't know what you're talking about," he said.

"I think you know exactly what I'm talking about. I think you know *who* I'm talking about, too."

Kevin pushed back from the computer and stared at the ceiling. At last, he let out a long sigh. "Thing is, I don't hang out with the dregs anymore. In case you haven't noticed, I'm now an official honor roll nerd. Not that there's anything wrong with—I mean, I'm not saying *you're* a nerd, Camy. I—"

"Sure. Whatever. No problem. Would you mind if I asked you what happened?"

"Nah. It's pretty simple, really. My dad promised to buy me a car if I could bring up my grades and keep them up for the rest of the year. Anyway, that's how it started. Once I tried it, though, I realized I actually *like* to learn."

"Even more than you liked being a slacker?"

He nodded.

"So what if I told you Sophie has serious nerd potential too? What if I said she's really smart underneath all that 'I don't care' attitude? Well, when she tries."

"Do or do not," Kevin said. "There is no try."

Whoa. The Yoda-speak-thing must be contagious. Either that or Kevin's transformation from slacker to dork was finally complete. I almost said something about it, but I looked down at my *Come to the dark side … We have cookies* shirt and changed my mind.

Really, I needed to do something about my wardrobe. Stat.

"But you like her, right?" I said.

"Yeah, but …"

"I know she'll say yes if you ask."

"She will?"

I hesitated before nodding. Promising anything about Sophie felt like guaranteeing a volcano wouldn't erupt.

"But homecoming's only a few days away," Kevin said. "I need a jacket or something. Do I have to wear a tie? Should I get her one of those wrist corsages?"

"So, you're going to ask her?"

"Well, I mean, I don't know. You think I should try?"

"Do or do not. There is no try." I stood up. My work here was done.

♡ ♡ ♡

Twenty minutes before first bell, I found Randall at his locker. "Maybe we should walk and talk at the same time," I said. That might look less suspicious. Also, I didn't think things would go as smoothly with Randall as they had with Kevin. As far as I knew, Randall's dream girl didn't even know he existed.

"I don't see you very much these days," Randall said.

"I still make it to all the games."

"Yeah. We know."

The comment made my head jerk up. For as long as I could re-member, Randall had been huge. He wasn't fat, but even when we were little, he'd been more like a mountain than an actual boy.

"You think any of us forgot about you?" he added. "Everyone knows you'd still be playing, if not for—" He nodded toward my knee.

I laughed. "I probably wouldn't be playing football anymore, any-way. You guys got bigger, or I got smaller, or something."

"We could've made you our kicker."

Randall was all about the "we". And for some strange reason, he thought I was still part of that. Or maybe he knew I just wanted to be.

"I do miss it," I said, "but it's not awful, being a fan."

"Look, Camy." He put a giant hand on my shoulder, stopping me before I could turn into the long hallway that led to the orchestra prac-tice rooms.

"I never said it back then, but … I'm really sorry." Randall sighed and his whole body shook with it. "I was showing off that day. I had no business being in that pileup."

"It wasn't you." The truth was, it *was* Randall, but it wasn't *just* him. I didn't say that.

"You're only telling me that to be nice. Inside, you hate me, don't you?"

"Absolutely not. If I hated you, I'd tackle you right here, drag you into the girls' bathroom, and give you a swirly. "

He laughed. That was another thing about Randall. His laugh was as large as he was. In the lobby behind us, everyone got quiet when they heard him. A few kids shot us suspicious glances, and I thought I saw one of Clarissa's minions scurry off.

"Shit. This is supposed to be a secret, isn't it?" he said.

"Yeah, but it's okay. We can tell people we were talking football or something."

As we walked down the hallway, we heard muffled notes from the members of the Olympia High Orchestra, all hidden away in their own practice rooms. We went from piano to French horn to cello. At the last door, Randall wiped his palms against his jeans, then smoothed his hair.

"How do I look?"

I almost said, "Fine." Except he didn't. There was nothing I could do about the silky blue material of his shirt. It might help if he fastened a few more buttons, though. And he'd have to lose the bling.

"Well," I began.

"Go ahead and tell me. I won't get mad." He looked at the door and his eyebrows rose when a sudden burst of music reached us. "She ... really means a lot to me."

"Okay, then, take the necklace off."

"What?" His hand flew to his neck.

I crossed my arms over my chest. "You want this to work, right?"

Randall reached behind him and unhooked the necklace. The chain jingled when he dropped it into his pocket.

"And button the shirt three more buttons."

"Two," he countered. "I gotta be me."

"Yeah, but she's a serious girl. You've got to show her Randall, the serious athlete, not Randall, the boy with the seriously bad reputation."

He buttoned the shirt.

I raised my hand to knock on the practice room door, but stopped. I had better sense than to interrupt Prudence Laramie in the middle of a song. Actually, I had better sense than to interrupt Prudence Laramie *any* time. I waited until I'd heard five seconds of silence, then I knocked. A violin let out a small screech of protest as if in response. I winced and felt Randall, behind me, do the same—a full body, linebacker kind of wince.

"Come in," Prudence called, in the same tone she might use to say, *This better be good.*

I stepped into the room alone since Randall was trying to cower behind me in the doorway. I reached back, grabbed his wrist, and tugged him inside. Then we all stood there and stared at each other. Or really, I stared at Randall and Prudence while they stared at each other.

"I know you," Prudence said.

Randall kicked one foot with the other. "Our lockers are pretty close."

Prudence shook her head and her incredible mane of red curls bounced. I'm pretty sure Randall forgot his own name in the wake of it.

"No," she said. "I *know* you. You were at the All-District Orchestra concert last spring. And you were at the City Youth Orchestra summer concert. You were there when we played the Aquatennial, too." Apparently, Randall Benson was hard to miss.

His cheeks turned dusky red. "I'm kind of a fan."

"How many of my concerts have you been to?" she asked.

"Except for a couple I had to miss because of football, um, all of them?"

The way Prudence looked at Randall, I thought she was trying to figure out if he was a music lover, or a giant, creepy stalker. "In that case," she said, "what pieces are your favorites?"

Randall looked like he was about to panic. This was a test, and he knew it. "I ... I ... like the stuff nobody really knows," he said. "Not all the music you hear in cartoons, but the other ... songs."

"Are you talking about atonal compositions?" Prudence took up her violin and drew the bow along the strings.

A haunting melody filled the room. It almost sounded as if the violin were crying. This wasn't the sort of music that you relaxed to. You listened to be challenged. My mom would've loved it. After a few moments, Prudence lifted her bow and the last of her notes echoed around us.

In their aftermath, she said, "Something like that?"

"Yeah," he said, his voice quiet, hushed, like he was standing in church.

"Why?"

That was when I knew: This was the *real* test. That other question had just been a warmup. I glanced at Randall, hoping he understood how important his answer would be.

"This is going to sound stupid," he said.

"Probably," Prudence replied.

"It makes me think about football."

Skepticism washed across Prudence's face. I shut my eyes. Clearly, that was not the answer she'd been looking for. But Randall wasn't done. Not yet.

"It's the way I feel on the field." He said each word slowly, like he was picking them carefully. "Like after the ball's snapped, then there's this crush of bodies, and the adrenaline, and it reminds me that I'm alive." He nodded toward her violin. "When I hear music like that, it makes me feel the same way. Especially when you're the one playing it."

Wow.

Prudence's mouth hung open, and I felt mine do the same.

Randall, being a jock *and* a player, recognized an opportunity to score a few points. "Want to go get a drink in the caf?" he asked.

Prudence dropped her violin into its case and they left the music room together. I started to follow them, but a twinge shot through my knee. I clutched the back of a chair to support myself. Minus the crazy fall I'd taken in front of Sophie, my knee had been behaving for weeks. Maybe it was all in my head. Maybe I was just reacting to Randall's talk about football and the pileup.

The thing was, I'd lied to Randall. On the day I got hurt, we were playing a team from another league. The game wasn't a really big deal or anything, but you couldn't tell that by the way some of the parents were acting.

It was hot, and I pulled my helmet off. Most of the time, I didn't do that. Like I said before, I wasn't the *only* girl who played youth football, but there weren't very many of us. It was easier to hide behind the helmet than to let your girl-ness be known. Someone on the other team always had something to say about it, and that something was never especially nice. But with the air so humid and thick that day, it felt like I could barely breathe. So I risked it.

It was a mistake. The next time I took the field, a mom from the other team stalked the sidelines. She followed every move I made, yelling the whole time, "Get her! Get her! Come on, boys! Get! That! Girl!"

Youth League Football is mostly a running game. If the quarterback can throw, and that's usually a pretty big *if,* the receivers still need to be in the right place to catch the ball. Even though a lot of people call football players dumb jocks, it's not a very easy sport to learn. It takes most teams a few years for everyone to get the hang of it. But our team had Gavin. And even back then, he could throw. Sometimes, when Coach let him throw to me, I actually made the catch.

No way would Coach let it happen that day, not with all the "Get her!" attention on me. But then someone fumbled on the snap. Gavin got the ball, but only barely. He had to scramble to keep the play alive. I ran into position and waited. It looked like Gavin might carry the ball himself but, just in case, I tried to keep eye contact with him. At the last possible second, he launched the football. It came across the field, heading straight for me.

I guess if you have to have a career-ending play, it might as well be a good one. I caught the ball and thought I saw a path through the defense. I'd made it halfway to the goal line when I felt a hand on my thigh. I tried to slip away, then I just tried to stay on my feet, but that wasn't happening. I was already falling when Randall reached us to throw a block. And, yeah, he really *was* showing off that day.

The hit Randall made was huge. It knocked my tackler off balance and caused the kid to grip my leg even tighter. He stretched it, pulled it, and, at exactly the worst possible moment, he twisted it. It was almost like he was offering my knee as a sacrifice. The four of us tumbled to the ground, the football and me on the bottom. The kid who was tackling me hit next. Then came Randall. I heard a loud pop and a scream when his extra weight landed on the pile.

The popping sound was the ligament in my knee tearing in half and letting go. I still don't know where the scream came from. Maybe it was my mom. Maybe it was me.

All I wanted was for everybody to get off of me so I could get away from the field. I didn't know how long I could go without crying and I didn't want anyone to see me do it.

Here's the weird thing about that: Boys cry too. I'd seen every kid on my team cry at some point. Really. Some of the biggest tough guys in school were the biggest bawlers on the field. They cried when they were hurt. They cried when they were frustrated. Sometimes they even cried when they were happy. By middle school, though, the tears had started to dry up. By high school, they were gone.

Sometimes I still wonder if that was a good thing.

I remember sinking back into the grass and waiting—for the boys to finally sort themselves out, for the referee, coach, and EMT guy to come dashing over, for someone to help me up. That someone turned out to be Gavin, who pushed his way through the adults. Between him and the EMT guy, I hopped my way to the sidelines. I saw my mother's crumpled face, and the worry lines on my dad's. Beneath all his equipment, I felt Gavin heave a sad sigh.

I barely heard the applause.

Chapter Fifteen

♡

ALL THAT DAY and the next, I looked for evidence of Rhino's "grassroots" campaign. I didn't see anything, anywhere. When I caught him texting with Elle, I wondered if he was really doing something for Sophie, or if he'd gone secret double agent on me. If Rhino wasn't really going to help, I'd have to do something myself.

Thursday morning, I came to school armed with all the pennies, nickels, dimes and quarters I could find. My haul was pitiful. I think Dad had already raided the usual sources. The only things left for me were my piggy bank and what I could scrounge up from beneath the couch cushions.

My search for change had been a waste of time, though. When I walked into homeroom, Mr. Moore had already packed away the homecoming canisters for Clarissa, Elle, Mercedes, and Sophie. He was holding one of the few "Camy" canisters I'd managed to put together.

He cleared his throat dramatically. "I suggest we all exhibit a little homeroom solidarity and vote for Miss Cavanaugh," he said, also dramatically. He shook the can and began walking up and down each aisle with it.

All the blood in my body rushed to my cheeks and I thought I might faint. I probably would have, too, if I didn't think that would call even more attention to myself. Instead, I stared at the spot on my desk where someone had tried to carve their initials. I didn't look up, not even when I heard coins begin to drop into the can. Not even when Mr. Moore gave the container a final shake and it sounded nearly full.

"Best of luck, Camy," he said, squeezing a little bit of extra drama into his comment. Then he dropped my canister into the box with the rest of them.

Two student council members appeared at the classroom door. They were pushing an AV cart loaded with boxes just like the one Mr. Moore handed them. When they rolled the cart toward the next classroom, I sighed and closed my eyes.

They were still closed when something brushed against my head. I hoped it was a ladybug. I wasn't sure if they really were lucky, but the way my plan was going, it sure couldn't hurt. I patted my hair but I didn't find anything.

The kid across the aisle from me shook his head and pointed to the floor. I followed his finger but all I saw there was a Minnesota Twins pencil eraser. I don't know why he thought it was mine. He rolled his eyes, reached down to pick the eraser up, then jerked his head to the other side of the room.

I looked left and caught a hint of Jason Abernathy's goofy grin. A second later, he flashed a note at me.

Hook me up?

I shook my head. Nuh. Unh.

"Come on," he mouthed. Jason gave me a classic puppy-dog look, all big eyes and pout. Did that really work on girls? I was pretty sure it didn't, at least not on any girl who'd read the wiki. I looked away.

DATING on the DORK SIDE

A second later something hit my cheek. Another note from Jason, this one folded into a paper football.

Pleez????? it said.

♡ ♡ ♡

There were three kinds of warnings at Olympia High School: tornado warnings, blizzard warnings, and Babette "Bing Bing" Riley warnings. In case of a tornado, we all hid in the hallways. In case of a blizzard, we all hurried home to hide out there. And in case of Bing Bing (an unfortunate nickname left over from grade school), we all just hid. Period.

It's not like Babette was unpopular, but I'm not sure anyone really liked her, either. I guess the best way to describe her is … dangerous. She was the editor of the school newspaper and her best friend ran the yearbook. Nothing happened without Bing Bing knowing about it.

It was a miracle she hadn't already figured out the whole boy boycott thing. And when she did finally hear about it? I was already bracing myself. I'd probably find my picture on the front page with a finger up my nose.

If a Bing Bing warning had gone out, I hadn't heard it. If others were ducking their heads, I hadn't noticed. But when Babette Riley slammed my locker door shut at lunchtime, she sure got my attention.

"So what does a girl have to do to get her own Hottie McHottie Pants?"

"What … who?"

"Look, I know you hooked up Prudence," Babette said. "She told me all about it. She also told me Randall asked her to the dance."

"That was fast."

"No kidding. And then there's Dalton, and Tim Lansing, and who knows who else. All of them have one thing in common." She stared at me over the top of her librarian glasses. "So, I'm back to my first question. How does a girl get her own A-lister?"

"Um, well, I have this spreadsheet," I said. It was no use lying to Bing Bing. She'd find out eventually, and the punishment would be even worse.

"Great," she said. "Who's still available?"

"Did you have someone in mind?" I asked.

"Oh, yeah."

I waited, wondering if she'd make me guess.

Instead, she looked me straight in the eye and said, "I want to go to homecoming with Jason Abernathy."

She wanted to ... *what*? "You want to go with The Ab?" I said, just to make sure I wasn't hallucinating.

"Yep. I do. But here's the deal. He has to dress up the same way he would for Clarissa Delacroix."

"Why would Jason dress up for Clarissa?" I said.

Bing Bing gave me a *Where have you been?* look and went on. "He has to agree to have one of those homecoming photos taken, too."

"You're going to memorialize the big night?" I laughed. I couldn't help it. The whole idea of Bing Bing and The Ab arm-in-arm under a crepe paper arch was just too ridiculous.

"Oh, I'm going to memorialize it, all right. It's going to be the center photo in the spread the newspaper is doing on the dance. It just might make the frontispiece in the yearbook, too."

Rarely does one encounter such pure evil genius. Babette could give Rhino some serious competition.

"The only way that could be any better," I said, "is if you went to homecoming with Aiden."

I still considered him my main suspect as the wiki's mastermind. Attending homecoming with Babette would be a fitting punishment.

Babette made a face. "Right. One, I can't stand being in the same room as that piss snake. Two, he'd never agree to do it. And three..." Her mouth turned up into a smile. "Jason is going to look really good." She touched her side. "Right here."

I felt sorry for Jason then. For about three seconds. Then I remembered the wiki, and the spiky paper football hitting my cheek. Maybe he deserved to spend a night as Bing Bing's arm candy.

"He's in the class next to me last block," I said. "Meet me in front of Mr. Moore's before the bell. He's never early, so we'll have to work fast."

"See you then."

She breezed off down the hall, pulling a stylus from her bun and making a note in a tablet she'd taken from her book bag, no doubt penciling in her dream date with Jason.

Even though he was one of the boys who, according to the list, would be willing to dance with a flagpole, I couldn't arrange this match on my own. I'd need Gavin to pull it off.

I looked for him everywhere that afternoon but never found him. Finally I pulled out my cell phone. They weren't allowed on in school. If you got caught, it meant a trip to the vice principal's office, where Mr. Jourdan would confiscate your phone and keep it until your parents came in to get it. I usually had mine in my bag but I was too chicken to start it up. Until now. I crouched in a bathroom stall and pecked out a text:

> **I need to talk to you right away. I have an idea for your flagpole dancer, the "stomach" problem. She's front page news, if you know what I mean.**

I hit "send" before I could change my mind, or change the message. All afternoon, I searched for signs of Gavin, while trying to avoid both Jason and Babette. But eventually final period rolled around and I couldn't avoid the situation any longer. When I turned the corner I found Bing Bing standing by the door to Mr. Moore's room. I didn't think there was a chance I could slip by her without being seen, but I gave it a try.

"Well?" she said when I tried to sneak past between two pom squad girls.

"Well," I said, and I kept on going.

Babette held out an arm to block me. "He doesn't know yet, does he?"

"Well ..." I said again. I glanced down the hall toward Jason, who was walking as if he didn't have a care in the world. He held up a paper football and smiled. I looked back at Bing Bing. I wondered if she already had something stored away to use against me. The look on her face made me think there were several exceptionally mortifying options she was considering.

Gavin skidded around the corner just as the bell sounded. "Mr. Moore, I need Jason and, oh, hey, Babette, you too, down in the gym for homecoming rehearsal." He flashed me a grin. "You, too, Camy."

I checked in and out of my own classroom, then the four of us walked down the hall toward the lobby and gymnasium. Gavin took a few steps in front of us, then turned around. He walked backward as he spoke. "So, Jason, I'd like to introduce you to your date for the homecoming dance tomorrow night."

"All right! Who's the lucky lay-day?"

"It's someone you're, uh, pretty close to."

Jason threw out the names of a few girls, starting with Clarissa Delacroix. Maybe Bing Bing was right about the two of them. I'd have to mention it to Elle.

"No, it's someone you're physically close to," Gavin said. "Like right now, here, walking next to you."

"Camy?" Jason's goofy grin spread across his face.

"No!" Gavin, Babette, and I all shouted at once. It's a good thing the theme song for the school-run afternoon TV show was playing, or we probably all would have earned detention.

Jason looked around, like some other girl might teleport in at any moment. When that didn't happen, he screwed up his face and said, "Bing Bing?"

"Bing-o," Gavin said. "Now for the rules: Jason, you will not disrespect or ditch your date. The only time you can leave her side is to perform your duties as homecoming escort." He turned to Babette. "Jason owns exactly one suit jacket, but I heard that he was slipping Swedish meatballs into the pocket of it at the country club a few weeks ago, so—"

"Dude. How'd you *know* that?" Jason interrupted.

"I have my sources. Anyway, Bing Bing, knowing that your date may smell like a month-old buffet, and considering the school only requires boys to wear a shirt with a collar to the dance, what is your preference?"

"I think I'll go with the shirt. But he has to wear a tie. A nice one. And I want a corsage."

"The dance is tomorrow," Gavin said. "It may be too late for flowers."

She sighed. "Okay. No flowers. But I require photographic evidence of the event."

"Huh?" Jason said.

"We're having our picture taken."

"Oh. Okay."

"So we have a deal?" Gavin asked.

They both nodded.

In the gym, student council members were working to staple blue and silver fabric along the edges of a big, temporary stage. Babette left to check the progress on the photo backdrop area. Jason sprawled across the bottom row of bleachers and closed his eyes. I took a seat beside Sophie while Gavin climbed past me to sit with the rest of the guys.

Ms. Pendergast came in a minute later. She clapped her hands together a few times, then called out, "We're going to run through the entire ceremony, from grand entrance to crowning. This includes all five girls and their escorts." She aimed an extra round of clapping at Jason until he finally sat up.

"I really got the prize when they handed out escorts," Sophie said.

"It could be worse. You could be stuck with Aiden."

She leaned in closer. "I heard about Prudence and Randall. Did you do that?"

"Actually, I didn't have to do anything. I just got them in the same room."

Sophie glanced toward Kevin Orrs, who was busy checking the audio equipment, and smiled.

"Sometimes that's all it takes. Speaking of which." She nodded at Gavin. "Any more visits to the boys' bathroom?"

She said it quietly, but I swear Gavin heard. He turned away from Aiden and toward us.

Before Sophie could say anything else, Ms. Pendergast resumed her instructions. I swear, I'd never been so happy to hear her voice.

"When the music starts, you will enter, taking slow, elegant steps up the ramp. You will continue to your spot on the stage. And boys, no rushing. We're not going for any forward passes here."

The girls giggled. The guys groaned. Ms. Pendergast cleared her throat. "All right, ladies," she said. "Get ready."

I stood and started toward the gym doors, but when I got halfway there, I realized I was alone. I turned to find Mercedes, Elle, Clarissa, and Sophie all sitting on the first row of the bleachers. They had all pulled out shoeboxes. And they were all slipping on the shoes they would wear tomorrow with their dresses. I studied the Chuck Taylors I'd pulled on that morning.

"Camy?" Ms. Pendergast said. "Don't you have your shoes? It was clearly stated in the packet that I gave to all of you girls." She flipped through the pages on her clipboard, then held it up. She stabbed at a section of the paperwork with her pen. "It's even in bold. Practice Thursday, last block. **BRING SHOES.**" The words came out of her mouth in capital letters.

I'd been so busy tracking comments on the wiki, matchmaking, and trying to turn the homecoming queen contest upside down that I hadn't paid much attention to the homecoming event itself. I'd barely managed to produce any canisters for my campaign, and I hadn't looked at Ms. Pendergast's calendar for more than a week.

But the truth is, even if I'd studied it that morning, I probably wouldn't have understood the significance. **BRING SHOES?** I still wasn't sure I understood it then, not until Ms. P made it horribly clear.

"I don't see how you can practice without the shoes. You don't want to fall on your face in front of the entire school tomorrow, do you?"

"I …" The words, the excuse, everything froze in my mouth.

"Ms. P?"

"Yes, Aiden?"

"I'm pretty sure those *are* the shoes Camy's planning to wear tomorrow."

Oh, ha ha. Just when I thought I couldn't hate him more. He *had* to be the one who'd started the wiki.

Ms. Pendergast fiddled with her hair for a second before turning back to me. "He's not … you're not really going to …"

I rolled my eyes, which didn't seem to score any points with her.

"I guess you'll have to manage." She sighed, as if my shoeless self was the bane of her existence, and went on. "Let's line up."

Everyone headed toward the gymnasium doors except Gavin, who fell in beside me.

"I'm sorry," I said.

"For what?"

"For being the worst homecoming queen candidate ever. Really, there should be a rule that gets you a better girl to escort or something."

"Just because you forgot your shoes?" he said.

I nodded.

"You remember the important stuff. That's what counts."

"Like what?" I asked.

"Well, did you ever forget your cleats?"

Then, despite the fact that the rest of the guys (and Clarissa too) were still snickering about me, and despite the way Mercedes and Sophie looked at me with pity, and even despite Elle's obvious disappointment in me, I smiled.

"Thank you," I whispered.

"Tell you what," he whispered back. "Meet me here early tomorrow, before school, and we'll practice with your shoes."

Chapter Sixteen

FRIDAY MORNING AT SIX FORTY-FIVE, I pushed open the front door of my house. I had my dress on a hanger, my book bag on one shoulder, and a tote bag filled with homecoming essentials on the other. I also had the phone glued to my ear.

"Pantyhose," Mom was saying. "Did you pack an extra pair? I always put a run in mine. That could be hereditary."

"I have two extra pairs," I told her.

Dad locked the door behind us, then headed for the car.

"Oh, baby, I should've come home for this," Mom said.

I froze on the steps. "Really, it's okay. Dad will take a ton of photos and shoot some video, and—"

"What kind of mother sends her little girl off to a situation like this over the phone?" She sniffed and I could tell she was starting to cry.

Dad started the car and pointed to his watch.

Gavin in ten minutes. Or Mom right now? I swallowed back a sigh that I hoped she didn't hear.

"Um, the kind of mom who has a job?" I tried, but that just brought on a fresh round of sniffles. "Look, Mom, I've got to go. Can we talk about this later?"

"Sure, baby. Camy? I promise I'll make this up to you. When you come for fall break, we'll spend some time on campus and … you *are* coming for fall break, right?"

I hadn't even thought about break, or about what I'd do when it came time to choose a college, for weeks. And I couldn't think about it now. "My signal is breaking up," I lied. "I'll call you tomorrow, okay?"

She was still apologizing and telling me how much she loved me when I hit the disconnect button. And, yeah, I know that made me the worst daughter ever. But what else could I do?

Dad pulled the car into the school parking lot and stopped in front of the main door. "I'll be back in time for the ceremony," he said. "Plus, as the father of a homecoming candidate, I get to sit in the grandstand for the parade."

"There's a grandstand?" I asked. Leave it to Dad to know more about homecoming than I did.

"No," he said. "I just made that up."

I groaned. "I'm leaving now." From the back seat, I grabbed my dress, my bags, and most importantly, my shoes.

I stood at the foot of the stairs, looking up at the school. My watch said five minutes to seven. Was Gavin in the gym already? Waiting for me? My heart sped up before my feet landed on the first step. The thought that maybe he wouldn't show made my heart beat even faster. Get it over with quick, I decided, and raced up the rest of the stairs, my dress fluttering behind me.

♡ ♡ ♡

The gym doors were closed. I wondered if I'd gotten everything wrong, not only with Gavin, but with homecoming in general. Maybe it wasn't today? I mean, I knew the parade was always on Friday afternoon before the game. And I knew that after the game, everyone went to the dance. Right?

I fought the urge to drop everything right in the lobby and pull out Ms. P's calendar to check. Instead, I cracked open one of the gym doors, just an inch. The space inside was lit with strands of twinkly blue and white Christmas lights. It made everything look different, like it was the kind of place where something magical could happen.

I set my bags and my dress on a bleacher seat. Even if Gavin didn't show up, I could still practice walking in my heels. I'd just kicked off my Chucks when the gym door flew open.

It was Gavin. When he saw me holding my shoes, he grinned. "They're not cleats, but I think they'll do. Ready?"

I wobbled a bit on the heels, then nodded. We started up the ramp and the plywood planks creaked beneath our feet. I placed each foot carefully, hoping I wouldn't stumble.

Instead, Gavin was the one who fell. I grabbed for the football jersey he was wearing when I felt him slip, but it wasn't enough. He landed hard and the thud echoed through the empty gym. My own landing wasn't much more graceful. I ended up sprawled halfway across his lap.

"Sorry," I said.

"I'm not."

Gavin moved a hand to my cheek and guided my head onto his shoulder. "There's something I've been wanting to tell you." His fingers traced my neck to my shoulder. The sensation sent sparks through the rest of my body.

I looked up into those amazing amber eyes. I'd imagined every detail of what it would be like to be this close to him a million times, but I was surprised at how soft his breath was, with a hint of cinnamon, and how right this felt, like we'd always sat like this.

"Yes?" I said. Whatever Gavin wanted to say, I was here to listen.

"Oh, Camy, there you are!"

I looked up to find Ms. Pendergast standing in the now-open gym door. Behind her, Elle, Mercedes, Sophie, and Clarissa were all standing, each lugging armfuls of dresses and makeup bags.

My face went hot. "We were just—" I began.

"Practicing," Gavin finished.

"Is that what they're calling it these days?" Under the twinkling lights, with the suggestion of a laugh in her voice and the start of a smile on her face, Ms. Pendergast looked almost friendly. Then she flipped on the lights and the magic died.

Clarissa's smile looked cruel. Elle seemed lost in thought. Mercedes bounced and made a silent clapping motion. Sophie gave me a thumbs up, not what I needed at the moment.

"Let's get this thing going," Ms. Pendergast said. "We need to take all the photos before this morning's assembly. So, it's off to the girls' locker room with you." She held her arms wide, like she was shooing a flock of chickens.

♡ ♡ ♡

I had to run by my math class first to drop off my calculus homework. By the time I made it back to the locker room, everyone else was in full homecoming prep mode. The air was hazy with hairspray and perfume. The combination of Juicy Couture, Cover Girl, and AquaNet stung my eyes.

Something else was floating in the air too, a conversation that seemed to stop in mid-sentence. About me and my lap-tastic moment with Gavin?

Both Clarissa and Elle were wearing hot rollers in their hair. Mercedes' braids were glimmering in an elaborate new pattern studded with silvery beads. Sophie had her hair pulled up in a twist and already looked like the queen I hoped she would be.

"I can't believe we get out of all our classes today," Mercedes said. Her words sounded loud and forced, like she was covering for someone.

Elle and Clarissa exchanged glances and rolled their eyes, but Sophie said, "Tell me about it. Hidden benefit of homecoming court."

"I know," I said, sounding just as forced. I sat on a bench and shook out a pair of pantyhose. I couldn't believe I'd be wearing those things for the entire day. "I'm going to have to study all weekend just to get back on track. Good thing Rhino is picking up all my assignments for me."

The locker room went silent. I was about to squirm out of my jeans, but with everyone staring at me, I was too self-conscious to move.

Then Mercedes laughed. "Oh, Camy, you're so silly. Besides, this weekend, we need to catch up in AcreRage. I haven't seen my sheep in forever."

Sophie snorted. Elle and Clarissa went back to work on their hair.

Something changed once we'd all wriggled into our dresses, though. It wasn't exactly a Cinderella moment, but everyone's eyes got a little wider.

"Oh, my God." Mercedes panted and waved a hand in front of her face. "I'm going to hyperventilate."

"Breathe," I said. With my dress on, and a mirror finally available, I swooshed over (no, really; I swooshed) and took out my supply of makeup. A little mascara, some lip gloss. What more did a girl need?

"You're kidding me, right?" Sophie said.

"What?"

"That." She pointed in disgust. Her eyes were all smoky; her lips were a sophisticated shade of pink. For once, that explosion of glitter that she always wore seemed like the perfect accessory. She looked amazing.

"We're getting our pictures taken," she said. "Are you even wearing any foundation?"

"Was I supposed to?"

"A little help here?" Sophie called out.

"What's up?" Mercedes bounced over as much as her heels would let her.

Sophie pointed to my face.

"Oh, wow, yeah." Mercedes nodded sagely. "This is an emergency."

Sophie pushed me onto the bench. "You. Sit." To Mercedes, she said, "If we mix some of my foundation with some of yours, we can maybe match her skin tone."

"I don't think—" I began, but Mercedes was already rummaging in her makeup bag.

"Do you want to look like a zombie?" Sophie swirled the two foundations in her palm until they blended, then she dotted my face.

"You're sure this will help?" I asked.

"Makeup 101. The flash from the camera will pull all the natural color out of your skin. I thought *everyone* knew that." She moved on, pulling out eye shadow, blush, and lipstick.

When she hauled out a giant brush and a big container of shimmery stuff, I held up my hand to stop her. "Geeks don't sparkle," I said.

"I thought that was vampires."

"Oh, no, Sophie. Vampires *do*," Mercedes said. "It's their skin. They have—"

Elle spoke up from across the room. "Actually, real vampires don't sparkle."

"Yeah, they do," Clarissa responded.

"Don't."

"Do."

"Don't."

"Do."

I was certain one of them was about to whip out her tweezers and start pulling eyelashes off of the other one when Mercedes interrupted.

"What about Ms. P? All the makeup she wears? She's got to be hiding something under there. Maybe *she's* a vampire."

Sophie laughed. "Or a witch," she said.

Just then the door of the locker room cracked open. "I heard that," Ms. Pendergast said. But if she was embarrassed by the comment, it was hard to tell. It didn't stop her from pausing in front of a mirror and adding an extra coat of lipstick. "All right, girls!" she said as she tucked the lipstick away. "It's time!"

I stared at myself in the mirror. I looked nothing like myself. Or maybe, I did look like myself, only if you jacked up the volume real loud.

I trailed after everyone else. Partly because I couldn't believe what I was seeing in the mirror, but partly because my book bag had gotten knocked over in the shuffle of dresses. All my folders, my assignments, and my textbooks were on the floor. It almost looked deliberate. I glanced around to figure out who'd done it, but everyone had already streamed out the door after Ms. P. I scooped up armloads of stuff, trying not to mess up my makeup or my dress, then hurried after them.

♡ ♡ ♡

"This time, I promise not to trip," Gavin said as he slipped his arm through mine.

That wasn't as easy as you'd think, considering that all ten of us were crammed into the athletic office. The smell of sweat socks mingled with perfume. Dresses rustled around me. Someone yawned.

"You nervous?" Gavin said. The sounds of the jazz band warming up and students stomping up the bleachers filtered in from the gym. I wanted to say something, but none of the other girls were talking to their escorts. The air in the office was thick and warm, but at the same time, the mood was icy.

"Yeah, I'm nervous, but not for me," I said quietly.

"So you don't want to win?"

I shook my head. "I'm hoping someone else will."

"Who?" he asked.

A finger poked the center of my back. I peeked over my shoulder at Mercedes. She nodded toward Elle, who drew a line across her throat. Either she wanted me to shut up … or kill someone. I turned back around and held my shoulders straight. I didn't even look at Gavin.

"I'm getting you in trouble," he said.

I didn't dare respond.

"Any rule against yes-no questions?" he asked.

I shrugged.

"Didn't think so," he said. "There's always a loophole. So, did I get you in trouble?"

I pretended to be checking my pantyhose and stole a glance at Elle. She looked like she was waging some kind of silent battle with Aiden and keeping her eyes on Jason, Kyle, and Lukas at the same time. I thought I was safe, but the girl was an expert multi-tasker. Just before I turned back to Gavin, she managed to toss a frown in my direction.

"Yes. You're getting me in trouble," I whispered.

"Do you mind?"

I thought for a moment and shook my head.

"Will you walk the track at tonight's game?"

I blinked, wondering how Gavin knew I did that. Wasn't he too busy warming up and going over the playbook to notice me before the games? I held out a foot and inspected my shoes. We were required to wear the dresses all day, so I was guessing we had to keep the shoes on too. By the time the game started I wasn't sure I'd be able to walk at all.

I nodded toward my shoe and shrugged again.

"I'd lend you my spare cleats, but I think they'd be too big."

I covered my laugh with a fake cough. Things got quiet again.

"Did you know it's tradition that homecoming queen candidates always dance the first dance with their escorts?"

Before I could even twitch in response, the door to the athletic office creaked open. Ms. Pendergast and Coach Cutter ushered us to a partition that hid us from the rest of the gym.

"It's time, everyone," Ms. Pendergast said. "Girls, today all eyes will be on you. Be elegant. Be regal. Be Trojans! And, boys, no tomfoolery."

From the corner of my eye, I saw Gavin mouth the word, "Tomfoolery?"

Again, I had to cough to cover my laugh.

Coach Cutter stepped forward to speak to the guys. I don't know what I was expecting him to say, but, "All right, men, remember, this isn't about you today. So don't screw it up," caught me by surprise.

We lined up in the order our names had originally been called. Jason checked me out from my toes to the top of my head, then shoved Gavin on the shoulder.

"*Dog*," he added before turning back around.

"Sorry, but I don't speak Ab," I whispered to Gavin. "Can you translate?"

Gavin cleared his throat. "He says he thinks you look monumentally hot and he wishes he was your escort."

"But Sophie's gorgeous."

"Yeah, and lethal. She'll probably kill him before the end of the day. He figures you're nicer."

"He shouldn't count on that," I muttered.

Jason threw me a wicked look at the same moment Ms. Pendergast hissed some last-minute instructions. The jazz band launched into something regal and processional.

We inched forward as each couple stepped onto the carpet that led to the ramp. Maybe I was biased, but I thought Sophie got the most oohs and aahs for her dress. I know she got the most applause. Gavin and I waited alone, and I found myself holding his arm so tight, I was afraid I'd cut off his circulation.

I let my fingers relax and whispered, "Sorry. And it's your throwing arm, too."

"It's not like I've been getting any good use out of it lately," he said.

I swallowed hard. The football team had lost every game this year and I couldn't shake the idea that it was all my fault.

"Another thing to apologize for," I said. Really, the list seemed endless.

Gavin turned me toward him then and took my hands in his. "Look, I'm the one who should apologize. It's something I've needed to do for a long time."

The junior class president picked that moment to call out, "And now, our fifth and final candidate for homecoming queen, Camy Cavanaugh, and her escort, Gavin Madison."

I swear, Gavin and I walked on air. I couldn't feel the floor, or even my own feet. I scanned the crowd for Dad and Rhino but saw nothing but a blur of faces, camera flashes, and Kevin's quick, steady movements as he filmed our climb up the ramp and onto the platform.

Midpoint in our walk, Gavin gave my hand a squeeze. "Hey, this walking thing isn't so hard."

I tried to let my smile absorb the laughter bubbling from my throat, and I caught his grin. A thought struck me then. Of all the couples on the platform, we were the only ones who looked happy.

♡ ♡ ♡

I'd witnessed three previous homecoming coronations. And while the view was different from my seat on the platform, some things never changed. Aiden seemed determined to carry on the lame emcee tradition of keeping us all in suspense. In fact, he was milking it for all it was worth as he ambled back and forth, back and forth, pausing behind each girl's chair, holding the crown over each of our heads.

Enough time passed that I spotted Dad in the audience, near the gym doors, two cameras and a video recorder around his neck. He rotated through each, filming and snapping photos. Once, he peered over the top of the camera and shot me a giant grin.

In the bleachers, Rhino had bypassed the chess club and was sitting with Sophie's crew. They looked restless without her there to anchor them. And although he'd perfected the art of not caring, today, I could tell Rhino did. He cared. If he bit a cuticle this time, it wasn't out of boredom. His gaze never left the stage. At one point, he lifted his hand in a wave. My smile in response froze halfway. I leaned forward to peer down the row at Elle, her face glowing, her lips pursed just slightly.

My throat tightened. I blinked a couple of times. That wave? He hadn't meant it for me. Moments before, I'd been jumpy and anxious, but now a wave of sadness struck me. How long did we have to sit here? How long did it take to crown Elle homecoming queen, anyway?

Longer than you might think.

"Why don't you get on with it?" Elle growled at Aiden through her smile.

"Why don't you bite me?" he replied.

All the charm of a Neanderthal? Check.

At last, he did the long, slow stand behind each chair. This was it. The stage seemed to vibrate with our collective nerves. The crowd went silent. He stood behind Mercedes, then moved on. Behind Clarissa. He stopped behind Elle. When a cruel smirk lit his face, I was glad she couldn't see him.

He skipped Sophie's chair and stopped behind mine.

"You might like to know," he said, his voice low and amused, "that the vote was closer than it has ever been in the history of the OHS homecoming queen contest. It came down to less than 400 points between the top three finishers, but a last-minute surge put one of these beautiful young ladies over the top."

He placed the crown on Sophie's head.

For a second, the world stood still. No one moved. No one clapped. I'm not even sure any of us breathed. Then Aiden's voice boomed throughout the gym. "Let me introduce this year's Trojan Warrior homecoming queen … Sophie Vega!"

Sophie's hands went to the tiara on her head, her expression blank with shock.

"No way," she said. "No. Way. This is a joke, right?"

"No, it's not a joke," I told her.

"Okay." She took in a deep breath and looked toward the ceiling of the gym. "Then is this the time where they dump the bucket of pig blood on me?"

I shook my head, but I snuck a glance at the ceiling, too, just in case. It wasn't a joke. And it wasn't a prank. That could only mean one thing.

"Sophie. You're homecoming queen." I sprang up and teetered on my heels. I kicked them off and threw myself at Sophie. I think I had my arms around her shoulders before the shoes hit the floor. "You won!" I said, and gave her a shake to emphasize the point.

"I'm the effing homecoming queen?" she said.

"You're the effing homecoming queen!"

It was then that I noticed the applause. The sound of it thundered through the gym, so loud that it threatened to knock us over. A second later, Mercedes nearly did, barging into both of us to form a group hug.

"Omigod, omigod, omigod. You know I voted for you," Mercedes said. "Omigod, omigod, omigod."

"No way," Sophie said. I suspected that might be her response to everything for the rest of the day.

"I did too," I added.

"Shit," she said. "I voted for you."

"Thanks," I said, a sudden spate of tears stinging my eyes.

Elle joined the group hug then, the perfectly poised student council president. She was beaming. You'd never know from her expression that she wasn't wearing the crown.

"Hey," Sophie said. Her voice cracked on the word.

"Hey, what?" Elle said, all breezy and light. "You won! You rock! Seriously, it's just what this school needed."

But something flickered in Elle's eyes. I wondered what happened when someone got knocked from the inevitable path that destiny had planned for them.

Clarissa was standing at the edge of our group. Without a thought to what I was doing, I stepped back, unlocked my arm from Elle's, and opened a space for her.

You know those beauty pageants on TV, at the end, when all the girls are crying? And you're certain it's got to be fake? Well, when

Clarissa stepped into the hug, we started bawling, all of us. We were one big, mascara-lined, girly mess of tears. Maybe we all cried for different reasons, but I'm here to tell you: The tears were real.

I glanced up then, my cheeks damp, my vision blurry, and realized everyone in the gym was standing, students, parents, teachers. Dad looked so proud, so happy, and clapped so hard, another thick sob formed in my throat.

And then I saw Rhino, because even *he* was standing. He didn't clap. Instead, he stood with his arms crossed, his eyes trained on our little group. When our gazes met, he brought two fingers to his brow and saluted.

And that little salute? That was for me.

In that moment, I believed. I believed in everything: Tinker Bell and Santa Claus and dreams coming true. You *could* change the world. This was proof.

All it took was a little genius help.

Chapter Seventeen

OF ALL THE PLACES ALONG the parade route to stop, the convertible I was assigned to halted right in front of Rhino's house. I was sitting on the trunk, my blissfully shoeless feet resting on the backseat. I'd arranged the fake fur stole behind me so I didn't actually have to touch it. I might need to wear it later, but that afternoon the sun was drenching the street and the temperature felt closer to August than October.

I tipped my head back and closed my eyes, letting the heat soak through me. Members of the marching band clomped by. The rattle of a snare drum and the reedy sound of a clarinet filled my ears. I didn't open my eyes until I heard something scrape along the concrete. That scrape was Rhino. And his couch. He'd hauled his coffee table out of the garage too and had arranged the furniture, nice and cozy, in the middle of his driveway.

"What are you doing?" I asked.

"What kind of friend would I be if I didn't show up to send you off?" He raised his can of Coke in a toast.

"The kind of friend who wasn't completely crazy?"

"Dude!" Jason called to Rhino from the car behind me. He gave him a double thumbs up. Possible Ab translation: *I highly approve of the new furniture arrangement.*

When I turned back to Rhino, he had a laptop open on the coffee table. He held it up, saying, "Smile."

"What?" I said before I heard the camera click. "My mouth was open!" I told him.

"Bonus! Your eyes were closed too. It's a keeper."

I sighed. "Are you going to torment me until the parade starts?"

"Actually, I thought I'd walk alongside and torment you the whole time."

I spotted the pom squad then. They were bouncing around nearby like a group of hyper puppies. "Hey, Lexy!" I shouted. "Rhino says you guys can practice your routine in his yard. There's plenty of room there!"

"Oh, Camy," Lexy squealed. "That would be awesome!" She clapped her hands and the entire Olympia High pom squad descended on Rhino's driveway. Girls flittered everywhere: in Rhino's garage, on his couch, and one girl even investigated the ladder to his loft. Rhino was standing in the center of all this, hair on end as if he'd dragged his fingers through it in frustration.

"I hate you," he mouthed.

"Karma."

"Ha."

"Something funny?" I hadn't noticed Gavin when he slipped into his spot next to me, and I jumped when he spoke.

I nodded toward the cluster of girls. "Rhino's just getting a little of what he deserves," I said.

"Why do you think I sent them over here?" Gavin said with a smile.

I laughed so hard then that I thought I might cry and mess up my mascara. Again.

Gavin glanced toward Rhino and some of the humor left his face. He pressed his lips together for a second. "I thought he was being mean."

"Who? Rhino?" I shrugged. "Nah, he was just being himself."

"Exactly."

The high school's drum major blew a long whistle, the official start of the homecoming parade. Someone from the local car dealership slipped into the driver's seat and the car rumbled to life beneath us. I let my hands rest at my sides, against the warm leather of the seat backs. When we reached the first stop sign, Gavin's hand covered mine. Halfway through the intersection, he laced my fingers with his. He didn't let go until the end of the parade.

♥ ♥ ♥

When the sun started to drop, so did the temperature. By game time, the five of us girls were sitting on a bench at the fifty-yard line, huddled in our faux furs. Elle sent complicated signals to the cheerleaders while Clarissa instructed the dance team's co-captain on what to do at halftime.

"I don't get it," Sophie said near the end of the second quarter. "Why are we losing?"

"Because we suck," Mercedes replied. "The guys haven't played decently since..." Her gaze darted toward Elle. "You know, since the boy boycott or whatever it is."

"It doesn't help that we're playing last year's state champs," I added.

The game wasn't awful, but if the Trojans didn't start scoring soon ... Well, twenty to zero would be a lousy end to homecoming. Only Gavin was playing with his trademark intensity.

CHARITY TAHMASEB AND DARCY VANCE

With each forward pass, each run down the field, I felt his frustration grow until it was almost like I could taste it on the air. I longed to pull on a pair of cleats and a helmet and join the guys on the field.

Most of the girls behind us in the bleachers left at halftime to get ready for the dance. A few of the parents and a lot of the guys disappeared too. Near the end of the fourth quarter, with the score unchanged, everyone but the most die-hard fans started streaming from the stands. Ms. Pendergast suggested we all go inside too. But even though my legs were freezing and my fingers had turned as blue as my dress, I didn't want to leave the boys out there on the field.

"The game isn't over yet," I said.

That's when Gavin did it. The center almost fumbled the snap. The wide receivers were blocked. But I saw the way he took in the whole field, the way he had a sense for where everyone was. His feet shuffled. Then, at full speed, Gavin "Mad Dog" Madison ran the ball straight up the field.

Randall knocked someone out of his way, and Gavin broke through the defensive line. He dodged one player, then spun away from another. I didn't realize I was standing until he zoomed past us. My "fur" stole slipped from my shoulders and I leaned forward, as if that would help him run faster. Gavin avoided one final tackle and charged into the end zone. He yanked off his helmet and stared up into the stands, right at me, his tractor beam gaze set on high. I couldn't have looked away even if I'd wanted to.

My heart seemed to stop; my mouth went dry. I forgot to cheer.

Once the screaming had died down, Sophie nodded at the field. "I hope you know that was all for you."

I shook my head in disbelief.

"And I can't wait to see what happens at the dance."

I wish I could say that was the start of an amazing comeback. It wasn't. We still lost the game. As soon as the last horn sounded, Ms. P herded us all into one of the girls' restrooms. Once we'd warmed up a little, we repaired our makeup and hair. Then we were led to the back entrance of the gym.

Precisely at eight, the boys entered from one side and the girls from the other, both Lukas and Gavin in clean football jerseys over dress shirts and ties. When we met up on the stage, the first thing he said was, "I'm sorry."

"For what?"

"For losing the game."

"That wasn't your fault."

"I'm not so sure about that. The thing is—"

But by then we had reached our appointed place at the edge of the dance floor next to Aiden (who scowled) and Elle (who gave me a warning look). Once Jason and Sophie had made it down the ramp, the music started.

The song was something slow and sugary. Gavin turned to me and asked, "Do you want to dance?"

Here it was. That princess moment I'd been waiting for since eighth grade. I nodded. He smiled and put a hand on my waist ... then Lukas tapped him on the shoulder.

"Coach Cutter is looking for you," he said.

Gavin groaned but turned to follow Lukas. "I'll be back for that dance," he called.

By nine thirty, I knew Gavin wasn't going to show. Actually, I knew at nine. To be totally honest, I knew it by eight forty-five. He didn't poke his head back through the gym doors once. I sat at the table reserved for the homecoming court watching Mercedes dance with Dalton all night long. Fast songs, slow songs; they even

CHARITY TAHMASEB AND DARCY VANCE

did the Chicken Dance. They were quite possibly the cutest couple ever.

Sophie sparkled under the twinkling lights. Halfway through the dance, Kevin started sparkling too. I guess he'd gotten a little too close to her glitter. Either that or he was just so happy to be with her that he was beginning to spontaneously combust. Clarissa flitted around the dance floor while Aiden tracked her every move.

When Elle danced with Rhino, it was like something out of a classic movie. All the other couples slowed, then moved away to clear the space. The humiliation of Rhino's dance lessons was finally paying off as he twirled Elle.

Maybe it wasn't my turn to be a princess that night, but at least my best friend got a chance to be Prince Charming. *Karma,* I thought for the second time that day. Rhino deserved this.

At one point, Kevin plopped into the chair next to mine.

"Hey, want to dance?" he said.

I looked at him, then toward Sophie, who was standing near the DJ. "She told you to come over here and ask me, didn't she?"

"She ... I mean, no." He shook his head.

"Tell her thanks, but I'm fine. Okay?"

"You sure?"

"Go," I said. "Dance with her."

I waited until after he'd stood up and walked back to Sophie before I let my smile fade. There I was, back where I'd always been, watching everyone from the sidelines. At least before, I'd had Rhino to keep me company. And sure, he came to sit by me a couple of times that night. He'd even snuck a Cherry Coke into the dance for me. But now he was sitting a few seats away, with Elle on the table in front of him, her feet in his lap. She bent forward to whisper something to him, and I watched as he leaned in to meet her, then brushed his lips against her cheek. The intimacy of it made me look away.

Just as I thought about leaving, Jason Abernathy tugged on a lock of my hair. "Wanna dance?" he said.

That was it. No, "Hello, how are you? You look nice." Just: *Wanna dance?*

"You make it hard for a girl to say no," I replied.

"Yeah." He gave me that slightly crooked grin. "That's what they all say."

I rolled my eyes, but my feet did something I hadn't expected. They followed Jason onto the dance floor. We caught the last few beats of a hip-hop song, then the music slid into low gear.

"Look, you don't have to—" I started to say.

He took my hand and pulled me close. "You can pretend I'm Mad Dog if you want."

"Why would I do that?"

"Who knows?" Jason shrugged. "Chicks dig him for some reason."

"Uh, chicks dig you too, Jason," I said.

"You think?"

I laughed. But really? I couldn't tell if he was serious or not. So we danced. And dancing with The Ab wasn't all that bad. I'd just started to relax and think of him as a possibly decent guy when a manicured hand shot between us.

"What do you think you're doing?" Clarissa yanked us apart.

I was speechless. Jason looked confused, just like he had after the SATs last year. I ran back to the table and tried to look like something tremendously embarrassing hadn't just happened to me.

A couple of songs later, the lights came on and the dance was over. I shielded my eyes and searched the gym for Gavin one last time, but the room looked as empty as I felt.

♡ ♡ ♡

If Ms. Pendergast had heard about the girls-only after party, she'd probably chalked it up to Elle being Elle. And she would have been right. But it wasn't school spirit that had motivated our student council president to invite so many people to her house that night. It was strategy, pure and simple. Elle didn't want anyone getting romantic ideas and hooking up after the dance. Not while Operation Lysistrata was still in effect.

The place was packed with all the Hotties of Troy, of course, but she'd also encouraged every other girl who'd been at the dance to come along, including Prudence, Babette, and even Tara Tanaka.

I roved the crowd, worried that Clarissa (or one of her clones) would start something. But it wasn't happening. Clarissa had vanished—to where, no one knew.

I had long suspected that removing Clarissa Delacroix from the equation = Instant Improvement. But maybe it wasn't just her absence that was setting things on a different path. Maybe, just maybe, it was the wiki. In some ways, it might have been one of the best things to happen to Olympia High. The evidence of it was everywhere I turned. In one corner, Mercedes and Tara were talking chess. In another, two pom squad girls were giving Babette a makeover. I even caught a group of cheerleaders discussing performance technique with Prudence.

It was weird. And wonderful. And I wanted to congratulate Elle. But I couldn't find *her*, either.

My quest led me through the rec room, to the kitchen, then upstairs to her bedroom. There I ditched the beautiful shoes in favor of my magnificently comfortable Chucks, then dug through my bag, pulled out my knee support, and wrapped it around my leg.

I met Mercedes at the bottom of the stairs. "Have you seen Elle?" I asked.

She nodded toward the living room. "On the porch," she said.

With so many people crammed inside, the cool evening air that greeted me was a welcome relief. I stepped outside, where a nearly full moon lit the lawn. A breeze blew a single oak leaf across the grass, inviting me to follow. Maybe Elle had felt the same pull. I decided on a walk.

The newer subdivision that Elle lived in had always seemed a world away, but I'd only walked a block or two when I turned the corner and found myself on Rhino's street. Had my feet automatically led me there again? I thought about turning around, but the truth was, I missed Rhino. I wanted to talk to him. About the dance. About everything.

I passed another house or two before Rhino's open garage door came into view. A flicker of blue caught my eye. I stepped closer and the blue took shape. I hunched behind parked cars and peeked around trees. I walked on tiptoes. Not that I needed to.

Music was floating from the garage. It was something slow but with enough of a beat that Rhino could twirl his partner. Once, he even dipped her. Elle's laughter rose above the song and Rhino pulled her close.

He kissed her then. It was like something you'd see in a movie. His thumb trailing along her cheekbone, her chin tilted just so, navigating the nose issue with finesse. I blinked, fast and hard, a strange lump in my throat.

I crouched in the darkness just outside the circle of light spilling from the garage and wrapped my arms around myself to stop shaking. I didn't like Rhino *that* way, I reminded myself again. I really didn't. Still, seeing him with Elle made me feel like he'd punched me in the stomach. He had her now. He didn't need me. And I had no one.

Rhino broke off the kiss with so much skill, it left me breathless. Then he took Elle's hand, and together they walked to the ladder that led to his bedroom loft.

The song faded and the gentle plunk of Elle's sandals hitting each rung echoed into the night. A new song cued up, but the music was lost in the scrape of the garage door closing. The last thing I saw was Rhino's dress shoes taking the ladder's rungs two at a time.

I don't know how long I stood there, staring at the door. Finally, my feet crept backward, one small step at a time. I stopped when I hit something warm and solid. A yelp strangled in my throat.

"Shh, Camy, it's me," a voice said. "It's just me."

I knew who that voice belonged to.

Chapter Eighteen

♡

HE LET ME GO slowly, and I turned around. The first thing I saw was the number fourteen. Gavin was still wearing his football jersey over his white dress shirt. The knot in his tie was loose, like he'd been tugging at it all night. I blinked, wondering what he was doing here.

"It's just me," he said again.

I nodded, breathless. I looked over my shoulder, at Rhino's garage. Had Gavin seen as much as I had? He followed my gaze, and his half-laugh made my heart squeeze tight.

"Does it bother you?" I said.

"I was wondering the same thing about you."

"Rhino's just my friend."

"I'm not sure that Elle and I were even that much."

Gavin fell silent, and in the quiet that followed, I started wondering again.

"What are you doing here?" I said, my words so soft, I'm not sure he heard me. It was almost like I didn't *want* him to hear me, didn't want to disturb whatever it was that had brought us together.

"You want to know something crazy?" he asked. He didn't wait for an answer. "I'm glad this happened. All of it. It sucked being dumped, but you know what didn't suck?"

I shook my head.

"Talking to you again."

There was so much I wanted to say, but I just stood there, staring up at him.

"I'm sorry about the dance," he said. "I would have been there, but Coach … he knows something's up. Or at least, he thinks he knows it. He and Pendergast have seen all the new, uh, relationships going on. And with the way the team's been playing…" Gavin sighed. "Let's just say he wanted to have a little talk with me."

"A little talk?" That was probably not a good thing.

"A little talk that lasted two hours."

Oh. "You didn't say anything, did you? I mean, I'd totally understand if you did."

He shook his head. "I'd rather have him mad at me for being a lousy team captain than for …" He shrugged. "You know."

It was almost funny. There we were, all alone in the dark, and *still* neither of us could bring ourselves to talk about the wiki out loud.

"You're not a bad captain," I said.

"Right. We haven't won a game all season."

"That's not your fault."

He raised his head and looked at me. "Then whose fault is it?"

I thought I should say: *Mine. It's my fault.* I even tried the words out on my tongue, but they stalled there. "Have you been walking around all night?" I said instead.

His gaze flickered toward Rhino's garage. "I needed to blow off some steam."

"Want to keep walking?" I asked.

Without a word, he took my hand. And, just like that, we left Rhino and Elle behind us. Neither of us looked back.

We each placed the toes of our shoes on the fifty-yard line. The field was quiet and dark, so different from how it had been a few hours ago. A chill ran over my arms, and I tried to keep my fingers from trembling.

"You cold?" he asked.

"A little," I admitted.

"Here." He pulled off the football jersey and helped me tug it on. The sleeves hit below my elbows, and the number fourteen swallowed me. He grinned. "Looks pretty good."

I laughed, but I stopped when Gavin's expression changed. "I have to tell you something," he said. "You asked me if I remembered the kid I was in eighth grade. The boy who couldn't pass a test? Well, once upon a time, my mom married a jerk." He shook his head like he was trying to shake away a memory. "Things got pretty bad at home. I started failing stuff at school. But you know that part. You were trying to help me."

I wanted to help him right then. I wanted to reach out to him and tell him that none of it mattered. That he didn't have to explain anything to me. But the thing was, *he did*.

I needed him to tell me what had happened. I needed to know why he'd suddenly stopped talking to me, then had spent most of the past three years pretending I didn't exist. I needed to know why he'd danced with Clarissa, why he'd hurt me like that. So I kept my hands at my sides and I waited.

"Anyway, I figured you must have said something to the guidance counselor about me," he said. "The next thing I know is, I'm sitting in her office with my mom. And the next thing after that, I've got an appointment to see a therapist."

He took a breath and let it out slowly. "I thought only crazy people needed therapy. I was embarrassed and angry, and I guess I blamed you for it, even though that didn't make any sense." He sucked in another breath. "I wanted to hurt you, like I thought you'd hurt me. Then the chance to do it came up at that dance with Clarissa and … and I took it." He looked down at his shoes.

The words in my mouth were thick, almost sticky. I wasn't sure what Gavin would think when he knew the truth.

"I *did* tell the guidance counselor about you," I said. "I didn't mean to do it, but things weren't so great at my house back then, either. My parents were fighting a lot, so I went to her office a few times to talk about it. When she asked if anything else was bothering me, I told her how frustrated I was because I was tutoring this really smart boy who couldn't pass any of his tests."

I waited for his verdict, but Gavin kept studying the grass. "I'm glad you told," he said finally. "The therapy helped. It took a while for me to see it, though. It took even longer to realize what a douche I'd been to you. I'm really sorry."

He stole a glance up at me. "You know what else helped? All those test-taking tips and study techniques you taught me."

I blinked.

"Turns out, they work. I'm still hoping to get some sort of athletic scholarship, but I already have a good shot at a few small academic ones."

"Academic?"

Gavin's smile made the night luminous.

"Do you have a school picked out?" I said.

"Wisconsin somewhere. I'd love Madison, but I'll take La Crosse, or Stout, or even Green Bay. Although I swear, I will *never* be a Packers fan." He held up three fingers, like a Boy Scout salute.

"Wisconsin," I said, like I'd never heard the word before.

"Yeah, it's that state just to the east of us."

Why hadn't I thought of that? I could go to school in Wisconsin. Big Ten football for Dad, socially conscious college campus for Mom. Not too far from either of them. Perfect.

"Wisconsin," I said again, not caring that Gavin would probably think I'd lost my mind.

"They have lots of cheese there," he said, his voice hesitant.

"Oh, I know where it is," I said. "You know what else I know? You just helped me solve a huge problem." On impulse, I threw my arms around him.

Maybe it was the relief of finally understanding what had come between us in the past. Maybe it was the joy of finally having a direction for my future. Or maybe it was how his arms felt wrapped around my waist. Or the moonlight. Whatever it was, I bounced up on tiptoes and kissed his cheek.

"Good form," he said, "but your aim is slightly off." He took my chin between his finger and thumb and bent his face toward mine.

Then, there on the fifty-yard line, Gavin "Mad Dog" Madison kissed me.

He tasted sweet and warm, like hot chocolate, or a Hershey's Bar, with just a hint of cinnamon thrown in. And I thought: As long as I live, I'll remember this, the sweetness of this kiss. His hands cupped my face and I felt like I could stand there forever, on the fifty-yard line, the perfect spot with the perfect boy.

That was when the stadium lights blazed on. At first, all I could see was the glare of the green grass and the field markers glowing white. Then a laugh echoed from somewhere in the stands, high-pitched and screechy. I squinted, my gaze drawn to the bleachers. I looked up at Gavin again and found a question on his face. *How long*, I was sure he was wondering, *until the smarty-pants tutor girl figures it out?*

And then I knew I'd been set up. This whole thing, all of it, the walk, the talk—the *kiss*—all of it was just a plan to destroy me, once and for all.

My eyes stung with tears, turning the lights into prisms. I did the only thing I could think of. I ran.

Chapter Nineteen

I HEARD GAVIN calling my name, but I knew the neighborhood better than he did. I didn't do anything obvious, like head for Rhino's. Instead, I circled around and took the back alley that led to my house and crept in through the garage.

I pulled off Gavin's jersey and tucked it into my leg support. As long as I didn't dance around the living room, it should stay put.

I was halfway through the kitchen when I heard Dad call, "Camy, is that you?"

"Uh, yeah."

The TV clicked off and he appeared in the doorway.

"I thought you weren't coming home for another hour. Are you okay?"

I nodded.

"You look kind of sick." The concern in his eyes made me feel guilty. I wasn't sick, I wanted to say. Unless being stupid was a disease. If that was true, I had a fatal case of it.

"I kind of have a headache," I said instead.

Head? Heart? My whole body hurt.

"It's been a big day," he said. "Want a cup of tea?"

"I think I'll just go to bed." Gavin's jersey slipped a little in my brace. I resisted the urge to check if the number fourteen was peeking out below the hem of my dress.

I was halfway up the stairs when Dad said, "Cams?"

I stopped, my hand gripping the rail. "Yeah?"

"You'd tell me if something was wrong, wouldn't you?"

"Sure," I said. I didn't like to lie, but I told myself the only thing that was *really* wrong was that I'd been dumb enough to trust a boy who'd already proven he wasn't worth trusting. Dad always wanted to fix things. There was no way he could fix that.

"Okay, then," he said. "Have a good night."

"You, too," I whispered.

It took five minutes to take off my dress, toss it on the closet floor, stash Gavin's jersey under my bed, and turn on my laptop. I probably could have managed all that in even less time, but I felt the need to rip my pantyhose into a dozen pieces first. Those things are stronger than you'd think.

With a scowl on my face, I went straight for the wiki. I was determined to discover all the answers this time. I was finally going to unmask the mastermind. When I did, I'd nail him, and Gavin, and all the other morons on the anti-hit list to the wall.

It ended tonight.

The first thing I did was scroll through the old messages in the chat box. I bypassed all the "Call of Duty throwdowns" until I found this thread:

> **Lukasn: How do we stop her?**
>
> **randallb: She has a weak spot. Everybdy on the football team knows that. Gotta play a little offense here. It's not that hard.**

When I'd first read those posts, I thought they were talking about Elle. I realized now, it was me.

jasona: o0o, tough guy. Say what, bro. Why don't *you* do sumthin about it?

It wasn't Randall, but Gavin, who'd done something about it. I checked the date on the thread. The next day we'd ended up in the boys' bathroom. The evidence was right there, in front of me. I'd just refused to see it.

When I clicked on the wiki's home page again, the list of Hotties refreshed. It was something I'd gotten used to, but this time, my name appeared at the top of the list. I clicked on it.

The picture took forever to load, but I recognized the stadium lights right away. I pulled my trashcan closer, just in case I needed to throw up.

There it was. Or, I guess, there *I* was. On the fifty-yard line. My mouth formed a perfect 'o'. My eyes reflected the light so I looked like I was possessed. My arms were held out like those of a puppet on a string.

Beneath the photo, jasona had written:

ha, ha, she looks like a dear in the headlights.

"It's d-e-e-r, you idiot," I said aloud. But really? Who was the idiot? The tool with the cell phone camera? Or the girl wearing the jersey of a guy on the anti-hit list?

Because even though you couldn't see Gavin's face, there was no missing the huge number fourteen draped over my dress. Elle certainly wouldn't miss it. And I couldn't explain it to her, not without ruining everything. Or maybe I should say, everything that wasn't ruined already.

In three seconds I'd made my decision. I was logged in as Jason, so technically, I wouldn't be deleting the picture, *he* would. Without comments, it might not leave a trail. But I didn't care if it did. All that mattered was getting it off the wiki before Elle logged on.

I clicked delete, then refreshed the page. I was right. The photo, and all evidence that it had been posted, vanished. I leaned back in my chair, thinking I should have had that tea.

It was going to be a long night.

At one o'clock, when I heard the creak of Dad's footsteps on the stairs, I switched off the desk lamp and huddled in the dark. After his bedroom door had clicked closed, I snuck downstairs. Forget the tea. I made a pot of coffee and carried the whole thing upstairs.

By three in the morning, I was feeling wired and my stomach hurt from anger and from all the caffeine I'd consumed. I'd read every single page on the wiki but I still felt like I was missing something.

Then it hit me. All this time, I'd never gone back to the secret page I'd found that first day, the one with the photo of Elle and Clarissa in Greece. I clicked through and held my breath during the second login. The first picture that came up didn't feature Elle, Clarissa, or a deep blue sea at all.

It was me.

For a long moment, my brain refused to believe what my eyes were telling me. The picture had been uploaded that afternoon. It showed me sitting on the trunk of the convertible. My dress looked beautiful. For once, my hair was behaving. It would've been a great picture. Except.

My mouth was open. My eyes were closed.

"A keeper," Rhino had called it.

Oh. Oh, no.

Only one person could have taken that photo. Only one person could have uploaded it. I checked anyway, hoping to see Jason's or Aiden's screen name. But no. Someone named Admin, without the asterisk, had posted it. He'd done it just before the homecoming parade started.

I clutched my empty coffee cup tight, just to have something to hold on to.

Rhino … was Admin?

I shook my head, and tears fell from my eyes as I did. Rhino was the wiki's mastermind. He'd known about it all along. Because he'd created it. I didn't want to believe it, not until I talked to him myself. Maybe there was some other explanation. I clicked back to the page and read the note Admin/Rhino had posted along with the photo:

A keeper.

Yeah, I thought. It was.

I made a backup of the picture and logged off. I couldn't stand another second of staring at the wiki. I climbed into bed and to my surprise, I not only fell asleep, but I slept hard. No dreams, no worries. At least, not until my cell phone rang.

♡ ♡ ♡

My hand groped for the phone. The display read twenty-five minutes after six. I squinted at the number. No way was I talking to Rhino. Not yet. Not until I was better prepared. But it wasn't him on the phone. It was Elle. My mind went to last night, to Elle and Rhino, together in his garage. Kissing like movie stars. Climbing up the stairs.

Then I thought about Rhino as the probable mastermind behind the wiki. I rolled onto my back and waited for the phone to stop. It chimed a minute later, letting me know a message was waiting for me in voicemail.

"Can you get in?" Elle's voice was frantic. "I thought maybe I had the caps lock on, but I tried again and nothing."

I stumbled out of bed, opened the login screen for the wiki and entered Jason's information. All I got was a warning telling me my user name or password was incorrect and inviting me to try again.

Uh-oh.

I tried again. And again. I even tried different passwords. Then I tried different user names. But if I couldn't log in as Jason, what made me think I could get in as Aiden? I picked up the phone to call Elle, but then I imagined how that conversation might go.

"What happened? Why can't we log in?" she might say.

"Jason probably changed his password," I would answer.

"But why last night?"

Because of me, I thought. Because of what happened with Gavin.

And that was when the doorbell rang. Downstairs, I heard the door creak open and Dad's voice, low but friendly.

"Camy?" he called up the stairwell. "You awake yet?"

"Sort of."

"There's someone here to see you."

At six-thirty in the morning? Who? Rhino? If not him, then who else?

"I'll be right down." I set the phone on my desk and pulled on a T-shirt and jeans. For the first time ever, I really hoped the person at the door wasn't Rhino. I was still hoping that when I walked through the living room. Dad was sitting in his chair, laptop open.

"Camy, quick, before you go outside, I need to show you something."

My feet froze. It was early. I hadn't had much sleep. I'd never been good at math, but I found myself adding up Dad + laptop + needing to show me something. Had he found *The Hotties of Troy*? Had he hacked into it, just like I had?

He turned the screen around. I closed my eyes.

"That's my girl, front page of the sports section."

He was reading the online edition of the *Olympia Weekly News*. And there, in the picture, was me. The photographer had snapped the photo during Gavin's amazing touchdown run. He'd caught me with my arms in the air, the fake fur stole slipping from my shoulders, Number Fourteen running past in the foreground.

"I've already emailed a copy to your mom. And outside?" Dad nodded toward our front door. "I'm not sure, but I think Number Fourteen is waiting for you." He gave me a look, which under normal circumstances would have been one of those annoying, know-it-all Dad kind of smiles.

I spun and headed back up the stairs.

"Hey!" Dad called out. "Where are you going?"

"To brush my teeth."

I let the sound of my feet pounding up the stairs drown out his laughter.

In seconds, I was on the floor with my cheek pressed against the hard wood. My fingers strained to reach Gavin's jersey, which I'd shoved way under the bed. I pulled it free, then just looked at it. How would I get this past Dad?

I opened my window. It was still dark out, not even a hint of sunrise showing. I wrapped the jersey in a tight ball and threw it. Then I brushed my teeth and headed down the stairs and out the door.

Gavin was standing in the driveway with his hands in his pockets. He opened his mouth to say something when he saw me, but I rushed past him and around the house. The lilac bushes had caught his football jersey and I waded in to tug it free. The first thing I did when I got back to Gavin was throw good ol' number fourteen right at his face.

"What the heck?" he said, fumbling with the jersey. "I'm sorry about last night. I had no idea that—"

"That what? That Jason just happened to be at the field? That he just happened to take my picture and upload it on the wiki? That he changed his password so now I can't log in?" I took a quick look at the house, hoping Dad couldn't hear me shout.

"What are you talking about?" Gavin asked.

"I can't log in. Sometime between last night and now, Jason changed his password, or someone changed it for him."

"I swear to you, I didn't do it. I haven't been online since …" He shrugged. "Wednesday, I think. And I had no idea Jason was going to be at the football field last night."

He sounded so sincere, and those amber eyes looked so honest. Part of me wanted to believe him, despite all the evidence.

"Okay," I said. "Then can you get me back in?"

"In where?"

"The wiki. Change his password again. Or give me my own login."

He stared down at his shoes. "I can't do that. It was one thing when you figured it out on your own, but I …" He shook his head. "I can't do that."

If I couldn't get a login, maybe I could get something else. Maybe I could at least get some information to make my life a little less awful. "Then how about this. Did Rhino start the wiki?"

Gavin's head shot up. "What?"

"Because I think he did. I think I found proof of it last night."

Gavin choked out a laugh. "Rhino? Why would you think that? It's probably something Jason did. He's an idiot."

"So, you're saying Jason took a picture of me. With Rhino's laptop. And then he posted it on the secret disclaimer page?" I asked, making my voice all syrupy sweet, the same way Elle did.

Even in the dim light from our porch, I could tell his face went pale.

"Why were you really at Rhino's last night?" Something clicked, another piece of the puzzle bringing the picture into focus. "It wasn't to see me," I said. "And I don't think it was for Elle, either." Gavin + Rhino = the wiki. It seemed too awful to contemplate. "You were there to tell Rhino about Coach Cutter's talk."

Gavin still looked pale, but his expression hardened, game face on. He wasn't budging, but I tried anyway.

"Get me a new login," I said.

"I wish I could."

"But you won't, will you?"

He shook his head.

"Then I don't have anything else to say to you."

"Camy, wait ..."

I turned my back on him and stepped inside. I shut the door behind me, then waited to hear the doorbell ring.

It didn't. And when I peeked out the front window, Gavin was gone.

I needed more coffee before I could even think about facing Rhino. I needed a shower. I needed a brain transplant too. And maybe something for my heart. But first, I had to get the coffeepot back downstairs before Dad noticed it was gone.

At least I managed to accomplish that one impossible thing before breakfast. I brewed a new pot, then drank a cup to congratulate myself. With renewed determination, or just too much caffeine, I threw on a jacket, then shoved my feet into a pair of Chucks.

What started as a march straight to Rhino's soon turned into a meandering stroll. I knew I needed to talk to him right away. Elle had already left two voicemails and three texts. I couldn't put off telling her forever. Still. Until I looked him in the eye and heard what he had to say, it could still all just be a big mistake, couldn't it? Rhino could still be the best friend he'd always pretended to be.

The door to his garage was closed, but I only had to stand in the driveway a few minutes before it opened. Inside, Rhino was wandering around with his hair all wild, wearing rumpled pajama bottoms and his chicken butt shirt.

He sure didn't look like an evil genius.

"Hey, Ladybug." He raised a hand in greeting. "You're up early. Have fun at Elle's party?"

"Funny thing about that," I said. "She disappeared partway through it. No one could find her."

"That's strange," he said.

After everything that had happened in the last twenty-four hours, I just wanted to get it over with. I was done hinting. I was done asking. There was no more try. Only do. I walked over to Rhino's laptop. I brought up the browser and typed the address for the wiki.

"You're going to have to log in," I said.

"I don't know what you're talking about."

"For real? Haven't you been tracking me every time I logged in as Jason?" I said. I heard the tiniest of exhales. Annoyance? Defeat? I couldn't tell.

"Actually," he said at last. "I have an app for that."

I stared straight ahead, at the wiki's login page, not daring to glance at Rhino. "Explain."

"What do you want me to say?" He sat on the arm of the sofa, directly behind me.

I swiveled in the chair to face him. "For a start, I'd like to know what made you think that this was a good idea."

"Good? I never thought it was a good idea. I thought it was a great idea. A brilliant idea."

"So all these things you guys write about us girls, you think it doesn't hurt?"

"Not when you didn't know about it," he said. "That was the whole point. You should be thanking me for rounding up the biggest jerks in our school and locking them up in their own online playground."

"*Playground*? It's more like you created the perfect Petri dish and then inserted a superbug into it. You took a wound and gave it a cozy place to fester." He bristled then, and I wondered. Did he really think that if a tree fell in a forest and no one was around to hear it, it didn't make a sound?

Words hurt even if the victim never hears them.

"What you've done, Rhino, it's … it's misguided at best, and at worst it makes you look like one of them. I never thought you could be such an assho—"

"I don't know what you're so upset about," Rhino said. Then he rolled his eyes. No. Really. He *rolled his eyes.* "And I don't know why I ever bothered to do everyone in our stupid school this favor, anyway."

"You still don't get it, do you?" I said. "Every mean post, every embarrassing picture, every stupid thing some jerk says about me or Elle or Sophie or Mercedes—"

He held up a hand. "That wasn't me. *I* haven't hurt anyone."

"You posted that picture of me yesterday," I snapped.

Rhino flinched. "You found the disclaimer page."

Oh, yeah. I'd found it, all right.

"That was childish. I took it down after a few hours."

"When? Before or after you were sucking face with Elle … and who knows what else last night."

"Is that what this is really all about?"

I crossed my arms over my chest. "No."

"You sure about that?"

Sure, I was sure. Mostly, anyway.

"Here's the thing," he said. "What if you never saw that picture of yourself? What if you'd never had access to the wiki at all? Would you be mad at me right now? Would we even be having this conversation?"

"So you're saying that ignorance is—" I was so angry that I couldn't even think of the word.

He cocked his head and scooted farther back on the arm of the sofa. "Bliss? Maybe. You have to admit, a lot of things would be better if you just didn't know."

"What things?"

He looked at me like I was the dumbest person on the planet and started waving his hands back and forth between us.

"Besides us, I mean."

"What about your beloved football?"

"Football? I don't see—"

"Think about the season we'd be having if not for you, and for Elle and her—what did she call it? Boy boycott?"

With Gavin as quarterback? I'd been counting on a great season, and Rhino knew it.

"What do you care about football?" I said.

"I don't, but you do. That's the point. And honestly?" He gestured toward the wiki. "Do you really care about any of the other girls on there? Elle? *Clarissa*?"

I started to say, "I don't," but that wasn't true. Not anymore.

"Look, I never meant for it to happen, but I do care."

Rhino raised his eyebrows.

"Okay, not so much about Clarissa, but I care about Elle, and Mercedes … and Sophie, too. That's why I'm here. Not because I'm jealous, or even because I was hurt by that stupid picture you posted of me. I'm here because I care about those girls, and I want to make things better for them." I looked at Rhino then, really looked at him. "Isn't there anything you care about?"

Rhino's gaze flickered around the room. It was like he was trying to look anywhere but into my eyes. Then a familiar expression settled on his face. It was the same one I saw whenever he tried explaining a math concept that I just couldn't get, frustration mixed with a little disbelief.

He sighed and pressed his lips together.

After a moment, he said, "If you really have to know … I did it for … for baseball."

"Baseball?" I said. I started to add *You've got to be kidding me*, but the evidence was everywhere—the Twins pennant on the wall, the framed photo of him and his brother Darren in matching uniforms, the RBI stats scattered across his coffee table.

"Yes, baseball," Rhino said. "And it was working, too. All I had to do was roll out the wiki, then, a little encouragement here, a little team bonding there, and voilà!" He threw his hands into the air. "Suddenly our team was winning the district championship, just like when Darren was playing. It was perfect. And it could have worked for football too, if you and Elle hadn't come along and screwed everything up."

"Baseball," I echoed, because I still wasn't 100% sure I could believe him. "Really?"

Rhino looked toward the ceiling. "You don't understand," he said. His words were surprisingly soft. "No one was supposed to get hurt."

"That doesn't make it right."

"Right. Wrong? Those words only have meaning because we say they do. Was it right that I gamed the system to get you onto the homecoming court? You didn't seem to mind that."

That was so unfair. "I never asked you to do it."

"You didn't complain about it, either, or when Sophie won." He pulled at the hem of his shirt. "I don't remember being thanked for *that* yet."

I'd known Rhino since preschool, but suddenly I felt like I had never met the boy who was sitting across from me. I stood up and pushed the chair in carefully.

Rhino didn't say a word until I took my first step out of the garage. "Cams, come on. Don't be like that," he called. "Where are you going?"

"I'm going to tell Elle."

He caught me at the end of the driveway and put a hand on my shoulder. I shook it off.

"You're going to do *what*?" he asked. He was squinting a bit from the rising sun, or was that worry I saw in his eyes?

"Depends. Are you going to shut down the wiki?" I asked.

The squinting stopped and Rhino's stare went hard.

"Then if you're not going to do anything about it, I guess I will." I turned onto the sidewalk.

"You know your precious Gavin was in on it from the start, don't you?" Rhino called after me. "From. The. Start. And he thought it was a good idea. No, a great idea! He thought it was the most brilliant fucking idea he had ever heard!"

I knew I shouldn't listen. I shouldn't let it hurt me; that was the only reason he was saying it. I kept walking, not looking back, not once.

And I pretended it didn't hurt at all.

Chapter Twenty

ELLE TEXTED ME two more times before I found her in the school gym, helping the student council members take down decorations from the dance.

What's up with you and rhino? the first text said.

He says you're mad read the second one.

I should have figured Rhino would go straight into damage control. Hadn't I always told him that the best defense was a good offense? I probably should have replied to Elle right away, too, but I thought this was something I needed to do face-to-face.

"We need to talk," she said, then crooked her finger.

I followed her to an empty classroom in the language hall. As soon as we stepped inside, she opened a cabinet, took out a TEST-ING, DO NOT ENTER sign and stuck it to the outside of the door. The move reminded me of Gavin and our meeting in the boys' bathroom.

She sat on top of the teacher's desk and squared her shoulders. "Okay, first, I'm sorry that you're mad about Rhino and me, but you should've said something. I asked you straight out, remember? And you were all, 'we're just friends.'"

"I'm not mad about you and Rhino."

"That's not what he said."

Of course.

"I don't care what he said. It's not true."

"Whatever." She flipped her hair. It was obvious she believed Rhino over me. "We still have that other problem to deal with. Can you get into the wiki?"

I shook my head. I didn't think I could trust myself to talk about the wiki and Rhino's part in it yet. I knew I would have to choose my words carefully.

"So," she said, "whatever the reason is, you're ticked at Rhino, but I've been thinking." She picked up a pencil from the desk and beat it against her thigh like a drum. "You were right all along. We should totally bring him into this. I mean, he's so smart about this kind of thing. He could hack the system. Easy."

I shook my head again, not sure I could hold back much longer, but then Elle's phone chimed. "Hold on," she said. Then, "Oh, good lord."

"What is it?" I asked, both curious and afraid to hear the answer.

"Nothing that I can't deal with later. Just another one of those stupid girls who can't keep it in her panties. Recognize this one?" She turned the phone's screen toward me.

I tried to swallow the bile that was rising in the back of my throat because there, on Elle's phone, was a photo that I was intimately familiar with. It was me. And Gavin. On the fifty-yard line. The *'dear' in the headlights* shot.

She turned the screen back around and started pinching and swiping, trying to enlarge the image. "Ugh. This phone," she said. "Anyway, it's probably one of the pom squad girls. Or, no, one of Sophie's skanks."

Maybe I should have been relieved that her suspicion hadn't fallen on me, but really? How does a girl who climbed the stairs to my best friend's (okay, former best friend's) bed get to call some other girl out as a skank? It wasn't fair. In the interest of self-preservation, I tried to rein in any anger I felt and stick to the facts.

"Back to Rhino," I said. "He's … he's not what you think he is. Or I guess I should say that he is who you think he isn't."

"What are you talking about?"

"Remember that disclaimer page we found that first day on the wiki?"

"The one *you* found?"

"Right," I said. "I hadn't been checking it."

Elle shook her head. "Me neither. I totally forgot about it with all the homecoming drama."

"I checked it last night." I took a breath. "Something I saw there—it sort of leads to only one person."

"You found the mastermind?" She gave me a smile. "It's Aiden, isn't it?"

"No. I thought it was him at first, but it isn't."

"Then who?" Her brow crinkled. "It can't be Jason. He's not smart enough. If someone gave that kid a penny for his thoughts, he'd have to give them change back."

She looked at me like she expected me to laugh. When I didn't, she said, "It's not Gavin, is it? I mean, it doesn't seem like something he'd do, but come on—" She waved the phone around again. "That's his jersey in that photo. Apparently his standards aren't as high as they once were."

"What?"

"Any slut in a storm," she said. "I guess boys will be boys after all."

That did it.

"It's Rhino," I said, the words coming out like a slap.

"Camy, girl. You need to get some sleep or something. You know Rhino doesn't have a football jersey. And he certainly wouldn't be screwing around with some little—"

"He's the mastermind."

"You're lying," she said. "You're mad at him because we have this … connection." A flicker of doubt lit her face for a moment. "And … and you're just trying to get back at both of us." She squeezed the pencil in her hand so hard that I thought it might break.

"No. Elle. I'm—"

She held up a hand, but I didn't stop.

"I'm not lying. Don't you think I wish I was? He was my best friend." I let out a breath. "I found a picture on the disclaimer page. It was a picture that I saw Rhino take. It's him, Elle. Your boyfriend. He's the one."

She pushed herself off the desk and walked to the door. She yanked it open by the knob. "Get out," she said. "Get. Out."

So I did.

♡ ♡ ♡

Hav u seen elle?

The text from Mercedes surprised me. I hadn't known she had my phone number.

Try the language hall, I responded.

I might have been angry with Elle, but there was no sense taking it out on anyone else.

K thnx

I didn't know what to do with myself. I'd worked all these weeks to find the mastermind of the wiki but, without Elle, I wasn't sure what to do with the information now that I had it.

I turned toward the football field. Maybe walking the fifty-yard line would jump start my brain. I'd only made it as far as the gate when my phone buzzed again.

Halp! it said, again from Mercedes.

Huh? I answered back.

We need u n the langauge hall, STAT!!!!!!!!!!!!!!!!!

I assumed the "langauge" hall was the language hall, and the "we"? Clearly Mercedes was included; she was the one who'd sent the text. Like I'd told Rhino earlier, I'd do just about anything to help that girl, but if Elle was also involved? Eh, whatever.

My phone was insistent.

Ssly the next message said. **Its teh end of the world as we no it.**

Despite my misgivings, I headed back toward the school. Mercedes met me at the entrance to the language hall.

"This is serious," she said. "I've never seen her like this."

We walked back to the classroom. The TESTING sign was still posted. I cracked the door to peek inside. The lights were off. The shades were pulled.

A voice from inside said, "Can't you read, moron? The sign says: Do. Not. Enter."

That couldn't be Elle. She wasn't the kind of girl to toss out random insults. Specific insults, occasionally, but never random ones.

I flipped on the lights.

She was sitting cross-legged on top of the teacher's desk. Her eyes were red. Dark streaks of mascara ran down both cheeks. Half her hair had escaped its blue and white clasp. And it looked as though she might have used the hem of her OHS Trojan Pride t-shirt to wipe her runny nose.

"Elle?"

"Go away."

"Come on. It's not that bad."

"You don't understand!" she wailed through a fresh batch of tears.

Twenty minutes later, Elle was still crying. When I looked into her eyes it seemed like she was lost. No, I thought; worse than lost. Elle looked broken. I'd wondered what happened when someone got knocked off destiny's path. Now I knew. And I'd been the one to give the final shove.

Mercedes and I tried everything: talking, patting her back, promising her a Diet Coke. Still, over and over, she howled, "You don't understand."

"If we can't get her to calm down, then we need to get her out of here," Mercedes said.

I knew what she meant.

A grainy cell phone photo of Elle going native by the Grecian sea might not be enough to topple the goddess of Olympia High from her mighty perch, but if Aiden, Clarissa, or any of the rest of the piranhas on the student council caught her in this shape, I was sure they'd leave behind nothing but bones.

We needed more help to get Elle out of the school unseen, but who? I'd always counted on Rhino to come to my rescue. That wasn't happening. Not today, and maybe not ever again. I blew out a breath and blinked back a few tears of my own.

Once more, I relied on my tutoring experience. Who knew about both boys and sneaking out of school? Almost immediately, a name popped into my head. I chided myself for thinking it, but I knew I had my answer.

"Sophie," I said out loud. "If only I had her phone number."

"I do," Mercedes said.

Under any other circumstances I would have wondered at the strangeness of a contact list that connected the school's most spir-ited with the school's most … misunderstood. But there wasn't time for that. Instead, I tapped in the number as Mercedes read it off and touched Call.

A little girl answered. She sounded all of six.

"Is Sophie there?" I asked. I heard the phone thunk and the patter of tiny footsteps. Then I heard something more ominous. The clip-clop of Ms. Pendergast's high heels. The corridor was clear, but I ran to the end of the hall and ducked into the stairway.

"Yeah?" Sophie said a few moments later. The sound of her voice in my ear made me jump.

"Hey, it's Camy."

"Oh ... hi."

"Um, we have kind of a problem," I said. "A boy problem." I figured it was best to get it all out there.

"Ooh." Sophie's voice perked up. "It's Gavin, isn't it?"

I gave her the SparkNotes version of events, talking around what I thought might have happened between Elle and Rhino the night before. At the end of it, I said, "We need to get her out of here and we don't know how."

Sophie arrived in less than ten minutes. She took one look at Elle, blew out a breath and said, "Okay, here's what we're going to do ..."

If I thought Rhino was an evil genius, he was nothing compared to Sophie. Her plan was amazing, and simple too. All we had to do was wait until the coast was clear, then walk out the door one at a time.

"The most important thing I've learned about getting out of school without being seen is to look like everything is completely normal. You know, like you're doing what you're supposed to be doing."

We spent a few minutes cleaning Elle up, then Sophie threatened to kill her if she cried again before we got out the door. Mercedes acted as lookout. As soon as she gave the signal we stepped out the classroom door. Sophie walked on one side of Elle. I took the other. When we got close to the office, Mercedes motioned for us to wait.

"Hi, Clarissa!" she gushed in a loud voice.

I couldn't hear the response, but the conversation between them seemed to take forever. When it finally ended and Mercedes signaled to us again, it looked like Clarissa had drained most of the perkiness right out of her. I fought the urge to chew my fingernails.

"I'll go first," Sophie said. "Wait two minutes, then send Elle out with Mercedes. You come two minutes after that. We'll meet up by the gates to the football field."

I nodded.

"And whatever happens, don't stop walking once you start."

I watched Sophie stroll right out the front doors like subterfuge was an everyday occurrence for her. I started counting backward from one hundred twenty. When I got to one, I gave Elle a push. "Go."

She wasn't as convincing as Sophie, but somehow she managed to meet up with Mercedes and scoot out the door. That left just me. I rubbed my sweaty palms on my jeans and tried to calm my heartbeat. I took a quick drink at the fountain, then started toward the door. I had my hand on it when I heard that ominous clip-clop and someone saying, "Camy? Camy Cavanaugh?"

I had twelve years of goody-two-shoes experience behind me. I couldn't help it. I stopped and turned around—and found Ms. Pendergast standing there.

"What are you doing here on a Saturday?" she said. "Not tutoring, I hope." She rolled her eyes.

Like I said before, I don't like to lie. And I'm usually not very good at it. But all the secret double agent wiki stuff I'd been involved in over the past few weeks had improved my skills.

"I just stopped by to see if the student council needed any help," I said.

Ms. P reached up to pat her hair. "That's wonderful, Camy. I'm so glad you took my advice and started interacting with your fellow students more. That Elle." She smiled. "She sure is a good influence on—"

Whatever she said next was lost in the sound of my internal barfing. The next thing I heard was, "Speaking of Elle, have you seen her?"

"N-no," I stuttered. I felt the start of a twitch forming beneath my left eye.

A look of distrust washed across Ms. Pendergast's face, but she dismissed it quickly enough. "Well, if you see her, tell her I'm looking for her, would you? And, Camy, I have a little project I was hoping you might help me with. It's kind of a puzzle and—"

"Sure! Great!" I said, but that wasn't what I was thinking. And then I wasn't thinking at all. I pushed open the school door, walked calmly until I was out of sight of Ms. Pendergast, then I ran like hell for the football field.

♡ ♡ ♡

We ended up at my house. Mercedes wasn't sure if her mom would be home, Elle didn't offer, and Sophie said my place was closer, but I got the idea she didn't want us to see where she lived. Besides, my dad had circled an ad in the newspaper for a tech swap that day. I hoped there would be enough widgets and what's-its there to keep him occupied until we got Elle straightened out. And if there weren't? Well, freaky hermit girl inviting actual friends to her house? He'd probably hug himself and buy us pizza.

Once we got inside, I grabbed bottles of water for everyone out of the fridge. We sat down in the living room.

"All right, then," Sophie started. "Who wants to tell me what's going on?"

Elle looked down at her water bottle and concentrated on peeling off the label. Mercedes was busy hyperventilating. I guessed I would have to be the one to explain.

Sophie interrupted when I'd gotten most of the way to the end.

"Is that all this is about?" she said. "Jeez, Camy, I told you there was no such thing as Prince Charming. And you." She zeroed in on Elle. "*You* should already know better. You've had boyfriends before. You know how guys are."

Elle stuck her water bottle between her knees and started sobbing again.

"Quit being a baby," Sophie said. But that just made things worse.

I jumped up to find some tissues. Remember what I said about Dad and shopping? Right. I couldn't find a box of Puffs anywhere, so I went into the bathroom and brought out a roll of toilet paper.

I don't know what kind of magic Sophie worked while I was gone, but things were a lot calmer, and less damp, when I returned.

"So I just don't get what the point is," Elle was saying. "You practically kill yourself trying to be perfect, trying to do everything right. Grades, looks, cheerleading, student council, your parents ... boys." She sighed. "You wait and wait for the right one to come around, the *perfect* guy, and then—"

"Hold on a second. You're kidding me, right?" Sophie said. "Are you trying to tell me that Elle Emerson, *the* Elle Emerson, has never done anything with a guy before?"

Sophie's eyes were huge.

So were Mercedes'.

Mine were too.

"No!" Elle said. "That's *not* what I'm trying to tell you. Of *course* I've done things."

We all let out a breath at the same time.

"I just never did *it*. I figure the other stuff doesn't count."

I shouldn't have been shocked that she felt that way. Not really. The rules for girls like Elle Emerson had always been different than they were for the rest of us. Apparently, that included sex too. She had this idea that her first time should be something epic.

And she'd almost had it, too. I thought about last night in Rhino's garage. How they'd danced. How, when they kissed, it really had seemed like something from a movie.

Elle looked at me then. "One thing. You've got to be totally honest. I promise not to freak, but I've got to know if he was lying or not. Was it really his first time too?"

"He said it was?" I formed the words with my mouth, I know I did, but they felt weird and foreign. "I wish I could tell you," I said. Because in that moment, I had no idea. The old Rhino, the one I knew better than anyone else, had ceased to exist.

Sophie kicked my ankle. "The answer is yes," she said. "God, Camy, you really do suck at this."

"Why do you think I called you?"

The three of them stayed the night. Just as I'd predicted, Dad ordered pizza when he got home from the tech swap. We watched *Pride and Prejudice* together downstairs. Then we went up to my room. Sophie gave me tips on how to control my crazy hair. Mercedes treated us all to mayonnaise facials, and Elle flipped through the clothes in my closet. She held up my *Star Wars* Come to the Dark Side shirt.

"Never. Wear. This. Again," she said, and turned to Sophie. "You weren't at the party," she said in her debater's voice. Even with a broken heart, Elle Emerson could still go a few rounds.

Sophie raised an eyebrow. Actually, I did too. I mean, Elle had hardly been at the party.

"I had to work the late shift." Sophie shook her head, a momentary flush covering her cheeks. "Denny's never closes."

"And that Kevin guy? You didn't…?" Elle asked.

Now Sophie really blushed. And then her face turned to glass again, all sharp and fragile.

"I don't see how that's any of your business," she said. "Kevin's not on your anti-hit list, but if you really need to know, he came to work with me. He stayed for like half my shift, and ended up drinking two pots of coffee."

"Is he still awake?" Mercedes asked.

Sophie grinned. "I switched him to decaf after the first pot. He never noticed."

"And that was it?" Elle almost looked like her old self, but it was more like a gauzy, watercolor version of herself, one that could wash away at any moment.

"Well, no." Sophie stared at the ceiling. "He kissed me." She touched her cheek. "Right here."

"I should've stopped there," Elle mused.

"And Dalton should have started there," Mercedes said. "The boy is sweet, but I'm ready to get on with the making out already!"

We talked and laughed until the sun came up.

Overnight, the temperature dropped from chilly to frigid. The first true frost of the season was glistening in the morning light. Sophie's car refused to start, so Dad offered to drive to her house so she could pick up the battery charger she stored there. We stopped at Elle's for the bags I'd left there on Friday. Then we dropped Mercedes off near her car at school.

I don't know why Sophie was so embarrassed about her house. Sure, it was a trailer, but it was really nice. A deck ran across the front of it, with a big pot of mums sitting on it. And her sisters were playing in the leaves that her mom was raking in the yard.

When we got home, I wasted two hours trying to hack back into the wiki. It proved impossible. I took a nap, then dug out all my folders and homework. Everything was still a mess after being knocked over in the locker room on Friday. I found my calculus. I found my earth science. I found my French. The only things missing were the spreadsheets I'd made for the wiki and the ones Gavin had given to me.

I dumped everything on the floor and sorted it. While I was super organized after that, I still didn't have either of the spreadsheets. *My locker*, I thought. *They must be in my locker.*

And if they weren't?

I didn't want to think about that.

.

Chapter Twenty One

MONDAY MORNING WAS one of those days that make you glad you live in Minnesota. The sky was blue. The air was crisp. The leaves on the trees were dressed in gorgeous colors. Despite everything that had happened, I was … happy. Hopeful, even. It felt like the first day of school all over again, like anything was possible.

Okay, so Gavin had turned out to be a jerk. But I'd spent the last three years not talking to him and it hadn't killed me yet. And, yeah, my best friend since preschool had ended up being more Prince of Darkness than Prince Charming. That still hurt. A lot. But at least I had Elle, Mercedes, and Sophie to take his place. Sort of.

The problem with the wiki wasn't solved yet, either. But with the homecoming drama over, we could take our time and figure out a way to really get our revenge. I felt so good that it was almost impossible to keep from whistling as I walked into school.

I don't know what I was thinking.

Actually, I *do* know what I was thinking. I needed to check both my locker and the girls' locker room to find the wiki spreadsheets before the wrong person got hold of them. I was stacking stuff next to my locker door when a shadow fell across the floor.

I heard a rattle of paper first, then, "Looking for these?"

I looked up to find Elle … and Clarissa. My knees felt like water, but I stood and faced them.

"A dating spreadsheet? Really?" Elle slammed the papers into my chest. "I don't know what's worse, this, or what you have going on with Gavin."

She took another paper from Clarissa's hands and held it up for me to see. It was a photo of two people standing on a fifty-yard line. The boy had his back turned to the camera. The girl was wearing a jersey.

"You lied to me," Elle said.

"It's not what you think. I don't have anything going on with Gavin," I said. *Not anymore.*

"Right."

"And those." I pointed to the spreadsheets. "I was trying to find out who was behind the wiki. Which, oh, by the way, I did. Remember?"

"Yeah, great job with that," Elle said. "No, really. Thanks for ruining my life. And thanks for waiting all of three seconds before going after Gavin too."

"Hello? You and Rhino?" What? Did she want it both ways? "You get all the guys and the rest of us get none?"

From down the hall, someone said, "You tell her!"

Elle sent a withering look in their direction and they shut up pretty quick. She turned back to me but she didn't say anything else. And Elle *always* had something to say. Instead, she shook her head like she couldn't stand to look at me for one more second and walked away.

Somehow, that was worse.

But even worse than that, Clarissa *didn't* leave. She stayed behind with a satisfied look on her face. Something clicked then. I remembered what Bing Bing had said about Clarissa and Jason.

I remembered Clarissa's reaction when she caught us dancing. My knocked-over book bag in the locker room while we were all getting ready. The missing spreadsheets. Clarissa's disappearance from Elle's party Friday night. The stadium lights.

Suddenly it all made sense.

"So," I said, "what were you doing with Jason at the football field the other night?"

Her cheeks colored, just slightly, but she tossed her head, letting her hair swing back and forth.

"You should've just given me the login to begin with," she said, "and saved yourself all this trouble."

Yeah. Right. I stared at her.

"Would that have been so hard?" Her smirk went all syrupy sweet. The smile told me she wasn't through, not yet.

Later that morning, I was sitting in calculus, my eyes pointed in the direction of the short, student-run TV show that played twice each day, once before lunch and once before last block, but I wasn't really watching. I was just glad it wasn't the special homecoming edition. Kevin probably wouldn't finish editing that until the end of the week. I wondered if I could come down with something contagious between now and then.

A gasp sounded behind me. Then a snort of laughter to my left. I tried to focus on the screen but my eyes didn't register what they were seeing right away. An amazing blue. Warm, sunlit sand. The blur of skin.

I sat straight up and leaned across my desk, like that would give me a better view. It was the photo of Elle and Clarissa from Greece. It had to be. Sure, it was blurrier, and pixilated. But if you knew what it was—and some of the guys seemed to know—then it was obvious.

My heart thumped hard, but slowed as I glanced around the room.

Sure, some of the guys were snickering, Aiden in particular. But the mathletes all looked at each other and shrugged. The substitute at the front of the classroom barely gave the screen a second glance before going back to the newspaper on the desk.

I don't know how Elle ended up at the door to the classroom three seconds after the bell rang. But she did. She stiff-armed me into a locker. Her eyes narrowed and her mouth got tight and fierce. I had never thought Elle Emerson could look ugly, but in that moment, she did.

"What the hell do you think you're trying to pull?" she demanded.

"It wasn't me," I told her. "I can't even log in anymore. Remember?"

"But you have a backup."

True. I did. "I didn't do it," I said. "I *wouldn't* do it."

"How do I know you're just not saying that?" There was a threat in Elle's voice. "Get me proof."

She didn't add, "Or else." She didn't have to.

As I walked to my locker at lunchtime, it hit me: Who was I going to sit with? Rhino? Not likely. Elle? Only if I wanted a lasagna rollup smeared in my face. Sophie? Maybe. If I could find her.

I stumbled on Mercedes instead. She was at my locker, tears streaming down her cheeks.

"Oh, Camy," she choked out when she saw me.

Tears were bad, but at least she was talking to me. I ran the rest of the way to my locker and hunkered down next to her. "What's wrong?"

"Dalton. He … he found out."

"About what?"

She gulped a few breaths. "About the whole dork dating thing. And he got really mad. He said, 'Why don't you just dump me already?' since that was the plan all along. I tried to explain that at first it was a setup, just for homecoming. But then I got to know him. I really like him, Camy. Lukas is nothing compared to him, but Dalton won't … He won't believe me."

I didn't know what else to do, so I hugged her.

"Could you talk to him?" she asked.

I said I would. I was halfway to the cafeteria to find him when I tumbled into the lockers for the second time that day. This time, it was Prudence Laramie on one side, and Babette "Bing Bing" Riley on the other.

"What's this stuff about a spreadsheet?" Prudence said. "What did those guys do? Did they rank us? Rate us? Decide who was good enough to date?"

"Yeah," Babette said. "And she helped them. She *helped them* rank us."

"Look," I said, turning to Prudence first. "You're right. There was a list, but Randall had only two words on his request."

Prudence crossed her arms over her chest.

"Your name." I turned to Bing Bing. "And you. Why do you even care? You only went to homecoming with Jason because … I *still* don't even know why you did it."

"Fair warning. I'm doing a newspaper article on this," Bing Bing said. "I've got a lot of people who are willing to talk."

Like the chess team, I thought, and the mathletes, and everyone else who had ended up as a dream dork date. They both pushed away from the lockers and headed for the lunchroom.

Babette threw a last glance over her shoulder at me. "Fair warning," she said again.

The second I walked into the cafeteria, I knew that talking to Dalton was out of the question. He was sitting at Rhino's table with Tim Lansing and the rest of the chess club. Rhino looked at me with a chill in his eyes that sent a shiver to my heart. I took a step back, tripped over my feet, and crashed into someone in the doorway to the caf.

That someone was Tara Tanaka.

"We need to talk," she said.

Of course we did. I was the most popular unpopular girl at Olympia High. She dragged me into the girls' bathroom.

"I don't know what the hell is going on, but you need to fix the part that involves Dalton," she said. "We start the chess tournament next week, with Prairie Stone. If he doesn't stop playing like an idiot, they're going to kick our asses."

"I …"

"I took him out in five moves in study hall today. Five moves. Freshmen play better than that."

I nodded. What more could I do?

She left me alone in the girls' bathroom. I stayed there for the rest of lunch.

♡ ♡ ♡

When school finally ended for the day, I climbed the stairs to the tutoring room, but I stopped on the third floor landing. Ms. Pendergast was standing near the door to the room. I'd forgotten that she had something she wanted to talk to me about. I wasn't sure what that "something" was. Considering the way my day was going, though, it probably wouldn't be anything good. I hunkered by a water fountain until I heard her clip-clop down the stairs.

Byron and a few freshmen boys were the only ones in the tutoring room. No Lexy. No pom squad. Not even a single leftover strand of pom-pom fringe on the floor. If Lexy's quote wasn't still glittering up on the wall, I might've thought the whole pom squad invasion had been a dream.

The boys squirmed in their chairs, and I didn't even try to stop them when they said they had to leave early. Only Byron paused at the door on his way out.

"Hey," he said.

Down on the practice field, Gavin called, "Hut!"

"Yeah?" I said.

Byron shook his head. "Nothing. I just wanted ... I mean, I just wanted to say I got a B on my last algebra test." He shrugged, and then he left too.

I sat alone in the tutoring room until the rattle of shoulder pads ended and the players abandoned the field.

♡ ♡ ♡

Tuesday morning, I convinced myself that I was sick and needed to stay home from school. Dad put on his worried face and made me promise to rest.

I tried watching TV, but every show seemed to be about some kind of drama or other. And even though I wished Judge Judy would show up to straighten out the mess I was in, I didn't feel like watching her help anyone else. I turned on my laptop instead. That was when I realized I wasn't just locked out of the wiki. Almost all of my new "friends" on Facebook had blocked me too.

I looked for something to read, but I'd been too busy to go to the library lately. All I had was my online copy of *Lysistrata*.

After school, Sophie showed up at my door, out of breath, face flushed.

"You've got to help me," she said.

I couldn't even help myself, but I invited her in anyway. "What's wrong?"

"What isn't?" She frowned and flopped into a chair. "I got called down to the office today."

"For what?"

"They accused me of cheating on my *Grapes of Wrath* report. I knew something like this was going to happen last week, but I wasn't really worried. It's not like they can prove anything. And then there was homecoming and—"

"Did you do it? Did you cheat?" I wasn't entirely sure I wanted to hear the answer.

"Hell, no! This is all Clarissa's fault."

I was perfectly willing to believe that Clarissa Delacroix was the root of all evil. I just couldn't see the connection between her and *The Grapes of Wrath*.

"What did she do?" I asked.

"You know how Pendergast has been busting my ass about English again this year?" Sophie said. "I'm in the same class as Clarissa. And I was talking to this girl about how you helped me before. Then, remember that Sunday when I was over here for the football game? Just talking to you brought back all that tutoring stuff you showed me. You're like some kind of miracle worker. Anyway, that's what I told her."

"And Clarissa heard you?"

Sophie nodded. "She popped right up and went straight to Pendergast's desk."

"I still don't understand," I said.

"She took what I said and made it sound ... well, you know Clarissa."

"So what did you say?"

"If I could pass with your help, then anyone could. Anyway, like I said, I wasn't that worried, but since it was Clarissa, I thought she deserved a little ... payback. Especially after what she did to you at homecoming, when you were dancing with The Ab."

"Sophie, what did you do?"

"I went into the wiki and found that picture of Clarissa and Elle. I was the one who put it on Trojan TV yesterday."

"You were the ... what?" For a second, I couldn't speak. "It was you? You realize Elle is about to kill me for that. She thinks I did it."

"Yeah, well, we cropped her out of the picture, but somehow the image reverted to the original. I'm real sorry about that."

Sorry? She was sorry? She was going to be even sorrier when Elle found out. "Wait. Who is *we* and how did you get into the wiki?"

"That's the worst part."

"There's a worst part?"

"Yeah. The school knows something about the Hottie site and they think Kevin is involved in it."

"What do you mean?"

She stood and started pacing. "They called me back to the office this afternoon, to talk to me more about the cheating thing. Then they started asking all these other questions. They wanted to know how Kevin and I 'got together' and how other people 'got together' too." She kept making air quote motions. "Then they asked if I'd ever seen anyone access an unauthorized webpage on a school computer."

"What did you tell them?"

"I lied, of course." She stopped pacing and turned to face me. "So, anyway, when I left the office, they were calling Kevin down there. And ... and after school, he wouldn't talk to me." Her face crumpled.

I wondered if I looked like that, like I was on the edge of falling apart.

"But Kevin didn't have anything to do with the wiki. They can't touch him for that," I said.

"Right. But—"

"He's the one who got you in, isn't he?"

She nodded and sniffed. "He hacked the site. Like you did. And if they find out he was in it, it's all over for him. Goodbye car. Good-bye scholarship. Goodbye Sophie." Tears welled in her eyes and spilled down her cheeks.

"Do you still have access?" I asked.

"I guess so." Sophie shrugged.

I blinked, the enormity of the idea knocking into me. It was one of those wonderful, terrifying notions that I didn't have the courage to voice. Not yet.

"I think I might have a plan," was all I said.

Chapter Twenty Two

THERE'S STRESS, like when you haven't studied for a test that you really, really need to do well on. There's dread, like when you know something is going to go from bad to worse. And then there's the absolute terror of being called to the office first thing on a Wednesday morning.

The first bell was still an echo in the air when Mr. Moore set down the phone and turned his gaze in my direction.

"Ms. Cavanaugh, it seems you're wanted in the office."

Murmurs rose around me. If Jason had been called to the office, no one would've noticed. But in my case? It was news.

"And take your books," Mr. Moore added.

A chorus of *oohs* rose around me. Heat stung my cheeks and I blinked fast, working to keep tears from my eyes.

"Save me a seat," Jason said.

I ignored him and rushed from the room. There was no reason to worry, I told myself. They could be calling me to the office for something good. Maybe I was getting some sort of award for maintaining decent grades when the whole school was falling apart around me.

Except it hadn't been that kind of week.

In the office, I spent an eternity in the world's most uncomfortable chair. Finally, the principal's door opened. Clarissa danced out and gave me that smile, the one that said she wasn't done with me.

"You can go in now," the secretary said without looking up. I took in a deep breath and pushed myself out of the chair.

I wasn't sure if Principal Miller's office was small or if it only looked that way because there were so many people crammed inside it. Principal Miller was sitting behind her desk. Vice Principal Jourdan, Ms. Pendergast, and Ms. Wilson, the school social worker, were in chairs along the wall.

"Have a seat, Camy." Principal Miller pointed to a chair directly across from her. "It's been brought to our attention that there may be a plagiarism ring in our school."

My shoulders relaxed; at least I knew what this was about.

"It's possible some of the students you've tutored might be involved." She paused to adjust a paper on her desk. "And that you may have assisted them."

"But—"

Ms. Pendergast spoke up before I could say more. "Camy, when I talked to you on the first day of school and encouraged you to be more involved with the other students, this was not what I had in mind."

"But I would never—" I started to say, but Ms. Pendergast interrupted me again.

"You know, dear, Ms. Wilson was just telling us that it's not unusual for children of divorce to seek support from inappropriate sources."

My cheeks felt like they were on fire. "But that's not … Most of the students I tutor don't need to cheat. They just don't have good study habits. That's all I give them. That's all I've ever given anyone."

"Right." Ms. P used a manicured fingernail to corral the lipstick at the corner of her mouth.

"Perhaps you did it without even knowing it," Principal Miller added softly. "Did you lend someone a paper you wrote, so they could see an example of how one should be written? Or maybe you left your own work unattended, where someone could see it?"

"No," I said. "Principal Miller, I know that Sophie Vega didn't cheat. She worked hard to write that paper."

"Unfortunately we have a witness who says she heard Ms. Vega state differently," Principal Miller said.

"And, anyway, it *is* kind of interesting that so many of your … poorer … students have seen such a dramatic turnaround in their grades," Pendergast added.

The fire in my cheeks went into nuclear meltdown. "No one cheated in my room."

"It's not *your* room, Camy," Ms. P said, her words an arctic blast. "It's the school's tutoring program."

Principal Miller gathered the papers on her desk. "I want to believe you, Ms. Cavanaugh. But until the investigation is complete, I'm afraid I have to suspend you from tutoring."

"What? You can't. I—"

"Sorry I'm late." The door opened and Coach Cutter stepped inside the already crowded room.

"That's all right, Fred. We're just getting ready to move on to the next issue. Would you like to begin?" Principal Miller asked.

Coach settled himself into a chair and looked right at me. "Camy, you know I used to watch you play youth football? You've always been a team player, so I'm sure you'll be happy to help us out of a certain, uh, situation we find ourselves in."

Don't bet on that, I thought.

"Apparently there's been some unauthorized computer activity going on here at the school and we think you might know who's involved. We'd like you to confirm that information." He waited a heartbeat. "Now, please."

My voice trembled with anger but I fought to get myself back in control. "What information do you want me to confirm, Coach?" There. That was better.

"Well, Camy, did Kevin Orrs use the school's server in any way to create an illegal website? All you need to do is nod your head."

I shook my head instead.

"I don't think you heard me. I said—" Coach leaned forward. It was a move I'd seen him do a thousand times on the sidelines when he wanted to get a particular point across. "Did Kevin Orrs access the school's server to create or maintain an unauthorized website?"

I shook my head again.

"She's lying," Ms. Pendergast said.

Ms. Wilson let out a gasp. Principal Miller said, "I'm not sure that was called for, Julie. Please refrain from—"

"Oh, come on," Ms. Pendergast said. "We all know that Sophie Vega and that slacker, Kevin Orrs, got to Camy. I don't know what they did, but—"

"They didn't do anything!" I said. "They're good kids. Kevin's on the honor roll!"

"Yes, well, leopards and spots," Ms. P said, as though those words were the last on the subject.

I stood up. I was probably already going to get suspended. I might as well make it worth it. I spun toward Ms. Pendergast.

"You and your *witness* just can't get over the fact that someone like Sophie was elected homecoming queen. And you." I turned to Coach. "You're just mad because your football team can't win a game."

"That is quite enough," Principal Miller said. "From all of you."

"May I say one more thing?" Coach Cutter asked.

"Is it respectful of everyone in this room?"

Coach nodded. "Camy. You may be right. I may be frustrated because *our* football team can't win a game. But if the team can't win because of some big, secret thing that has gotten out of control, something that is hurting people, then it's not just about football anymore, is it?"

I sank back into my chair, tears pricking my eyes. The adults talked back and forth. I nodded when they seemed to expect me to, but I didn't really hear what they said. When the bell rang for second block, everyone stood.

I made it through to last block by telling myself I would not cry. I would not talk to anyone. I would not worry that the school might call Dad. I'd go to class, I'd take as many notes as possible, and I would wait for the end of the day.

When it finally arrived, it took longer than usual to sort through the books and assignments in my locker. I tried to make myself believe that I was waiting for the hallway to clear out. But when it did, and I shut my locker door, I knew the truth.

I was lost.

Without thinking, I turned toward the staircase that would take me to the third floor, the tutoring room, and my skybox view of the football field.

What happened when someone got knocked off the path destiny had planned for them?

I was afraid to find out.

So I stood there, like a total dork, holding back tears, and stared at the flight of steps until I heard the stomp of serious boots against the linoleum floor.

"Hey," Sophie said.

"Hey," I said without turning around.

"Do you really have a plan?"

The idea that had popped into my head the day before had come with so much potential and so much terror, it had made me dizzy. I'd spent hours poking holes in it the night before. It was hardly a sure thing.

For one, the plan meant getting up in front of the whole school. Not exactly my forte. But just a week ago, I'd stood there as a homecoming candidate and survived. It meant being sneaky too. But considering the last month, sneaky should be an elective at Olympia High. At least this way, we'd all get credit for it. If the idea worked, it just might fix everything. And if it failed? My heart lurched at the prospect. I took a breath.

"I guess so." I shrugged. "Will you help me?"

Sophie gave me a grin. "Do you even have to ask?"

♡ ♡ ♡

My throat tightened a little every time I thought about it. I came close to hanging off the chain link fence until practice was over, then begging Coach Cutter for his help. Here's the thing: I was pretty sure Coach would do the right thing if I told him Kevin Orrs was behind the wiki. But if I told him it was actually his star quarterback?

I was nearly certain Coach was one of those rare members of the male species that maybe, just maybe, you could trust. But I didn't know that for sure, and somebody needed to do something, and that something needed to be real.

A week ago, I would've said that somebody was Elle. But with everyone knocked off of destiny's path, maybe it didn't matter so much *who* did something, as long as *someone* did.

I only had one problem. Or maybe it was two.

Thanks to my years of watching football practice I knew, with stalker-like precision, exactly which door Gavin used. Twenty minutes after the guys left the field, they started pouring out the side door. I waited until Gavin broke away from the group and hurried after him.

"I need your help," I blurted.

He stopped, then turned around slowly. "Oh, yeah?"

"I want to do something about the wiki," I said. "I want to set things right without getting anyone into trouble."

Gavin took a few steps forward. "And you need me?"

I nodded. "I can't do it alone. You're doing the football highlights thing at the pep rally on Friday, aren't you? That's what it said on the school website."

He studied me for a second. "In case you haven't noticed, highlights have been a little hard to come by this year. The thing I'm doing Friday should probably be called 'Two or Three Plays That Didn't Totally Suck.'"

I knew he was trying to be funny, but I couldn't force myself to laugh.

"So, what do you need?" he asked.

I told him the plan. When I finished, he rubbed his face and scratched his head. "I don't see how you're going to get Rhino to help."

"If you come with me now, he will." I nodded toward the street that led to Rhino's house.

"I'm in," Gavin said. His voice was loud enough to make me jump. He took a few steps across the grass, then turned to look at me. He held out his hand.

I glanced around, worried someone might see us. But really? There was no more boy boycott. Tomorrow, there might not even be a wiki. There were no rules anymore. There was no one to tell me *no*. My fingers stretched toward Gavin's, and he held my hand.

We walked all the way to Rhino's like that, my fingers laced with his.

We dropped hands at the foot of Rhino's driveway, though. Before we did, I felt the muscles in Gavin's arm stiffen. He looked like he was about to try for a forward pass.

I probably looked like I was about to hurl.

"Pre-game jitters?" he said.

I sucked in a breath. "I'm okay."

Even with the afternoon sun, it was cool enough that Rhino's garage door was shut. I tried not to think of it as an omen.

"Come on," I said to Gavin.

I inched open the door, grabbed Gavin's hand, and yanked him through the back hall. The second we entered Rhino's space, he greeted us with a scowl.

"I don't even want to ask," he said.

I stepped forward until I was standing with the couch between us. "We need to do something about the wiki," I said.

Rhino walked around the couch and touched a finger to the tip of my nose like I was a little kid. "No, Ladybug, we don't."

I was seriously reconsidering my whole "no violence" stance. "It's time, Rhino. The school already knows, and—"

"You told them?"

It was like he spit the question at me. I had to back up. "No. But they know there's 'unauthorized computer activity'. I don't think they know what it is, exactly, and they don't know who's behind it, but they think it might be Kevin Orrs."

Of all the words that had passed between us, I think those last hurt him more than anything else.

"Kevin Orrs?" he said. "He couldn't code his way out of a bag."

"I thought you'd be glad for the warning," I said, "so you can shut it down before anyone gets into trouble."

"What if I don't?" he asked.

"I'll tell them everything I know."

Behind me, Gavin cleared his throat. Yeah. I hadn't exactly told him that part of the plan.

Rhino snorted. "Please. Now that I know they're looking, I can make the wiki vanish whenever I want. No, I wouldn't even have to do that. I could move the whole thing to another server. So, thanks for the heads up."

"The Internet is forever," I reminded him.

He shrugged. "True. But it'd take an expert to track down any evidence. An expensive one, too." He turned from me and went back to working on his laptop. "I've seen the school budget. Trust me, they don't have that kind of money. It would be your word against mine, Ladybug."

"No." Gavin took a step closer to me. "It would be your word against *ours*."

Rhino clutched his chest. "Bro, you're killing me."

"You know," Gavin said, and he nodded toward me. "We could always—"

Rhino pointed a finger at him, stopping his words. "No, we couldn't."

They stayed like that, locked in a silent battle of wills, until I opened my book bag and pulled out a pile of paper. With Sophie's help, I had gotten back into the wiki. I hadn't had enough time to get it all before football practice ended, but I had enough. I'd printed screen shots, the source code behind them, and anything else I could think of. I handed a few of them to Rhino and waited. "Does that change your mind?"

"You've been busy." He flipped through the sheets, then touched a few keys on his laptop. "Let's see ... logged in as Aiden?"

There went any chance of ever getting in again. I hoped I wouldn't need to, but it was hard to tell.

"You're not going to give this up, are you?" he said.

I shook my head.

Rhino gave the papers a shake, then, to my surprise, handed them back to me. They crinkled in my grip, and I shoved them back into my bag, not caring that they crumpled.

"You're serious," he said.

I nodded.

Rhino glanced at Gavin. "And you?"

"Unless ..." Gavin began.

Rhino shook his head, and to my relief, Gavin nodded.

"You know what this means?" Rhino began. The words hung in the air.

It means what? I wondered. That we couldn't be friends anymore? But were we now? I'd already lost the Rhino I'd thought I knew. I could sacrifice this one. Take one for the team. Elle would be proud.

I nodded one last time.

"All right. You win." He sat in his chair and leaned back. "What do you need me to do?"

Chapter Twenty Three

♡

FRIDAY MORNING, I left homeroom with only minutes to spare, a hall pass from Mr. Moore clutched in my hand. I went straight to the gym and staked out a spot on the first row of bleachers near the podium.

Rhino had rigged the laptop so a single click would take us from football highlights to the wiki. Gavin and I had practiced handing off the microphone.

The bell rang and students wandered in for the last pep rally of the football season. I stared straight ahead, not daring to catch anyone's eye. Soon the gym was packed. The band played. Principal Miller talked about something—school spirit, I think. At last, she cleared her throat and said, "And speaking of spirit, please give a big Trojan welcome to your quarterback and football team captain, Gavin Madison."

Everyone clapped and a few people called out, "Mad Dog!" When Gavin stood up, I panicked. I was no longer sure I could do it.

He must have been reading my mind. "Don't worry," he said. "I'm going to lull them with boredom."

Then he walked to the podium, hit a key on the laptop, and his slide presentation appeared on the screen behind him.

My mouth dropped open. The first slide was titled "Beginnings" and beneath that was a photo from the third grade youth football league. That photo included me, number twenty-three. I was also in the next two pictures. I shot a look at Gavin, but he was staring into the crowd. He seemed to pick out one person, then another, daring them to hold his gaze.

He gave the clicker a little shake. "Excuse me. It looks like we have a slight technical difficulty," he said. "Hang on. It'll only take a second."

That was my cue. Gavin aimed the remote at the screen again. It switched from his presentation to a sample of the wiki. I'd compiled a "worst of the worst" from the comments I'd read over the past month and sent them to Rhino. He'd promised he could make all the names anonymous. My heart was beating so hard that it hurt, but I stood, took the microphone from Gavin, and turned toward the screen.

There it was, *The Hotties of Troy*, in all its Neanderthal glory.

Murmurs rippled through the audience as they realized we had left football territory behind. Someone said, "What the hell?" A wave of whispers flooded the gym. It didn't start receding until understanding had settled over most everyone in the bleachers.

"Some of you know what this is," I said above the dying noise. And, yeah, my voice shook, but only at first. "Some of you have probably heard about it, or at least heard rumors of it. Maybe you wondered if it was true, if it really existed. It does. Let me introduce you to *The Hotties of Troy*. It's like Wikipedia, only all the pages are about girls right here at Olympia High." I scrolled so the screen contained only posts and comments, then picked up the laser pointer Gavin had positioned next to the laptop.

"There are a lot of words up there," I said. I turned the pointer on, and highlighted a few:

Muffin Top.

Dog Face.

Bitch.

Dyke.

Whore.

There were others, but I couldn't bring myself to highlight them. Just knowing they were on the screen made my face burn as red as the laser's tip.

"Like I said, so many words. And each one was written by a boy in this gym. By those same boys that we used to play with at recess." Or on the football field, I thought. "They were written by boys we sit next to in classes and work beside at jobs, by the same guys we thought we knew our whole lives."

At the moment, those guys were looking toward the ceiling, or at the doors and windows, as if desperately seeking some method of escape. Good. They deserved to squirm.

"Just because someone wears a sports bra instead of a jockstrap, it doesn't make her any less of a person." I paused, just for a second. They were still squirming. I still had everyone's attention. I tried not to rush, but fear that someone—a teacher, Principal Miller, even one of the boys—might try to stop me had the words pouring from my mouth.

"It doesn't give anyone the right to talk about her like she's some kind of product you can buy or reject in a store. And it certainly doesn't give anyone the right to pass on things she might have shared or done with you privately, in a moment of trust."

I looked up into the stands again, this time to find Rhino. In a show of male solidarity he'd chosen to sit with the baseball team today. Unlike the rest of the players, though, he refused to look away. Instead, he was staring straight through me. Okay, if that was how he wanted it …

"Someone once told me that right and wrong only have meaning because we say they do," I said. "I think he was both right and wrong about that. Like him, you might think the wiki was okay because, for a while, the girls didn't even know these words existed. But *you* knew. And maybe you thought about us differently because of it. Those words took away all chance of a real relationship between us. Because there's nothing honest about saying things behind someone's back."

I drew in a breath and shook my head. "Some crazy things happened because of the words on the wiki. First, all the girls got mad about it, but then we got together. We made new friends; we joined clubs." I glanced at Jason, in his seat beside Rhino. "We danced with guys we'd normally never even speak to. Those words caused all of that."

The gym was so quiet, I was afraid to shift my feet or readjust the microphone. If I did, whatever spell everyone was under might shatter. "For a while I thought the good they caused might be worth all of the rest, but words can hurt too. I think we've all seen that this week."

Jason's face, and Rhino's, and all those around them, blurred when tears came to my eyes. I blinked them away and sniffed. "I wish we could have the good without the bad, but I don't think that's possible any more. It's not up to me, though." I paused again. "I can make sure these words go away. Or I can give the information I have to Principal Miller, and I'm certain she'll make sure no one sees them again except for maybe our parents."

Principal Miller nodded from her seat at the side of the bleachers and a groan spread through the crowd.

I thought for sure the pulse in my throat would choke me, but my voice had a will of its own. "But even if she does that, the wiki, and all the harm it does, will still live on if we refuse to believe that words have power. They have the power to hurt. They have the power to heal. It's your choice."

I looked around, at kids in the bleachers, at the section where the teachers were sitting. All of them looked a little shocked. "Thank you," I said before returning the mic to its stand. "Thank you for listening."

I took a step back and bumped into something solid and warm. Gavin was standing behind me, then moved to my side. He slipped his hand into mine and gave my fingers a squeeze.

A clattering came from the stands. Jason landed with a thud on the gym floor, then strolled over to stand next to Gavin.

"*Dog.*" He shook his head and shoved Gavin's shoulder.

Even after all this time, I still didn't speak Ab.

Next, Elle picked her way out of the cheerleaders, followed by Mercedes. Sophie's boots thunked their way down the stands until she landed next to me. To my surprise, Clarissa came up next. Our eyes met and something shifted between us. We'd never be friends again. To tell you the truth, I'm not sure we ever were, not really. But in that moment, at least we understood each other.

Rhino slouched his way down the bleachers. He held out his hand, not to me, but to Elle. The tears streaming down her face made my own eyes sting all over again. She took his hand. He must have been too close to the mic, because his whisper reached us all.

"I'm sorry," he said. "I'm so sorry."

I think we all were. I know I was.

Up on the screen, the wiki blurred and faded. At first I thought it was from the tears in my eyes. But I caught Rhino gazing at the projection over Elle's shoulder and I knew.

The wiki was gone.

I gave Gavin's hand a final squeeze, and his fingers slipped through mine as I started for the gym doors. I was amazed they let me leave. Amazed that, when I reached the threshold, applause was thundering behind me.

♡ ♡ ♡

For the second time in a week, I found myself sitting in the most uncomfortable chair in the world. I waited in the office for hours. A ridiculous number of people passed by me while I squirmed on the seat. I recognized a few members of the school board, the superintendent, Ms. Wilson, Coach Cutter.

Dad.

I started crying when he came in. He knelt beside my chair. "You okay?" he asked.

"That depends," I said. "Am I grounded forever?"

"Probably." At least he kissed the top of my head before following the crowd down the hall.

I thought I heard his voice once. I thought I heard Mom's, but that had to be my guilty conscience. I was sure she would have plenty to say about what happened, but there was no way I could hear her all the way from Iowa. I heard a lot of other voices too. A few of them *did* get loud enough to hear from Iowa.

Finally, Ms. Bentley sent me in. We were in a different room this time, a larger one, with enough seats that no one had to perch on the radiator. I looked around at all the sober faces. Someone was missing. "Ms. Pender—" I started to say under my breath.

Principal Miller looked at me and said, "Ms. Pendergast will not be with us today. She is on a leave of absence. Ms. Cavanaugh, I want you to know that at Olympia High School we believe that *all* students can change for the better and we do not single out students for special negative attention. That wouldn't be fair."

Of course, a few minutes after that, she did single me out for special negative attention. How fair was that?

In the end, I got a whole lot of lecturing and five days' detention for failure to cooperate with an investigation of behavior that could prove harmful to (a) student(s) or the school environment.

Whatever.

And I *had* heard my mom. They'd Skyped her in for the meeting. It was both wonderful and terrible to see her, and I realized how much I missed her.

Dad filled me in on the details on the way home. Principal Miller had pushed for a massive suspension for everyone who'd been involved, but Rhino had made the images we'd used at the pep rally—and the rest of the wiki—vanish. There was no evidence that *The Hotties of Troy* had ever existed. Without that, the school board members felt they couldn't hand out any punishment. Except to me, of course.

Dad said he wasn't sure what would have happened even if there *was* still proof. A lot of people at the meeting had thought the wiki was just "boys being boys." He breathed heavily out of his nostrils when he said that part.

He also said that he and Mom had agreed I should have some "special negative attention" at home too. I'd have to talk to Mom on the phone later. She had her own lecture she wanted to deliver. Plus, I had to write an essay for them. The topic was: How to tell when a problem is too big to solve on your own. (Insert eye rolling here.) And I was grounded. I couldn't go anywhere, have friends over, or use my phone or the Internet until I'd served all of my detention.

"That starts now," Dad said.

"But tonight is the last home game of the year," I said. It might be the last time I'd ever get to see Gavin play. I felt like crying all over again.

"I don't think you'll be missing much," Dad said. Then he told me that, even though there wouldn't be any formal punishment, Coach Cutter had decided to bench all the players on the Varsity team for that night's game.

Maybe I *could* have counted on Coach to do the right thing.

There was a bright side. Sort of. Actually, there were two bright sides.

First, the plagiarism investigation against Sophie, me, and the other kids that I'd tutored was over. They hadn't found a single incident of cheating. That meant Sophie would pass English and I could go back to tutoring as soon as I'd served my detention.

Second, apparently Aiden Tuttle hadn't thought saying hurtful things on the wiki was quite enough. He'd been caught passing an actual paper note about Clarissa in homeroom that morning.

"You can look forward to seeing that young man sitting detention with you, Camy," Dad said.

Like I'd look forward to anything that involved Aiden.

Things were weird between Dad and me in the car. They were even stranger when we got home. Even though I knew I had disappointed him by getting into trouble, I caught him grinning at me. And twice he sort of punched my shoulder.

We were in the kitchen, cooking breakfast for dinner, when he said, "Look, Cams, you should have told someone about the wiki earlier. The principal, a teacher … your father, maybe?" He raised his eyebrows at me and gave me his most serious dad look then. "But I'd be a liar if I said I wasn't a little bit proud of the way you handled yourself today, princess."

"Dad, I'm not the princess, remember?"

"Queen, then."

"I'm not the queen, either."

"Right here you are." He tapped the spot over his heart. "You're the queen of right here." And he gave me a hug.

♡ ♡ ♡

Serving detention wasn't as bad as you'd think. Really. Except for having to see Aiden's face every afternoon, it was a lot like tutoring. The only thing missing was the skybox view. On the first day, I worked on the essay for my parents. The next day, I did some extra-credit work for my classes, hoping it would be enough to bring me back to my pre-wiki honor roll nerd status. The rest of the time, I helped the other detention students.

Outside of detention, I kept to myself. I didn't volunteer answers in class, and I spent my lunch periods in the hallway outside the science labs. If someone tried to get my attention, I pretended I was blind and deaf and walked on. It was a little lonely. The truth is, it was a whole lot lonely, but it was easier that way.

I didn't know what to expect from the kids at school. Sure, there had been a show of support at the pep rally, but what if they'd changed their minds once they'd really thought things through? Retreating to the sidelines felt familiar, comfortable, and safe.

On Thursday after detention, I spotted a piece of printer paper, folded in thirds, sticking out of my locker's air vents. It reminded me of something, but I couldn't say exactly what, not until I noticed Clarissa standing in front of her own locker, a few yards down the hall. The combination of girl and note brought back memories of Clarissa's over-the-top campaign for homecoming queen, with its posters, pins, and flyers stuck everywhere, and I almost laughed.

But the homecoming contest was long over. I pulled the note from the vent and opened it carefully.

I still didn't know what I was looking at. It appeared to be a screen-shot, off a website like YouTube. The title at the top read: *Hotties v. Notties Ep. 7*. The picture beneath it looked sort of like a diorama, the kind we'd made in sixth grade social studies class. You know, with shoe-boxes and stuff? But this one didn't depict a random capitol of Europe.

It looked more like a crude representation of a boxing ring.

And inside the ring?

Dolls. One tall, thin, blonde Barbie type in a cheerleader outfit and one shorter doll, flat-chested, with big dark eyes. The second one was naked except for the toy football helmet scotch-taped into its crazy black hair. I'd seen that kind of doll before; I think they're called trolls.

Even with the speech bubble above the troll's head saying, "Hut! Hut!" I still didn't understand. But things became devastatingly clear when I read the subtitle printed in bright blue across the bottom: *Elle Emerson v. Camy Cavanaugh.*

The video had received two hundred and thirty-seven views since it was uploaded last spring. Someone had wanted me to know that; the date was circled in green marker. It was one of a series of eight. You could see them all by subscribing to the channel TrojanMan.

I wondered if this was the type of video that could be reached by typing my name in Google. I thought about college admissions offices and scholarship boards doing searches. I thought of every last employer I might work for. Everyone I might meet. Even my own children in some far-flung future. Heat rose in my face. If the Internet really was forever, I didn't want to go through life as the Troll Doll Girl.

Another thought occurred to me. Since I was obviously the Nottie in the picture, did the other seven episodes feature me as well? How many views did those videos have? And who else was I "hut-hutting" against? Lexy? Clarissa?

Speaking of Clarissa, I'd been so focused on the printout that I hadn't even noticed her moving in my direction. She'd almost passed me when she stopped and touched my arm.

"Don't bother looking it up," she said. "You won't find them anymore."

"How would you know?" I choked out.

But instead of answering, Clarissa pointed upward and said, "Hey! I guess we forgot one."

I looked up. Above our heads, a *CD 4 HQ* poster was still hanging, those jade eyes looking down on me with mock benevolence.

"Damn, I look good," she said. With that, she sashayed down the hall and disappeared around the corner.

I fought the urge to chase her and show her what a real *Hotties v. Notties* throwdown would look like. Not that it would change anything. I folded the screenshot and was about to stick it into my calc book when I noticed writing on the other side.

Once again in green, someone had carefully penned: *You might have overlooked something about your nosy friend.*

Now I was totally lost. The only "nosy" friend I could think of was Rhino. Besides the fact that we weren't actually friendly these days, what could he possibly have to do with this latest humiliation? He might not be the superhero I'd thought he was, but I still couldn't imagine him doing something so deliberately cruel.

♡ ♡ ♡

The next day in French class, Madame Bourg-Schmidt assigned partners for conversation practice. "*Mademoiselle Cavanaugh et Mademoiselle Emerson*," she commanded.

"*Merde*," I said under my breath, but when I glanced at Elle she didn't seem too upset about the pairing. We scooted our desks together.

"*Bonjour*, Camy," Elle said, giving me that dazzling I-should-have-been-homecoming-queen smile.

"*Bonjour*," I said back.

"*Ça fait longtemps*," Elle said. (Long time, no see.)

"*Oui*."

"*Il s'est passé beaucoup*," she said. (A lot has happened.)

"*Oui.*" I figured it was best to stick to one-word answers.

"*Au de sujet, je regrette rien.*" (By the way, I have no regrets.)

"Really?" I said, reverting back to English. "That's not what you said a couple of weeks ago. I seem to recall a few tears and plenty of regrets." I pointed toward the classroom door. "It was just down the hall. Remember?"

For a second, Elle frowned. But the dazzle returned for Madame Bourg-Schmidt when she said, "*En francais, les filles.*" (In French, girls.)

"*Parlez-vous de Rhino*?" Elle asked as Madame walked away.

"*Oui.*"

"Well, okay, yes," she started. "We should have taken more time to really get to know each other and trust each other before we … how do you say it?" She shrugged, and even that looked French. "You know. But I'm not sorry about the rest. Not one bit."

At least I think that's what she said. It was in French and, like just about everything else, Elle's grasp of the language was a lot better than mine.

"*Et vous? Des regrets?*" she went on. (Did I have any regrets?)

I sighed. "*Oui.*"

"*Que?*"

What did I regret? It wasn't taking down the wiki. Looking across the desks at her now, I couldn't say I regretted my friendship with Elle, either. And as pathetic as it might sound, I wouldn't take back a single moment I'd spent with Gavin. Not the plotting and scheming. And definitely not the kiss.

No, if I regretted anything, it was …

"Rhino." My voice caught in my throat when I tried to say his name.

I missed him so much. Even through everything, I'd held out hope that somehow we could fix things and get back to what we had once been.

"*Il n'a pas à être de cette façon,*" Elle said. (It doesn't have to be that way.)

And maybe it didn't. At least not until yesterday, when that YouTube screen shot had shown up. The "nosy" friend couldn't be anyone else but Rhino. The idea that he'd betrayed me for so long, even before the wiki had come into existence, was too much to get over. Too much to forgive.

"*Ici.*" Elle handed me a tissue.

I hadn't even noticed I was crying.

"What's going on?" she asked, in English this time.

I unzipped my book bag and pulled out the folded sheet of paper. I pushed it across the desks to her.

She opened it and her jaw tensed. "Haven't I told you that what people say about you doesn't matter?"

"Even when that person is Rhino?" I reached across both desks, turned the paper over, and pointed to the note in green marker. The one that said, *You might have overlooked something about your nosy friend.*

Elle straightened in her seat and dropped the paper into her lap. "*Les pomme frites sont délicieux.*"

The fries are delicious? Either my French was worse than I thought or Madame Bourg-Schmidt was standing right behind me. She walked past us, pausing to raise one eyebrow. Elle waited until she was a few desks away before leaning forward and whispering, again in English, "This doesn't seem like something Rhino would do."

"Did the wiki?" I countered.

"Who gave you this?"

"Clarissa, I think."

Elle's blue eyes went icy. But before she could say anything else, Madame Bourg-Schmidt clapped her hands together.

"*Exam improvisée*," she said.

Pop quiz? Oh, sure. Why not?

♡ ♡ ♡

Jason showed up that afternoon, the last day of detention. He plopped into the desk next to mine.

Mr. Moore picked up a piece of paper and looked at it twice. "Surprisingly, Mr. Abernathy, you are not on my list."

"I know," Jason said. "Kind of amazing, isn't it?"

"So, why are you here?"

"My mom's going to kill me if I don't bring up my grades, and I heard Camy's a genius at that kind of stuff."

I've had five days to think about this (seven if you count the weekend), and if you ask me, the last day of detention should come with a checklist:

You find a jock asking for tutoring?

It's still a sign of the apocalypse.

Or maybe not. After Mr. Moore dismissed us, Jason followed me back to my locker. "So, we're okay and everything?" he said.

"Sure."

He held out a fist. My own fingers curled and I found myself bumping his fist back. Then Jason Abernathy did something I didn't expect. But really, after everything, I should have. He leaned forward, head tipped toward me, and sniffed.

He grinned. And then he was off, racing down the hall, body slamming lockers.

Jason "The Ab" Abernathy: the jock that half the school loved and the other half feared. The jock that I kind of, sort of … thought was okay.

♡ ♡ ♡

I shoved the rest of my books into my bag. I was in a hurry to get home. A week is a long time to go without a phone or the Internet. I wanted to catch up with the world. Besides, I needed to check out that troll video. Clarissa might have given me her weird assurance that it was no longer available, but I wanted to see for myself. I'd almost made it to the doors when I heard the rustle of pom-poms.

"Camy! There you are! Come on!" Lexy disappeared up the stairs.

I was too curious to leave without following her. My knee hurt a little when I got to the second floor landing, so I slowed down. I took the last set of steps carefully. By the time I made it to the third floor, I didn't see Lexy anywhere. The tutoring room was dark too. That made my heart hurt.

In the days since the pep rally, Ms. Pendergast had decided she wasn't coming back to teach at OHS, I had been banned from tutoring, then I'd spent a week in detention. I wasn't sure there was a tutoring program left to go back to.

But I missed my room. I missed my skybox view of the football field, even though that would be empty too. Tonight was an away game, the last of the season. According to the announcements this morning, there was hope that the team might even win.

The second I opened the door to the tutoring room, the lights flashed on. There was an explosion of blue and white pom-pom fringe and flying ponytails and ... almost everybody. Byron and his friends. Lexy and the entire pom squad. Mercedes and Dalton. I glanced around; the only ones missing were Elle and Rhino. And Sophie.

But a moment later, Sophie skidded into the room. "Surprise," she said, giving my arm a gentle punch.

Lexy rushed up to me. She was holding a long sheet of paper in her hands. "Camy, look." She shoved the paper at me. "I took your speech from the pep rally and … look!"

I held the paper carefully. "Aww, it's in glitter glue," I said. Pink, purple, and electric blue.

A lot more things happened in the tutoring room that afternoon, but studying wasn't one of them.

♡ ♡ ♡

I smiled all the way home. I was still smiling when I pulled open the cover of my laptop and turned it on, then I remembered my mission.

I opened the browser and typed in the address of the *Hotties v. Notties* video. Nothing. I searched as many ways as I could and came up with several candidates. Each of them turned into a dead end, though. I tried typing the account holder's name, TrojanMan, and found about what you'd expect: tons of sites devoted to condoms, and one notice that a video posting account had been suspended for reported violations.

Just in case, I punched in my own name, Camy Cavanaugh. What I found then surprised me. In the past week, the citizens of the Internet had been busy discussing me. My name popped up in blogs and feeds, a whole page's worth. And none of it had anything to do with a troll doll.

Instead, from Olympia to Prairie Stone, to Bear Head Lake and back, the *"uplifting," "inspiring,"* and *"OMG totally AwEsOmE"* story about a former football player turned homecoming candidate who'd stood up for girl power and against rumors … had gone viral? Well, viral in a small town Minnesota kind of way.

Wow.

When I opened my inbox and Facebook wall, they held so many emails and posts that I wondered if I'd ever have enough time to get through them all. Most of them were quick messages of support. Mixed in were new friend requests, invitations to Halloween parties (Mercedes) and harvest festivals (Lexy). Prudence had suggested I "like" the OHS orchestra, and Bing Bing wanted to know when I would be available for an interview and photo shoot. The investigative article she'd threatened me with earlier was going to be a "Trojan Treasure" feature instead, whatever that was. Sadly, my AcreRage chickens had passed away from neglect, but I thought I might be able to nurse a few of the sheep back to health.

I sorted the posts between the ones I needed to respond to right away, and the ones that could wait a while before I did something with them. One from the first category had come from my mom. The subject line said, Fall Break Plans.

I sighed.

Mom had been great about what she called "the situation." Sure, she'd lectured me, but she'd also really talked to me about respect, between guys and girls, and between girls and girls too.

"You're growing up," she said at the end of it. And it'd felt like she meant it.

That didn't mean I was all fired up about visiting her over fall break, though. I mean, I *do* love my mom. I miss her and I wish I could spend more time with her. But I wanted to spend time with my friends too. When I opened her email, I realized that both of our school breaks were at the same time. I wrote to her:

> **Mom, I'd really like it if you spent fall break with me here. That way I could introduce you to some of my friends and talk to you and Dad about my college plans. <3 Camy**

Five minutes later, she responded:

Camy, Sounds like a great idea! See you soon. ~Mom

I had one more email to sort and I couldn't decide if it was a *do it now* or a *pretend you never saw it*. Someone with a screen name I hadn't seen before had sent a link to me:

Hotties of Troy2! Check it out!

I held one hand over my eyes and clicked the mouse with the other. When I finally found the nerve to peek, I saw a new wiki. An open one where anyone could post—as long as the message was positive. A wiki where someone called Adm*n kept everyone in line. Mercedes had left one of the first messages:

mercedes: We won the chess meet! We pwned the pawns! Dalton and Tara are so hot, it's like their brians are on fire!!!!!!

Beneath that, Dalton had posted a response:

daltonr: Mercedes swept the novice division. Her "brian" is on fire too.

I was still laughing when the doorbell rang downstairs. I opened the door expecting to see Boy Scouts selling popcorn, or third graders hawking wrapping paper for the annual PTA fundraiser. Instead, I found Elle. And she wasn't alone. She had a death grip on Clarissa's upper arm.

"Somebody has something to say to you," Elle said.

"I wasn't trying to make things worse. I swear." Clarissa yanked her arm out of Elle's grasp. "Remember Homecoming?" she began. Like it was a night either Elle or I could forget. "That night, I tricked Jason into leaving his laptop at my house so I could get into the wiki and see for myself. Well, I did, but I also found that video, and a bunch of other ones, saved on Jason's hard drive. They were funny, and actually kind of clever."

"Really?" Elle said. "Even the one of you?"

A blush blazed up Clarissa's cheeks, but she recovered quickly. "Anyway, I asked him about them the next day and he got all freaked out. He made me promise I wouldn't tell anyone that he had them. I pushed him about it and he finally caved." The memory of her conquest brought a smile to her face. My stomach started to churn.

"Here's the deal," she said. "When Jason saw the videos last spring, he sent a link out to everyone on the baseball team, and guess who that included? Yeah. Rhino."

Obviously it made sense to Clarissa. And from the way Elle nodded, she'd understood as well. But, frankly, I was lost.

"I still don't get it," I said.

Elle pulled a fresh copy of the YouTube print from her jacket pocket. "Look at the date on the video. It's just before the wiki got started, right?"

"And?"

"Don't you see? When Rhino found out what they'd done to you in that video, *that's* when he built the wiki. He made the guys all promise to stop posting things anywhere else, and in exchange, they could have free rein inside *The Hotties of Troy*." Elle paused and spoke her next words slowly. "He did it to protect *you*."

I studied the paper in my hands. "Why didn't he just tell me when I found out about the wiki?"

"He didn't want you to know about this," Elle said. "He didn't want you to be hurt."

In my mind, I heard the echo of Rhino's protests that day I'd confronted him about the wiki: *No one was supposed to get hurt.* I thought about the strange exchange between him and Gavin when we convinced Rhino to help us shut it down.

"Was it that bad?" I asked. After all, I'd survived the wiki. How awful could a troll doll in a football helmet be? Enough to ruin a friendship?

Elle cast a glance at Clarissa. She went pink again, shrugged, and wouldn't meet my eyes.

Okay. Pretty awful. I sighed. Rhino. Wasn't he always riding to my rescue, whether with an ugly orange skirt, the cash for the perfect homecoming dress, or a crazy scheme to protect my online reputation?

"Still," I said, turning the paper in my hands. "Two wrongs don't make a right."

"Look around you, Camy." Elle said. "This isn't your tutoring room. It's the real world. People take risks to get what they want. They make mistakes. Try factoring that into your problem and see what answers you come up with."

I nodded, then sighed again. "I think I need to go work on some math."

Clarissa's forehead crinkled, but Elle snorted and tugged her down the steps. When they reached the car, I called out to her.

"Hey, Elle?"

She looked up.

"Thanks."

"What are friends for?" She grinned. "Let me know when you figure out that equation."

I nodded, my eyes drawn once again to the paper in my hands. Could I solve this one? Math had never been my best subject, but it was kind of like a test, and I was good at those. Still, it would take some work.

Camy + Rhino = what?

♡ ♡ ♡

I woke up early the next day. The sun hadn't risen yet but I could already tell that something felt different.

I gathered up all the printouts I'd made of the wiki and carried them to the outdoor fireplace in our backyard. On top, I placed the screen shot from the troll video. I lit a match, then stood there, under the last of the night's stars, and watched them burn. When the only thing left was ashes, I scooped them into a jar, washed the smell of smoke from my hair, and walked to Rhino's.

The cold air nipped at my cheeks, enough so that I'd wrapped a scarf around my neck before I left the house. It was still early, and Rhino's garage door was shut. That was okay. I'd planned on leaving the jar with a note, anyway.

The second the glass touched concrete, the door creaked, and I stepped back to let it open. Rhino was standing in the center of the space. His hair was a mess, and he was wearing an oversized Twins sweatshirt with a pair of plaid pajama bottoms.

He pointed to the jar. "What's that?"

"The wiki," I said. "And a screen print from something called *Hotties v. Notties*."

His face tensed. I held still, held my breath, and waited. It didn't happen right away, but at last I saw the crinkles around his eyes deepen and that rare, warm Rhino smile appear.

"We okay, Ladybug?" he asked.

"I hope so."

"You were right, you know."

"I thought you said there was no such thing as right and wrong."

"I was ..." His lips twitched. "Wrong."

I laughed.

He held open his arms and for three glorious seconds, Rhino let me inside his personal bubble.

"I missed you," he said, but my throat was so tight, all I could do was nod.

"What are you doing up so early?" I asked a few moments later.

Rhino gestured toward the driveway. "See for yourself."

A cherry red Mini-Cooper pulled in, and Elle rolled down the window. Her face brightened when her gaze landed on me, and she waved.

"It's about time you two made up." She looked over at Rhino. "Well? Anything new on Todd the Toad?"

"He has some extra evidence, but nothing you don't have a counterargument for," Rhino said. "Plus, he's doing this thing where he touches his nose, but he's just trying to fake everyone out. Don't fall for it."

Elle nodded. "You're the best."

I expected Rhino to agree with that. Instead, he leaned toward her window. "No, you are," he said and gave her a quick kiss.

"Let me guess," I said after Elle had driven away. "Another debate with Prairie Stone?"

"We both like the challenge."

"I'm glad you two are working things out," I said. "She's nice."

"Please, Ladybug. *You're* nice. She's … Elle. But speaking of nice…" He raised an eyebrow. "What about you and a certain football player?"

I took in a deep breath and shrugged my shoulders as I let it back out.

"Did you know he was willing to take the blame for the whole wiki? He knew how much it would hurt if you found out I was behind it."

I shook my head. But it sounded like Gavin.

"Call him or something."

"I might," I said. "Right now, I'm just going to take a walk."

♡ ♡ ♡

I didn't do it on purpose, I swear, but my feet led me to the football field. The toes of my Chuck Taylors had just touched the fifty-yard line when I heard the pounding of sneakers behind me.

I turned, and froze.

It was Gavin. His breath was coming out in clouds and he had a football tucked under one arm. "Hey," he said. "Rhino told me you'd be here."

"He did?"

"Well, he texted, and said I should take a walk."

That sounded like Rhino. "I'm glad you're here," I said.

"You are?"

I nodded. "I've wanted to tell you how sorry I am for everything."

"Like what?"

"Like the lousy season. I—"

Gavin interrupted. "It's not like any of us deserved to win, anyway. Except for the last game. I wish you could have seen it, Camy. Randall was awesome."

"I bet you were pretty awesome too."

"Nah." He shrugged, then a smile snuck onto his face. "Actually, I wasn't too bad. Coach Cutter set up a meeting with a recruiter after the game. Guess who's playing college ball next year?"

I gave him a high five. "That's great."

"Randall too. We're pretty stoked about it." He tossed the football in the air and caught it. It was good to see him show some confidence. Maybe Rhino was rubbing off on him.

"So, I was thinking about it. You know how the high school quarterback always ends up with the best girl in school and stuff?" he said.

Maybe a little too much of Rhino's confidence was rubbing off on him. I squinted, trying to make my face look fierce. I was about to repeat a little of my mom's speech about boys and girls and respect and … when he laughed.

"So, anyway, I hear there's this party coming up and I thought maybe you'd go with me and you could practice."

"Practice what?"

"Practice being my girlfriend. I mean, if you want to." Gavin kept his eyes on the football in his hands.

"Girl … friend?" I asked.

"You're a girl, right?"

He looked up and I nodded.

"And we're friends."

"I hope so."

Gavin glanced at the football in his hands one more time. Then he looked up at me again. "So, friend. Want to go long?"

Without answering, I ran. I ran with the cool October air against my cheeks and the turf beneath my feet. I ran, and for once, my knee didn't hurt at all. I spun around just in time to find Gavin throwing the most beautiful pass I'd ever seen. I caught it and clutched the ball to my chest. I held on until Gavin tackled me.

He swung me around by the waist. I might have squealed. He might have laughed. We definitely tumbled to the ground. And there, beneath the goalposts, Gavin "Mad Dog" Madison kissed me.

This time, there were no interruptions.

Acknowledgements

Have you ever wondered why so many books include a page that begins: No one has ever written a novel by themselves? It's because it is true. Our characters, their world, and the words that describe what they say and do may seem to come straight from our brains to your page or screen but that is an illusion.

We would like to thank Jennifer Klonsky for believing in this story enough to sustain our belief in it all these years later. We'd also like to thank the fans of The Geek Girl's Guide to Cheerleading, for continuing to ask if there would be another book. We offer our gratitude to Sara Bennett Wealer for reading and offering her amazing advice on everything from tech advancements to how to keep all of you turning the pages.

If not for Carol Davis, our talented editor, this book would have been filled with so many inappropriate ellipses, dashes, em-dashes and misplaced commas that it likely would have been many pages longer. What do you do when your last language class was in another century but your characters have a grand desire to parlez the Francais? You contact the lovely Mlle. Brittany Mazzola and Mme. Heather Christianson to ask for their advice. Merci beaucoups, ladies! And we can't picture this book becoming real without the talent of our fabulous cover artist, Aaron Andersen.

Darcy would like to thank her mother, Luanne Jarvis, for being the Best. Cheerleader. Ever. She'd also like to thank her husband, Doug/Niles for the countless times he's answered the question: she's or she is, which sounds better? And her children, Matthew and Sara, for learning to be resourceful during all those years that their mom sat in front of a computer screen saying, "I'll take care of it as soon as I finish this sentence/ paragraph/chapter/novel.

Charity would like to thank her entire family for putting up with this writing thing, with special thanks to her daughter Kyra who has a wealth of story ideas.

Together we would like to express our appreciation for all of the wonderful writing friends we've made through the years, including those at Writers Village University, on WordPress, the 2009 Debutantes, and on Facebook. And finally, we would like to thank YOU, the reader. You are really what all of this is about.

About the Authors

Charity Tahmaseb has slung corn on the cob for Green Giant and jumped out of airplanes (but not at the same time). She spent twelve years as a Girl Scout and six in the Army; that she wore a green uniform for both may not be a coincidence. These days, she writes fiction (long and short) and works as a technical writer for a software company in St. Paul.

Her short speculative fiction has appeared in UFO Publishing's Unidentified Funny Objects and Coffee anthologies, Flash Fiction Online and Cicada.

Darcy Vance is the slacker half of the author duo of Charity Tahmaseb and Darcy Vance. She didn't start writing seriously until she was 40, and didn't publish her first novel until she was 50. Even then, she needed a co-author to get the job done.

While Charity was busy slinging corn for Green Giant and jumping out of airplanes for the Army, Darcy was busy making out with boys and perfecting the art of the doodle. She only makes out with one boy now (her husband) but she still doodles wantonly.

Their novel, The Geek Girl's Guide to Cheerleading, was a YALSA 2012 Popular Paperback pick in the Get Your Geek On category.

www.ingramcontent.com/pod-product-compliance
Lightning Source LLC
Chambersburg PA
CBHW031213120726
47905CB00002B/315